P9-CLR-964

DISCARDED

ROCK BOTTOM

ERIN
BROCKOVICH

WITH CJ LYONS

ROCK
BOTTOM

A NOVEL

Vanguard Press

A MEMBER OF THE PERSEUS BOOKS GROUP

Copyright © 2011 by Erin Brockovich

Published by Vanguard Press
A Member of the Perseus Books Group

All rights reserved. No part of this publication may be reproduced,
stored in a retrieval system, or transmitted, in any form or by any means,
electronic, mechanical, photocopying, recording, or otherwise, without the
prior written permission of the publisher. Printed in the United States of
America. For information and inquiries, address Vanguard Press, 387 Park
Avenue South, 12th Floor, New York, NY 10016, or call (800) 343-4499.

Designed by Brent Wilcox
Set in 11.5 point Adobe Caslon Pro

Library of Congress Cataloging-in-Publication Data
Brockovich, Erin.
   Rock bottom / Erin Brockovich with CJ Lyons.
      p.   cm.
   ISBN 978-1-59315-625-1 (hardcover : alk. paper)
   ISBN 978-1-59315-667-1 (e-book)
   1. Women environmentalists—Fiction.   2. Single mothers—Fiction.
3. Environmental lawyers—Crimes against—Fiction.   4. Mountaintop
removal mining—Environmental aspects—West Virginia—Fiction.
5. Mining corporations—West Virginia—Fiction. I. Lyons, CJ, 1964–
II. Title.
   PS3602.R6325R63 2011
   813'.6—dc22

                                                       2010036852

Vanguard Press books are available at special discounts for bulk
purchases in the U.S. by corporations, institutions, and other organizations.
For more information, please contact the Special Markets Department
at the Perseus Books Group, 2300 Chestnut Street, Suite 200,
Philadelphia, PA 19103, or call (800) 810-4145, ext. 5000,
or e-mail special.markets@perseusbooks.com.

10 9 8 7 6 5 4 3 2 1

4/11
BdT

To Evan and Abby,
who both have the heart of a hero

Home is the place where,

when you have to go there,

they have to take you in.

ROBERT FROST

ACKNOWLEDGMENTS

Dear Reader,

Many people work hard behind the scenes to bring a story to life, and *Rock Bottom* is no exception.

We'd like to thank all the wonderful folks at Vanguard Press/Perseus Books Group, including Roger Cooper, Georgina Levitt, and Amanda Ferber. Also Kevin Smith, our editor, as well as our agents, Mel Berger (Erin) and Barbara Poelle (CJ). Of course, we can't forget our first readers who kept us on track: Toni McGee Causey, Kendel Flaum, Kim Howe, and Caroline Males.

For their expertise and research advice, a big thank-you goes out to Carl Causey, for the dragline insights, as well as to Wally Lind and Lee Lofland for providing the inner workings of a small-town sheriff's station. We also had help from several print resources: Michael Shnayerson's *Coal River*, Jeff Goodell's *Big Coal*, and *Coal Country*, edited by Shirley Stewart Burns, Mari-Lynn Evans, and Silas House.

We very much appreciate the efforts of all the groups working to educate the public about mountaintop removal mining. Special thanks to the online resources provided by ILoveMountains.org, EndMTR.com, EarthJustice.org, and Ken Ward Jr.'s coverage of all things coal mining for the *Charleston Gazette*'s Coal Tattoo blog.

Most of all, we'd like to thank all of our readers. We're glad you shared AJ's story and hope you enjoyed it. Never forget: there's a heroine inside us all.

We'd love to hear your thoughts. You can reach us through www .cjlyons.net.

Best wishes,
Erin and CJ

━━━━━ O N E ━━━━━

"Hi, you're on the air with AJ Palladino, the People's Champion." I couldn't help but cringe every time I chirped the greeting, but the station manager insisted on using the title foisted on me by *People* magazine, so I had no choice.

Unlike my freelance research work, this radio gig kept food on the table and a roof over our heads. Small price to pay. Didn't mean I had to like it.

"AJ, hi again!" came a woman's voice. Happy, unlike many of my callers. "It's Martha. Martha from Pennsylvania."

The computer screen in front of me lit up with Martha's history and her previous calls. But I didn't need to read the details. As soon as I heard her name and voice I remembered. "Martha from Deercreek. You were having some problems with a fish kill in your stream, if I recall?"

"You remember! Thanks to you, we've been able to finally get things put right."

"We found you a contact with your state Department of Environmental Protection, and I think the local Ag-extension was going to help set up monitoring for your well?"

"The Ag-extension folks were so helpful. Turns out we weren't the only property affected. Two more farms downstream were as well. And the DEP, well, there was some hassle there at first, but I did what you

1

said, I kept calm and just insisted that they do their jobs and investigate. And you know what? Turns out it was a dry cleaner from in town. Too cheap to pay to safely dispose of all those chemicals, he thought he could come out here and pump them into our creek! But they caught him, red-handed. And now he's paying to clean it all up—him and the state. Anyway, I wanted to thank you for all your help. It means the world to me and my neighbors."

It wasn't often that people took the time to call back and say thanks, so of course I smiled and gave my producer a double thumbs-up. "Thank you, Martha. Without people like you being willing to take a stand for what's right, guys like your dry cleaner would get away with destroying our environment and our communities just to save themselves a few bucks. You're a real people's champion."

My producer cued the cheers, applause, and celebratory sound effects. We signed off from Martha and took the next call. "Hi, you're on the air with AJ Palladino, the People's Champion."

"You're the one who took on Capital Power, won all that money for those folks?" This guy didn't sound near as happy as Martha.

"I helped. It wasn't about the money, though. It was about helping the people whose families suffered after their water was contaminated by Capital Power." I chose my words judiciously. The court case was famous, over and done with for four years, but every day someone just had to remind me of it—and of how far I'd fallen since.

Cinderella, the day after the ball. When she learned the prince didn't put the toilet seat down, the royal horse stalls needed mucking, and glass slippers weren't the most practical attire when running your ass off all day long in a palace with marble floors.

"What about helping all us people out of work now that Capital declared bankruptcy? You gonna go to court for us? Fight for our right to feed our families?" His words skidded together, building momentum like a NASCAR driver spotting the checkered flag.

"Sir, I'm not a lawyer—"

He drowned me out before I could finish my routine disclaimer. "No, you're just the bitch who took my job and my house, and now I can't even look my wife and kids in the eye. We're living in a tent. A goddamn tent! All because of you—"

I signaled my producer to record and trace the caller's location. Sitting up straight, I pressed my headset hard against my ear, as if I could channel the intentions behind his words.

"Sir, tell me more. How many kids do you have?" I tried in vain to engage him. Some were like that—they'd phone in to rant and vent and call me names that had the producer tapping the bleep button faster than a telegraph key. Those shows always made the station manager grin as ratings spiked. Usually I gave as good as I got. But something about this guy. . . .

"What do you care? The People's Champion, my ass. This is all your fault. Remember that, bitch. All your fault."

A blast thundered through my headphones. I tore the headset off, my ears ringing so loud I didn't realize I was shouting. "Sir, sir! Are you all right? What happened?"

The ON THE AIR light faded to black. I climbed off my stool, my balance wobbly. "Did you find him? Is he okay?"

"We've called nine-one-one. There's nothing more I can do." My producer was calm as he switched out PSA spots to fill the dead air.

"That was a gunshot."

The switchboard lights danced like firecrackers. He ignored them. We wouldn't be taking any more calls. Not today. Maybe not ever.

Sinking into the chair beside him, I cupped my ears, trying to muffle the screeching echo still rattling my fillings. "He's dead, isn't he?"

The direct line rang. He answered it, listened, then said, "Thank you," and hung up.

"Tell me." I wanted to throw up, needed to throw up, just to have an excuse to curl up alone in a bathroom stall, but instead I hung on to the arms of the vinyl chair, squeezing all my hope into their faux-leather padding.

"You can't blame yourself," he said in a tone meant to be kind.

I squeezed my eyes shut, blocking out the sight of his lips moving, letting the echo of the gunshot stampede through my brain.

"He's dead."

Four months later. . . .

The tug-of-war in my stomach was a tractor pull pitting an eighteen-wheeler against a Panzer tank. My blinding headache as I hunched over the steering wheel of the van and peered through the equally blinding rain didn't help. Once we'd left the concrete tangle of highways surrounding D.C. and made it over the West Virginia border we were on two-lane switchbacked highways crossing through the Appalachians.

Home. The word filled me with dread—and yet also offered a tantalizing feeling of anticipation. Maybe this time. . . .

When we were kids, we used to whine that Scotia, West Virginia, was the town where dreams went to die.

But I'd escaped.

I'd lived my dreams. Lost most of them. Except the most important one, the one sleeping in the backseat, his corduroy snores harmonizing with the beat of the windshield wipers.

David. Almost ten years old and going to meet his grandparents for the first time. Not to mention his first trip to the mountains. First time leaving D.C. since he was an infant in my arms.

Was I crawling back, a failure, a fool for returning to the town that had tried so hard to assassinate my dreams? Or was I really still just a kid myself, coming home at twenty-seven to be healed?

Lord, how I wanted it to be the latter, that Walton's Thanksgiving special where John Boy reunites with his father and everyone ends up safe and sound, wrapped in a crazy quilt of love. . . .

I passed the WELCOME TO SCOTIA, POPULATION 867 sign and noted the bullet holes that had blown out the center of every "o" and dotted every "i." Nothing changed. Good-bye, Walton fantasy—hello, Scotia reality.

With all the finesse of a roundhouse punch, that reality hit home when I pulled up in front of my parents' house and saw that the only light on was upstairs. Last week, when I'd called to let her know I was coming home, my mom had been so excited by the idea of getting to know her only grandchild that she'd insisted I stay with her and Dad instead of with my grandmother, as I'd planned.

She'd gushed about preparing a room for us to share, said it would be no problem to accommodate David, none at all. Of course, she'd also poured on the guilt about me keeping David from her for so long—as if it'd been my idea.

Goes to show how low I'd fallen that I'd taken her at face value. Of all people, I should have known better. Usually I'm the biggest skeptic in a crowd, too guarded, barricaded even, but she'd suckered me into trusting her. And stupid me, I'd told David about it.

"Is the ramp around back?" he asked, his voice still ragged from sleep. "If they don't have it ready, I could use my crutches."

David was so excited about making a good impression on his grandparents—he'd changed clothes three times before we left D.C. I glanced in the rearview mirror and saw that he had his face pressed against the window. A kid on Christmas Eve, searching the sky for Santa.

And I was about to give him a lump of coal. Courtesy of my folks, Frank and Edna Palladino.

"No crutches. Not in this rain and mud."

"Mo-o-om." He dragged it out to three syllables. "I can do it. You're not going to carry me." The horror!

"Let me run in first, see what's going on." See if I could salvage anything, protect him from having all his familial fantasies crushed.

I jumped from the van before he could protest and dashed through the rain to the front porch of the only home I'd ever known. The doorknob was icy cold. I stopped myself before turning it. Going on ten years since I left—should I knock first, like a stranger?

The doorbell echoed through the darkened downstairs. After a few minutes the hall light came on, and my father came tromping down the steps. He looked surprised to see me, but long experience told me he was faking it. Denial, our family's drug of choice.

"Angela, what are you doing here?" He opened the door. He didn't invite me inside but instead stood there filling the doorway with his broad shoulders, barricading the entrance.

"Did you forget we were coming today?" For David's sake, I didn't lash out the way I wanted. Instead, I played along with his delusions. "That's okay, we can sort things out in the morning. Mom said she'd have the downstairs bedroom ready for us." It was a tiny room, called the "maid's room" back ninety years ago when the house had first been built, but it had its own bath and wouldn't need a lot of work to accommodate David's wheelchair.

"Well, see, we just didn't realize how much work it would take. . . ." He peered over my head to the van, trying to make out David's face. But the windows had steamed up, and all you could see of David was a black blob bouncing in anticipation. "It's just not fair to your mom, asking her to care for a crip——, a handicapped child. And not fair to you or David," he added, as if he was doing us a favor.

As much as I'd have loved to punch him in the nose and take David away from this town, we had nowhere to go. If there was one thing I'd discovered in the years I'd spent away from Scotia, it was that as long as I had breath in my body, I'd do whatever it took to protect my child.

Didn't matter if it meant facing down a grizzly with its tail caught in a hornets' nest or groveling to my parents. David was my heart and soul—everything I did, I did for him, so he'd have a future better than any I'd ever dreamed of, so he'd have a present that was the best I could give him, so he'd never look upon his past with dread and anger and fear like I did.

I dug in for one last try. "Is Mom around?"

"She's having one of her spells." Pain shadowed his face as he shifted his weight from one leg to the other, still blocking the doorway.

It was Mom he was protecting. The "spells" started after my brother died, fifteen years ago. Our family secret. As if grief was something to be ashamed of. He stepped forward, forcing me to step back.

"Okay. I guess we'll spend the night in the van." I wasn't serious, of course. But venting some of my anger made me feel a little better.

He actually nodded, his gaze not quite vacant—I gauged it as a two-thirds-of-the-six-pack-consumed stage. His own nightly trip into oblivion.

Then he got this wistful smile that made me remember swinging off a rope into a pond, his strong arms stretched open to catch me. A younger me, trusting him, making the leap.

"Does he have your eyes? Those green Costello eyes? You get that gypsy blood from your mom's side of the family, that's why you couldn't stay put here."

Memories unearthed themselves like zombies clawing their way out of a freshly dug grave. I held on to the door, the wood gouging my palm, and fought to bury them once more. I couldn't "stay put" in Scotia because I'd been LifeFlighted out ten years ago, half-past dead. Me and David—although he hadn't been born yet. That had been another rainy night.

"Try your gram. Edna said something to her about your coming back." I noted that he didn't say "coming home."

With that, he turned and climbed back up the steps, turning the light off when he reached the top, leaving me standing just outside the threshold, in the dark.

A familiar dread and uncertainty roiled over me, making me feel off balance, unable to remember the life I'd built for myself as an adult, feeling dwarfed, diminished. Meaningless. Nothing.

I was definitely back home.

TWO

David, little genius that he is, said nothing as we pulled away from the curb and I made a five-point turn to head the van in the direction of my grandmother's farm.

Sometimes my fury and exhaustion make me rant. Sometimes his frustrations and anger make him rave. Thankfully, we rarely rant and rave at the same time. Good thing, since he inherited my take-no-prisoners temper.

A temper that had gotten me fired from my past two jobs before the radio station. After my initial success with the Capital Power case, I'd been assigned to assess the viability of another class-action suit against a chemical company accused of contaminating ground water when it illegally disposed of a now-banned insecticide called toxaphene. I'd gotten close to the potential clients—too close. Got caught up in my passion to find them justice and spent millions of the firm's money trying to find the "smoking gun" that would prove our case.

When I found nothing, again and again, and the firm decided to drop the case, I lashed out at the senior partners during one of their monthly golf outings. Actually dumped a gallon of toxic sludge from one of our clients' backyards into a golf bag with brand-new thousand-dollar titanium-whatever-hoopla clubs.

It wasn't a big surprise when they spread the word to other law firms, effectively blacklisting me. After that, I vowed not to let my temper or passion get in the way of doing my job.

Of course, that was before I slapped the congressman.

So sue me, I'm a work in progress. At least I'm trying. Coming home, facing my family and everything I'd fled ten years ago, I was going to have to try harder than ever. Dad's response was proof of that.

Gram Flora's house was across the hollow, on the edge of town, as far away from the coal mine as you could get. Situated in the middle of a twenty-acre apple orchard that had been in my grandfather's family, the Hightowers, for generations, it had always been my safe haven.

As we steered through the rain, the van's threadbare tires slipping on the gravel drive winding up the hill to Gram's house, I saw that some things never change.

"Mom, you're smiling," David said in wonder. Like he couldn't remember the last time I'd smiled. The thought knifed beneath the joy uplifting me at the sight of the lights on throughout Gram's two-story traditional farmhouse. She'd even left the porch light on for us.

More than that, there were two aluminum truck ramps aligned over the porch steps and a sheet of plywood leading up to the front door, covering the small step there.

"Thank you, Flora," I said, my breath escaping in a rush as I stopped the van and sat in silence, enjoying the moment of peace.

The front door opened and Gram Flora emerged, beckoning like an orchestra conductor, waving us in out of the cold and rain. She was a scrawny thing, bent and crooked from her seventy-three years, but always in motion despite the fact that she was pretty near totally blind. At her side appeared a handsome man who looked to be a few years younger than me, maybe twenty-four or twenty-five, black, with a shaved scalp and a smile as welcoming and full of amusement as Flora's.

Ignoring the rain, he dashed out to the van and opened David's door. "Hi! You must be David. I'm Jeremy. Did I get the ramps spaced okay?"

I could have kissed him, the way he put David in charge. David craned his neck out the door, scrutinized the ramps, calculating the angle and pitch and traction, then smiled and said, "Let's give it a try."

No arguing about risking his crutches on the slick porch steps, and he even let Jeremy help him into his chair while I unfolded my achy bones from the driver's seat and came around the van to oversee.

"Angie." Gram Flora was the only person on earth I allowed to call me Angie. I was "AJ" to just about anyone I was on speaking terms with. "The boys will be fine. You come in out of that rain before you freeze." Even though she couldn't see me, somehow she seemed to know that while David was bundled in a hooded parka, I wore only jeans and a sweatshirt, my coat buried somewhere in the recesses of the van.

As a kid, I thought Flora's blindness was really some kind of magical second sight, like Superman's X-ray vision. I wondered and worried that since I had her weirdly unsettling green eyes—like looking up through the water from the bottom of a pond when the sun was directly overhead—I might also grow up to be blind and all-seeing.

Now I know it was years of diabetes and not taking proper care of herself. Unlike most fairy tales, reality is worse than any wicked witch or evil stepmother.

But that doesn't mean that there isn't still such a thing as magic—or magic incantations. Because then Flora said, "Come on in. I've got coffee and hot cobbler."

We talked until past midnight before I finally went to bed.

Ever wake up in the morning, waiting for the coffee to finish brewing as you pour your kid's cereal, feeling like you've wandered into *The Sound of Music*, the sun is shining, the birds are humming, and so are you?

But then the dream ends with a crash, and it's the kid shaking you awake, the alarm is blaring, there're no clean socks, it's five minutes till the school bus, he needs lunch money, all you have is a quarter and two cough drops, and all you want to do is crawl back into that dream world?

This morning was not like that.

I couldn't remember ever having a morning like this. Waking up with the scent of clean sheets in my face, all warm and cozy under a fluffy stack of blankets and quilts. Rolling over and letting myself drift back into oblivion. Opening my eyes again an hour or so later and realizing it wasn't a dream—it was whitewashed walls and gingham curtains and Murphy's Oil and blessed silence.

A glimpse of heaven.

The first full night's sleep I'd had in ten years. I was a scared seventeen-year-old kid when I'd had David, surviving a trauma only to give birth to a premature baby. The little sleep I had in the hospital was in the rocker beside his incubator; then I was set loose in the world alone with a special-needs baby; then he was a special-needs and exceptionally gifted little boy while I was a single, working mom; and always he embodied my hopes and dreams and worries and fears and future . . . so really, there just wasn't room for sleep in my life.

Gram had put us up in the summerhouse—a square, single-story cottage with a wraparound porch and large windows that pushed out to welcome the breeze from any direction. She and her husband—my Grandfather Hightower, who died the month I was born—had built it to house migrant workers while the orchard was still going. When I was a kid, one of my favorite traditions was joining Gram, my folks, and Randy, my big brother, to "air out" the summerhouse and get it ready for the workers.

We'd slap on a new coat of white paint—Randy and me getting more on us than on the walls—hang fresh gingham curtains, wash the oak floors, and air out the bunk-bed mattresses and the braided rag rugs.

The inside of the house used to be one big open area, with the kitchen and bath in the rear of the house, but over the years it got partitioned into a front room, two smaller bedrooms behind it, and the wide-open kitchen and a large bathroom/laundry room. It had no heat except for the fireplaces and wood burner, but now that I wasn't blurry with exhaustion, I noticed a space heater, its grill glowing, standing in the hall between my room and David's.

I luxuriated in the shower without rationing hot water. David was an early riser and had grown fiercely independent with his morning routine; I was sure he'd been up for hours. Slipping into sweats and my sneakers, I hugged my arms to my chest to keep warm as I stepped out the backdoor.

The March wind scurried along the ridge as if it too had overslept. The sun was above the hemlocks already, and the rain the night before had scoured the air, leaving behind the crisp spark of winter and spring colliding.

It was freezing, in the midthirties at most without factoring in the wind, but I couldn't help it, I just had to stop and drink in the view that had filled my heart for the past ten years every time I closed my eyes and thought of home.

Gram's place was halfway up Hightower Mountain. The vista swept out beneath my feet like a magician conjuring yards and yards of green silk from his outstretched hand. For the first time in a decade, I remembered how to breathe. Not just filling my lungs with air, but filling my entire body.

A hawk pirouetted in the air over the valley—no, not a hawk, I saw, but a turkey buzzard. No matter, it seemed to enjoy showing off to the earthbound human, dancing along an updraft, then diving below the ridgeline, out of sight once more. My blood soared along with it, my heart racing to catch up.

Home. I was home.

Finally, the wind and cold drove me away from the ledge and up the back porch steps. As soon as I opened Gram's kitchen door I was greeted by the smells of a wood fire, coffee, and biscuits. Even better, making me feel as dizzy as if my feet had temporarily escaped the bonds of gravity, was the sound of my son laughing. I would crawl through fire for that sound.

Suddenly my parents and their deficits in the welcome-home department seemed irrelevant, petty inconveniences. Before I left Scotia ten years ago, I'd learned not to let Frank and Edna gnaw away at my soul—I'd simply have to rebuild my defenses, extend them to protect David as well.

Don't get the wrong impression. My parents aren't mean and cruel on purpose. They're just damaged. Ever since my big brother, Randy, died. Putting up with my endless questions and my tagging after him, he was my hero.

Randy was sixteen when he got mono. So handsome—you should have seen the girls squabbling about who would bring him his homework or bake him cookies while he was home sick. Then he got better, went back to school, and back to football.

The doctors said it sometimes happens. Mono leaves the spleen enlarged, vulnerable to the slightest hit from the wrong direction. He collapsed during practice, died in the back of the ambulance as they rushed him over the mountain to the hospital in Smithfield. By the time my parents arrived, he was cold and gone.

I was a little older than David is now—a stubborn, difficult child who loved to argue and question everything and who never shut up. Pretty much the same as I am now. But my folks, they needed me to just shut up, to just go away, to just stop being. At least long enough for them to finish grieving.

Guess they've never finished. I pretty much took care of myself from then on—Randy's ghost took up too much room in their lives for me to find a way back in.

That's probably why I am the way I am. Any guy I've ever dated more than once says I'm a control freak. Can't argue with that. But when you've lived a life as out of control as mine, who's to say that's a bad thing?

It's like suddenly looking at your hand scratching your arm without even realizing you had an itch—it's that much in your nature. I see a problem, I have to fix it. No, not just have to. Need to.

"How do you spell your name?" David was asking Jeremy, Gram's personal care assistant, as they sat at Gram's kitchen table, a massive plank of oak that could seat a dozen hungry farm workers.

"J-e-r-e-m-y," Jeremy answered.

A mischievous grin squinted David's face, a favorite look of mine that I hadn't seen in a while, not since I lost my job with the radio station. "Wrong. Y-o-u-r-n-a-m-e."

"Argh. . . ." Jeremy rolled his eyes and collapsed with his head on the table, acting like he'd been mortally wounded. He was twenty-four, had his LPN degree, and talked with a Pittsburgh accent that sounded ruler-flat alongside Gram's rolling mountain cadences. After talking with him the night before, I wondered why an openly homosexual black man would move to an insular and unforgiving small town like Scotia, but it was obvious that he adored my gram and they enjoyed each other's company, so I hadn't asked.

Jeremy sat up again. "Okay, my turn. There's a priest, a rabbi, and a monkey out fishing. . . ."

I indulged in a little hope to sweeten my coffee, waltzing through the kitchen and grabbing a mug from where they hung from beneath the cabinets, joining David, Jeremy, and Gram Flora at the table.

"Good morning!" I practically sang the words.

"Morning was a few hours ago," Gram said with a crack of laughter. Not derisive, more appreciative. She was typing away on a small laptop equipped with a special keyboard with raised characters, listening through an earbud in one ear as the computer read her her e-mail. "But you sound human again."

"Thanks. I feel human again." I rumpled David's hair—he hated it, shied away as always, but it was a mother's prerogative. "How'd you sleep?"

"Great. The birds are noisy in the morning. One of them came the whole way up to the porch to eat, right there in front of me."

"Boy acted like he'd never seen a finch before." This time there was a hint of disapproval in Flora's voice.

"Guess we'll have to remedy that," I matched my inflection to her singsong dialect that wandered up and down the scale like the mountain switchbacks. I finished my coffee and sighed with satisfaction. The clock said 10:08. Scandalous. "I'd better call Zachariah Hardy and let him know I won't be in until this afternoon."

Flora pulled the earbud out and closed her laptop. Jeremy rattled his spoon against his tea mug.

"Zachariah Hardy the lawyer?" Jeremy asked. He exchanged a lop-sided glance with Flora, his gaze fixing on her face and her blind eyes just missing his.

"Of course the lawyer," I answered, my radar pinging but my mood too good to pay it full attention. Hardy couldn't have fired me—I hadn't even set foot in his office yet. Plus, he knew all about my back-ground—why would he change his mind now? "You didn't think I came home to mooch off family, did you? It may not be much of a job—filing and answering phones and such—but it should be enough to pay our keep."

Jeremy stood. "C'mon, David, I'll show you the rabbits." He made his escape, David with him.

Flora was shaking her head, short little shakes like trying to scatter a swarm of gnats. "Honey, I would've told you, but I didn't want to risk you changing your mind about coming home. You may want to read the newspaper."

"Newspaper?" My short-lived serenity fled, replaced by familiar anxiety. "What happened?"

I grabbed the *Mountain Gazette*, thinner than a single section of the *Washington Post*, and unfolded it across the table. The front page was filled with photos of tree-sitters and environmental activists protesting Masterson Mining's latest project: a new coal-washing site it wanted to build on land just behind the school. It was an idiotic idea, and I couldn't help my eye-roll. Some things never changed. Old Man Masterson deserved any bad press he got.

"Isn't Hardy defending the protesters? Maybe I should get over to the office earlier."

"He was." Flora's tone was sympathetic. "But if you want to find out where Zachariah Hardy will be later today, turn to the obituaries."

Her words didn't hit me all at once, but more like hail pinging off a tin roof—little strikes here and there, followed by a major dent that shook my foundation.

"You're kidding me." The pages flew as I shuffled through to the obits. And there it was. Hardy's picture, funeral details, a short description of his work at a Philadelphia mega-conglomerate before he abandoned big-city law to turn to environmental activism here in his hometown of Scotia, West Virginia. Made it sound like he was single-handedly fighting the monster-truck political machine that was King Coal.

Until his untimely death, presumed to be from a heart attack.

Gram reached across the table, found my hand, and patted it. I was so numb, I barely felt her touch.

"Hope you brought something black to wear."

THREE

Elizabeth Hardy sat in the backseat of the black Cadillac, inhaling the scent of mothballs, cigarettes, and tears. The funeral director had insisted on driving her, didn't think it seemly that a grief-stricken daughter would drive herself. Plus, he had clear doubts about her ability to navigate her way "across the holler and up the hill"—everything in this place seemed to be up a hill—seeing as how she was a flatlander, as if Philadelphia was as far from Scotia as Samoa.

The funeral director jerked his head in a sudden twisting motion and spat tobacco juice into a Mason jar he kept in the cup holder. Scratch that last thought—she doubted he had any clue where Samoa was.

"We're here, miss," he said. "Let me check up on things, and I'll be back to escort you."

The funeral director–chauffeur–undertaker, who also owned the local florist-and-formalwear shop and a used-car dealership, popped out of the car like a pigeon bobbing for breadcrumbs, spry for a man who appeared to be in his sixties. He reminded her of the old character actor who was often Cary Grant's foil, Edward Everett Horton, one of her father's favorites.

Sniffing back tears, Elizabeth sat with as little of her body touching the seat as possible. The upholstery was supposed to be leather but definitely had come from no cow of earthly origin. And that smell . . . she opened the door, letting the scent of damp earth flood over her. She put one foot out, only to have her Kate Spade pump sink into mud and gravel. Great.

This was why she hated funerals. Not like anyone enjoyed them. But this one . . . she felt like she barely knew her own father, a man who had always been too busy and too focused on his career to be distracted by a little thing like a daughter. At least until three years ago, when he'd had his middle-aged breakdown and returned to his West Virginia roots to protect his "home." Since then, they'd slowly begun to connect, not so much as father and daughter, but as almost-friends.

Maybe she'd never really known him. Which was sad, but also no different than the relationship she had with her mother.

Her mother had insisted that Elizabeth come to the funeral—yet had excused herself, saying, "We've been divorced longer than we were married." So what did that make Elizabeth? The cast-off remnant of a marriage gone wrong between two people unsuited to share their lives with anyone?

She twisted the thought around her mouth—it tasted bitter on her lips. But truthful. No wonder she hadn't been able to salvage her own marriage.

That was why she hated funerals—they made people face the truth about themselves, and right now she could see the frightening parallels between her life and her father's. Both divorced before they were thirty-five, both deeply unhappy with their chosen "noble" profession of the law, both restless, wanting more, but too cowardly to define their dreams, much less dare to dream them.

No, that wasn't fair. Her father had dared to dream. Because of his dream, he'd abandoned everything. Funny how hard he'd worked to leave his small-town childhood behind, yet in the end he'd left his world of corporate wealth to return home and fight for this place.

She climbed the rest of the way out of the car, looking down the side of the mountain ("hill," her ass) to the scattered coal dust–covered roofs that freckled the countryside. Scotia wasn't big enough to be a town, maybe not even a village.

Her father had never brought her here to visit when she was young—his relatives were all dead or gone. He'd never invited her here after he moved back three years ago, at least not until she'd left Hunter and begun the divorce proceedings. By then, the last thing she'd wanted was to try to force another strained relationship back on track . . . and fail. Again. So she'd declined her father's invitations, although she did enjoy the letters—real letters, handwritten scrawls on yellow legal-pad paper—he'd started to send her.

The graveyard was hidden behind a row of large evergreens with a gravel path winding between them. Elizabeth began up the path, her usual stride hamstrung by the mud sucking at her heels, more rapacious than Bela Lugosi's Dracula—so much better than Chaney's or . . . her mind stumbled, forgetting the actor's name although she could clearly visualize his face. Lee. Of course, Christopher Lee. How could she have forgotten that? Her father loved Christopher Lee, thought he was one of the great unsung actors of B-movie history.

Pausing to clear her head, she drank in the chilled air. It smelled thin compared to the multi-layered heaviness of the city. She remembered phone calls with her father anchored in a safe topic—their mutual love of campy old movies—that had helped them avoid the awkward silences. She'd miss those talks. They were the only time she felt truly connected to her father.

When she'd gone into family law, she'd thought it would be about keeping families together. That she'd discover the secret she'd never learned from her own parents. How wrong she had been.

Then she realized that she was about to give the funeral director what he expected: a woman tottering along, bewildered and bowled over by emotion, forced to take his arm to steady herself, crying.

She straightened her posture and continued on her path, conquering the mud that conspired to unbalance her. Her father may not have given her much of his attention when she was young, but he had instilled in her a strict code of behavior: Hardys didn't totter, and they never cried.

The trail took her uphill through the rows of trees, opening up onto a wide expanse of brown grass and gray headstones clinging to the side of the mountain. Before she could register the spectacular view she was blinded by the glare of flashbulbs and cameras.

"Ms. Hardy." A reporter dressed in a Burberry overcoat shoved his microphone at her. "Are you going to take up your father's environmental crusade, preserve his legacy?"

"What about the Ladies?" another called, this one holding a small digital recorder.

The TV people jostled to get in her face, and a brunette reporter in a skirt three inches shorter than Elizabeth's, wearing no coat over her suit, sidled up. "Elizabeth, how did you feel about your father playing David to Masterson Mining's Goliath? Do you think it was the stress of the fight that killed him?"

Elizabeth blinked, the questions battering her from all sides. She was surrounded, not sure of which way lay escape.

Help came from a surprising source. A woman a few years younger than Elizabeth, with blond hair and green eyes—wearing black jeans, black cowboy boots, a black T-shirt that looked to be two sizes too small, and a black motorcycle jacket two sizes too large—shoved her way through the crowd, took Elizabeth's arm, and bullied her way clear.

"Ms. Hardy has no comment," the blonde shouted over her shoulder as the reporters protested.

The wind cut between the gravestones, rippling the hem of Elizabeth's lambskin coat, but the blonde paid it no attention as she marched them up the hill.

They arrived at the gravesite. At the sight of the hole in the ground where her father would spend the rest of eternity, Elizabeth's legs went wobbly. The blonde gripped her arm tighter, supporting Elizabeth more than anyone else would notice, as if she were used to helping someone suddenly swamped by grief.

"I'm AJ," the blonde told her.

Elizabeth barely heard her. She couldn't look up from the gaping hole, which seemed ready and eager to swallow her father. The artificial grass carpet attempting to camouflage it was torn in places, and mud squished through from beneath. One flap of the too-green-to-be-real carpet had fallen into the grave, revealing the winter-compacted red clay wall gouged by a backhoe's blade, the ribbons of earth leaving behind streaks like a trail of blood.

A shudder almost toppled Elizabeth, but the blonde held her firm. She forced her gaze away from the dark maw and discovered that twice as many people as she'd seen at the church had come to attend the burial. Had her father made that many friends here, despite crusading for such an unpopular cause?

Silent laughter flinched across her skin. More likely the people had shown up here because this was where the cameras were. Zachariah Hardy's final moments aboveground turned into a media circus.

Jeremy had offered me the use of his truck anytime I needed it, but it was such a beautiful day, I preferred to walk. He and Flora would have the van, in case they needed to go someplace with David. Plus, the way roads are around here, it's often just about as fast to walk cross-country as it is to drive down the mountain, follow the road around the base, and then twist and wind your way halfway up the ridge again.

I was too late for the church service. No surprise there—Flora always said I'd be late to my own funeral. Which, you gotta figure, isn't an altogether bad thing. But I arrived at the cemetery in time to save Hardy's daughter from a mob of rapacious reporters.

She definitely wasn't from around here. Brunette hair slicked back and smelling of exotic flowers, ankle-length shearling coat, designer suit and shoes, posture so rigid that she walked like she had a stick up her ass you'd need dynamite to blast free.

Couldn't be anyone except Hardy's daughter, Elizabeth. Besides, I could smell "lawyer" wafting off her—it's a smell that crawls under your skin so you can't wash it off. Get too close, it sometimes rubs off on folks like me who do the real work around law firms.

Hardy had sounded different from other lawyers when I spoke to him on the phone—my job interview, he called it. It was more like two old friends catching up, even though we'd never met. Said he'd been a high-powered corporate litigator in the city for thirty years before coming to his senses. We only talked a few times, but I'd liked him, was looking forward to working with him. Looking forward to getting back to doing work that mattered.

When the crowd of reporters ambushed the daughter, she said nothing, but her mask slipped for an instant, revealing the vulnerability of a child who has suddenly lost a parent. Then she straightened, as if girding herself for a battle.

I chided myself for misjudging her. It's a habit I'm constantly fighting to break, especially since I hate it when people judge me on my appearance or how I talk.

The only black clothing that had been easy to find while rummaging through my suitcase was a pair of black jeans and a Godsmack T-shirt that I'd turned inside out and wore under the black leather motorcycle jacket I'd stolen from a former boyfriend. Pushing through the crowd, taking the opportunity to kick some shins with the steel toes of my cowboy boots, I made it to her side and pulled her free. Seemed the least I could do—help her bury her father in peace.

We made it to the gravesite, and I saw why the media was here. A group of half a dozen girls danced on the lawn, all with hair down to their waist, dressed in gauzy flowing dresses with fluttery sleeves and gathered bodices, a cross between hippies and medieval ladies-in-waiting. I shivered for the Ladies—they had to be freezing in those thin frocks. Middle of March, but somehow they'd gotten fresh flowers for their hair. Probably from George McCoy, who would have charged them outlandish prices for a few stems stolen from funeral arrangements paid for by others.

Their dance was a hypnotic, slow-motion whirling dervish around a man who stood at their center. Yancey, the leader of Free Earth. I'd read about him in the newspaper that morning. He wasn't a tall man—most of his Ladies stood taller than he did—but he commanded your attention with his straight posture, full head of thick, brown hair that flowed Charles Manson–like to his collarbones, and dark, penetrating eyes that missed nothing. The kind of man who would come to show his support for a "lost friend" and use the opportunity to turn his dead lawyer's funeral into a public protest.

There I was, judging again, but all it took was one look. I didn't like Yancey.

There were also a number of men wearing Sunday suits and a scattering of women clutching handkerchiefs. A cluster of locals were dressed in jeans with T-shirts that had the Masterson Mining logo—two large Ms crossed like they were mountain ranges—inside a circle with a red slash across it. The homegrown protesters looked with disdain on the antics of the Free Earth clowns, who now swayed in time to a hymn to Gaia.

After glowering at Yancey's crowd, who simmered down to a low hum, the minister finally got started. The girls crowded around Yancey, all of them reaching out a hand to touch him on the arms or shoulders or back, as if he offered them sustenance.

As the minister intoned his prayers and read from the Bible, my attention drifted. I wished I had brought something to lay on my Grandfather Hightower's grave. He was buried several rows over, in a place of honor on the edge of the plateau, where he'd have a direct view of his beloved mountain.

It had been a Masterson from two generations back who killed him. Twenty-seven years ago, Absalom Hightower had tried to revive the coal miners' union and had come close to winning. But the night the workers were voting to strike, Absalom's truck had been forced off the side of the mountain. He'd been found at the bottom, pinned by the wreckage, his chest ravaged by a shotgun blast.

The coroner, a Masterson cousin, had ruled his death an accident, saying the shotgun was Absalom's and had gone off during the collision. The union was disbanded, and the strike ended before it got a chance to start.

Folks around here say I have a lot of my grandfather in me, which isn't necessarily a good thing—not here in Masterson country.

Elizabeth stood beside me, her body occasionally swaying in time with the minister's words, as if she was having a hard time staying anchored. Her eyes never left the hole in the ground, ignoring the casket resting on the rails above it. I don't think she even noticed Yancey and his harem.

Why Hardy had added them to his client roster, I had no clue. It didn't seem to fit the man who praised the grassroots local groups for their fight against Masterson Mining. Maybe he'd joined with Yancey to take the fight to the next level? Yancey's Free Earth certainly had drawn media attention that the local groups couldn't. Or maybe Yancey had gotten involved after he heard that Hardy had won a hearing before the State Supreme Court.

None of my business—not anymore. Unless I could convince his daughter to hire me.

Once the minister finished, the small crowd—reporters and protesters outnumbering mourners—dispersed. As they did, I spotted a dark-haired woman at the back of the group opposite me, almost hidden behind a Masterson grandsire's monument. A man stood close enough beside her for their sleeves to touch, but they were not holding hands.

Remember that carnival game where you swing the sledgehammer as hard as you can and ring the bell? That sledgehammer collided with my brain so hard that not only did I hear ringing, but I felt like my head was going to explode off my shoulders and land with a *thunk* on top of Hardy's coffin.

My knees sagged, and I held on to Elizabeth's arm. She was sobbing and probably thought I was offering her comfort. Far from it. I was trying to save myself.

What was *he* doing here? He was the last person I'd expected to see in Scotia. He'd sworn he'd never come back, promised me he would escape. Once upon a time, I thought he'd take me with him, rescue me.

He wasn't supposed to be here. Over the years, when I'd thought of him—reaching for the phone in the middle of the night and then dropping it, unwilling to disrupt his life and marriage or to cause him more pain than I already had—I'd always imagined him someplace warm and sunny. Belize, Santorini, Patagonia. Never here. Anyplace but here.

Anger flashed through my stunned surprise, leaving behind the ashes of despair. I'd braced myself to face disdain and derision—that was the price of coming home.

I hadn't prepared myself to face Cole Masterson.

To my anguish, he nodded to the woman, who stayed where she was, watching, and picked his way through the mud, shaking it from the hems of his designer slacks. He wore a black suit, white shirt, dark red tie, no overcoat. Polished, confident. Cole was only two years older than me, but I felt childish compared to him—and my clothes had nothing to do with the feeling.

I wanted to run, should have run, but I couldn't. My feet had sunk into the mud, and my stomach had tumbled even lower, spinning in free fall.

Elizabeth held out her hand as he joined us. "Mr. Masterson, thank you for coming."

I noticed an edge of contempt in her tone. Couldn't take the time to analyze it. I was too busy trying to find spit to swallow and the courage to meet his eyes. His face was as chiseled as those of the marble Masterson ancestors surrounding us. Colder than marble. Especially his eyes.

Used to be I could spend all day dreaming of those eyes on me.

No longer. Now they turned to me, offering nothing but a slap in the face.

"I'm sorry for your loss, Ms. Hardy," Cole replied, grasping her hand, his gaze locked onto my face.

He released her, stood silent, waiting for me. And I had nothing. Dragged down and out of my body, my voice had sunk into the damp earth like a mine shaft tunneling into the mountain.

He stared at me a moment longer, then flicked his gaze aside, casting me away as if emptying out the trash. Turned and walked away, his back stiffer than iron.

Elizabeth must have noticed the blood fleeing my face because suddenly she was the one squeezing my arm and holding me up. "What's wrong? Are you okay?"

What was I supposed to tell her? That that was Cole Masterson, onetime love of my life, the boy I'd almost died for, the father of my child?

I tried to suck in my breath to answer but couldn't get enough air. We were alone now in the cemetery, wide blue sky above us, air crisp and fresh, but there wasn't enough to fill my lungs. Just like ten years ago, I was drowning.

The memories sucked me down faster than the water had on that awful night. I felt my vision go black. Then both Elizabeth and George McCoy, the funeral director, were there, pushing me down onto a nearby stone bench, urging me to put my head down between my knees. The wind was freezing, but I was sweating, trembling.

"I had no idea she knew your father," George was saying over my head. "AJ hasn't even been back up to Scotia in ten years. Of course, her and Cole—now there's a tale to tell."

Bantering about my tragedy like beer-hall gossip. Fury cauterized my shock. I lurched to my feet, still unsteady, but by God I wasn't about to let anyone see it. "Mind your own business, George McCoy."

"Let us drive you home," Elizabeth offered, the rigid set of her facial muscles now softened by the idea of helping me. Seemed like my stupidity had taken her mind off her own worries for a few minutes.

Before we could move more than a few steps, the lady reporter and her cameraman hustled down the path toward us.

"Ms. Hardy, Ms. Hardy," she called, waving her hand like a schoolgirl who needed to use the restroom. They arrived in front of us, blocking our path. The reporter heaved in a breath, nodded to her cameraman, and said, "Elizabeth, would you care to comment on an anonymous tip we've received that your father was murdered?"

FOUR

Elizabeth stumbled back, her weight landing on my insole. I caught her, kept her upright. Her face had crumpled, twisted by surprise.

"What did you—who—why—" She pulled free from me and lunged for the reporter. "What are you talking about?"

The reporter sidestepped Elizabeth, taking care not to block the camera. I shoved myself between them. "Turn that camera off," I ordered. The cameraman looked to the reporter for instructions. "Now!"

The reporter nodded. The cameraman turned his camera off and lowered it.

"Why would you say that?" Elizabeth demanded. "Why would you think that about my father?"

As if the camera was still rolling and she was auditioning for a slot on a crime scene show, the reporter reached into her pocket and whipped out a piece of paper enclosed in a sandwich bag. Breadcrumbs slid along the bottom edge. Elizabeth reached for the paper, and I read over her shoulder. Stark, handprinted block letters lined the back of one of Hardy's funeral programs. Written in plain black ink, they appeared rushed but legible.

TELL THE DAUGHTER TO GO OR
SHE'LL END UP LIKE HER FATHER

"This doesn't say Hardy was murdered," I said.

"Might as well have." The reporter's eyes widened with delight, her hair not shifting a strand as she whipped around to face Elizabeth once more. "Who do you suspect, Elizabeth? One of Masterson's people? A local upset that your dad invited Yancey's Free Earth here? Maybe it was Yancey himself, trying to drum up more media attention."

"My father wasn't killed. He died from a seizure." Elizabeth's color had drained until she looked as gray as the headstones. I looked past her—George had gone to talk to the gravediggers, probably to tell them to hold off on filling in Hardy's grave.

"Who would do this?" Elizabeth asked, her voice trembling as much as her hand.

I took the note from her, snatching it away from the reporter when she reached for it. "Did you call the police?"

She frowned. "No, not yet."

"Do it now." Her smooth brow furrowed as she covered all the angles—how to make the most of the footage and inside knowledge she had without getting in trouble. I made up her mind for her. "If you don't, I will."

"Of course, it's our civic duty." She pulled her cell phone out, and a minute later she was talking with someone at the sheriff's department. I handed her back the paper. As she talked, I led Elizabeth away. "Hey, you can't leave," the reporter called after us. "Where are you going?"

"If the police want to talk with her, tell them she'll be at her father's house."

George joined us at the car, his expression almost as excited as the reporter's—it didn't take a lot to create a scandal in a little town like Scotia. Sad to say, this was probably the most excitement they'd had around here since, well, since I'd left ten years ago.

"Are you okay?" I asked Elizabeth as George eased us out of the parking lot.

She nodded, staring at her hands as she flexed and curled them. "Do you think she's right? That someone could have killed my father?"

"I don't know." How could I? I didn't even know Hardy was dead until this morning. "He didn't seem worried when we talked on the phone last week."

"I know, he seemed fine to me as well. Excited by the case." She smoothed the fabric of her skirt over her knees, playing with the hem. "But if someone did hurt him"—her voice stumbled as she avoided the "k" word—"if they did, why would they want to hurt me?"

The Cadillac lumbered its way down the switchbacks leading from the cemetery. "I lived in Philadelphia my entire life, and I've never known anyone who was a victim of serious violence," Elizabeth said, surprised at how casual she sounded as she discussed a threat on her life. "Two days here in my father's hometown and suddenly. . . ."

Her stomach lurched, and the taste of burnt coffee soured the back of her throat. She swallowed it down, rubbing her palm across the hem of her skirt. She didn't have enough information, so there was no use jumping to conclusions.

AJ shrugged. "Scotia has that effect on people."

Elizabeth wasn't sure if she meant that as a joke. If so, it wasn't funny. "You're not taking that note seriously? Who would want to hurt me?"

AJ didn't answer.

As the silence lengthened, anxiety fluttered through Elizabeth's nerves. The turmoil in her stomach felt like a boat about to capsize. If she had to breathe the rancid odor recirculating inside the car for one more minute she would hurl. She cracked the window, relishing the fresh air, and distracted herself by examining her traveling companion. So this was Angela Joy Palladino.

After her father had told her about hiring AJ, Elizabeth had searched out everything she could—part out of curiosity and part out of jealousy. Her father made AJ Palladino sound like Wonder Woman turned environmental crusader and had been excited about partnering with her, despite AJ's checkered past.

Elizabeth had pictured her more like the actress who had played her in the Lifetime movie: a buxom, blond, bimbo trailer-trash hillbilly taking on the Goliath that was Capital Power.

The real AJ, slumped against the seat, gaze unfocused, didn't seem at all like that. Well, she was blond. But she appeared young, vulnerable—a wayward kid pretending to be grown up.

Although she'd handled herself well at the cemetery, getting Elizabeth out of there, protecting her from that reporter.

"Do you think that note is real?" Elizabeth asked again, feeling weak for voicing the question. Denying the problem, returning home, thinking about it later—or never—would be so much easier. But she couldn't leave it alone. The thought of someone wanting to hurt her father or herself . . . it was outrageous. "Maybe it's just a publicity stunt."

"I don't know. Things happen around here." AJ frowned as she stared out the window. "Things that wouldn't happen anywhere else."

Elizabeth had just about convinced herself that the note was a prank, but something in AJ's tone made her tighten up inside all over again. "But I'm not from around here. I don't have anything to do with what happens around here. I only came to bury my father."

"You're not going to stay, finish his work?"

Elizabeth ignored the question. She knew what whoever wrote that sick note wanted her to do, knew what her father would have wanted her to do, knew what she wanted to do. What she didn't know was if she could do it. She needed time to think.

Desperate for something to take her mind off the note, and curious to understand why her father had been so impressed by AJ, Elizabeth changed the subject. "I heard about the guy who killed himself on your radio show."

AJ flinched, her leather jacket creaking with the sudden movement.

"That must have been hard."

AJ shrugged, turning to look out the window.

"So, you're from Scotia?"

Now a nod. Still no eye contact. As if the barren trees and mud-streaked boulders were more interesting than Elizabeth.

"I also heard about how you lost your job with Wykoff and Heath. No law firm would hire you after that, losing all that money on a no-win case."

That earned her a glare. AJ twisted in her seat, facing Elizabeth full on. "Don't forget the congressman I slapped after he pinched my ass."

Elizabeth had to chuckle. "Oh yeah, saw that on TMZ. The look on his face. I was actually surprised the lobbyist fired you. I would have given you a raise."

"That's what your father said." AJ's face softened. "I never had a chance to tell you how sorry I was for your loss. We only talked on the phone, but he sounded like a good man. Passionate about his work. Trying to make a difference."

It was Elizabeth's turn to stare out the window, inhaling the stale stench of the car, trying to regain control.

"Wish he'd been as passionate about his family," she murmured, immediately regretting the words, hoping AJ hadn't heard. AJ's reflection in the mirror showed she had, so Elizabeth kept her face turned away as town came into view.

Main Street was shadowed by empty storefronts on both sides. Ugly steel posts cut off at ankle height marked where parking meters had once lined the curbs—they were easy to see because all the parking spaces were vacant.

They turned right at the Methodist church onto her father's street. Instead of guillotined parking meters, it was lined with old sycamores and sagging picket fences. As if people here in Scotia were too worn out from fighting for their future to take care of their present—at least that's what her father had written in one of his letters, revealing a poetic side Elizabeth had never imagined he had.

Had someone here killed him?

She shivered. Maybe it had been a seizure, like the pathologist said. Maybe that note was some hillbilly miner's sick idea of a joke. Making sure that Masterson won his case by default by driving her away.

Anger warred with anxiety and doubt. Should she stay, finish what her father had started?

The Cadillac pulled up to the curb in front of her father's house. Elizabeth dreaded going in alone—alone except for the ghost of a man she'd never really known.

"Why don't you come inside with me?" she asked, tugging her skirt over her knees. "We'll talk business."

FIVE

Hardy's house was a large Victorian, sky blue with curlicue gingerbread at every corner and an inviting wraparound porch. I had to look twice before getting my bearings—when I was a kid this house had been gray, the trim black, and the porch uninviting.

"Your dad was living in Old Lady McGinty's house?" A hint of awe colored my voice. We'd been convinced that Old Lady McGinty was a witch, despite her Bible-thumping. She hated kids—any age, any sex, any color. Too bad she spent nine months out of the year teaching us English.

"She was an aunt on his mother's side," Elizabeth explained. "When his folks died, he let her live here. Then she died, and he decided to move on back himself."

"Did you ever come visit her?" I stepped from the car, half-excited to see what Old Lady McGinty's house looked like on the inside and half-afraid that her ghost would come rushing out of the cobwebs and force me to conjugate a verb.

"Never met her, never been here before until two days ago." Elizabeth joined me on the curb, looking up at the big house. George honked his horn as he pulled away. "It's a nice house, though. Back in Philadelphia, I'd never be able to afford a house like this."

"And now it's yours."

"If I decide to stay." Her sigh was part wistfulness and part resignation. She strode up the walk to the porch steps, her heels clitter-clacking in a businesslike way, and unlocked the door.

It wasn't anything like I'd expected: no cobwebs, no lace doilies, no broomsticks in the corner. The interior was sparkling white on the walls, traditional lace curtains open to the sunlight, and a few wool rugs in muted tones that allowed the maple floors to show off their rich, warm colors. The front room was set up as a waiting area, with chairs and tables scattered around. Leaded windows took up the front wall, and a large fireplace the far wall. Photos of trees and streams and fog over the mountains hung above glass-fronted bookcases on the opposite wall.

It didn't feel like a lawyer's waiting room. Instead, it felt like a room ready to host a book club or Sunday family get-together. Formal but not full of itself.

A lot like how Hardy had sounded himself during our conversations. I wished I could have met him while he was alive.

Elizabeth hesitated inside the foyer, as if not sure where everything was. She took off her coat, hung it in the closet beneath the staircase to our right, and held her hand out for mine. I shrugged out of my jacket and handed it to her. She stopped midstream, hanger in one hand, coat in the other, staring at me.

"Is your shirt inside out?"

I glanced down. Busted. She'd either understand or she'd go all hoity-toity on me and I'd be out a possible job. I pulled the shirt over my head and reversed it, then pulled it back on. "Didn't think Godsmack was appropriate for a funeral, but it was the only black I could find on short notice."

She froze, her mouth half-open, and I thought she was going to hand me back my jacket and kick me out the door. Then she burst out laughing. Not a twitter or a giggle, but a full-body guffaw that left her bent over, gasping for air, still clutching my jacket.

Sitting down on the staircase, resting her head against the polished banister, she finally stopped. When she looked up, tears streaked her makeup, but she was smiling. "My father would have liked you."

Recognizing that the tears were more real than the laughter, I rescued my coat and the hanger, slung them both over the banister, and sat down on the steps beside her. I wrapped an arm around her—David says I give the best sideways hugs of anyone, even if he insists he's outgrown them—pulled her close, and let her cry. She wasn't very good at it, all sniffling and choking and trying to deny her tears.

"It's okay," I murmured. "It's okay to cry."

"Hardys never cry." The words emerged as hiccups.

"So you're a pioneer. Breaking new ground." Laughter burbled through her again. She wiped her nose with her hand and sat up. "How's it feel?"

"Better. I guess."

"Sit. I'll go get you something to drink." I was much more comfortable taking action than trying to think of more small talk.

"No, I'll—" She half-stood, fluttering her hands in a hostesslike gesture, then collapsed back down. "Coffee, please. If you don't mind."

"I don't mind." She was older than me, probably in her midthirties, but at that moment she looked young, vulnerable. I felt sorry for her, remembering how it felt to grieve alone. Not to mention suddenly being threatened—even if the note was a prank, it was still frightening. I gave her another hug. "I'll be right back."

The kitchen definitely was a single-man, microwave-dinner type of kitchen. Dirty dishes sat in the sink, half-covered in soapy water. The coffeemaker pot had a few inches of thick sludge that would have been more at home in a garden as potting soil. I tossed the used filter and grounds into the trash, added a clean one, and rinsed out the pot. While fresh coffee bubbled, I made myself handy and did up the rest of the dirty dishes, leaving them to dry in the rack. I doubted that Elizabeth had had much to eat that day, so I made her a plate of some ham salad and Jell-O mold from the refrigerator filled with the ubiquitous home-cooked funeral offerings.

I was just turning to take her food out to her when she joined me in the kitchen. "People keep bringing food. Green bean casserole. And macaroni and cheese—I think I have four different kinds of it. I just keep shoving it in the refrigerator. I haven't really had the heart to touch anything in here." She made a face at the plate in my hand. "I don't even know what that stuff is."

"You never had ham salad?"

She shook her head. "I'm vegetarian."

I laughed. "That won't last long if you stay here."

Her face clouded again. "I'm not sure what I'm going to do." She poured us each a mug of coffee. "I don't enjoy being threatened. Or someone implying that my father may have been killed."

"People around here tend to defend themselves vigorously—especially if their families or livelihoods are threatened. But I doubt that one lawsuit about a coal-washing plant is enough to kill over. Even if your dad had won, Masterson would just move the plant to another site, right?"

She squinted her face at me as if I was speaking Farsi. "You don't know? I thought you were from around here."

"I am—but I've been gone. Just decided to come back when your dad offered me the job." Translation: when Gram Flora told me about him and I called and begged him to take me on.

"Come with me." She carried her coffee mug down the hall and into the front room on the other side of the wide staircase. Hardy's office, I supposed. "This is about much more than a single coal-washing plant."

I walked inside. The room had no desk. Instead, a large dining table sat in the middle of it. Spread out on top of the table was a map of Smithfield County with bright red crosses drawn in marker over several ridgetops. Lining the walls, instead of the law books I'd expected, were photos. Not serene nature photos like those that adorned the waiting room. These were the most unnatural photos I'd ever seen.

Explosions bringing down huge swaths of earth . . . a bulldozer felling trees by the dozens . . . an aerial view of what used to be pristine forest but had been turned into a dust bowl.

"Mountaintop removal?" It was a cheap way to extract coal by blasting off the tops of mountains, forests and all—what the miners called "overburden"—and dumping it into the valleys below while huge machines clawed at the exposed coal seams. Extracting coal this way was cheap, and it used half as many men as underground mining to get at coal twice as fast. But it was damned expensive in terms of the cost to the people and the environment—poisoned streams and groundwater, fish kills, flash floods, destroyed habitats, unemployment, housing values decimated, wells turned toxic.

But that happened in other places. Never here. Not in my mountains.

"Masterson started it on Black Mountain four years ago. Realized it was a moneymaker, so he's been buying up more land ever since—not too hard with the economy in the toilet and half his workers laid off when he closed the underground mine. He's about finished with his first site and is ready to move on to another, but he needs to have that road and the new coal-washing plant built first." Elizabeth traced the route of the road on the map with her finger. "My father's lawsuit wasn't about only the one plant—it was about shutting down Masterson's complete operation."

Finally, it was all making sense. Why Hardy had been so excited when I called, even after I disclosed my past. "That's why your dad wanted to hire me. To stop Old Man Masterson."

She looked at me, frowning. "Not Kyle Masterson. He's put his son in charge of the mountaintop removal project. It's Cole Masterson my dad was fighting."

I was lucky the chair was close behind me. Hardy was even smarter than I'd thought—he must have heard the gossip and probably knew exactly what he was getting when he hired me. Maybe he even knew about David—thought that would be his ace in the hole.

Like hell.

"What did your dad tell you about me?" As much as I supported any fight against Masterson and for the preservation of my mountains, I wasn't about to be used because of my personal history.

Elizabeth sat down at the table, smoothing the wrinkles in the map. "To tell the truth, I was a bit jealous. He couldn't stop talking about you—said you were a one-woman crusade, taking down Capital Power. His old firm had actually turned down that case as unwinnable, so you were his hero."

She swirled her coffee in her mug, seemed fascinated by it. "He was more excited about you coming to work with him than me."

I heard the pain in her voice. "The job I signed on for was file clerk, part-time research, answering phones, and doing legwork. I'm no lawyer. I didn't take your job."

"No. You didn't. I turned him down, every time he asked. Even though I hate my job, even after I divorced Hunter. Did you know divorce lawyers have a divorce rate higher than dentists? I was so angry at everyone and desperate for a change, but I just couldn't give up and go to work for my father."

"You worried it made you seem like a failure?"

She shrugged, still searching her coffee mug for answers. "Guess I kind of wanted to hurt him—he risked everything when he left corporate law, tossed away everything that I was taught mattered. Yet he'd never sounded happier than when he talked about the cases he was working here. Said he was finally doing work that mattered, that made a difference." She looked up. "But then, after I'd spent my entire life following his and my mother's footsteps into a high-powered corporate job, what did that make me and the work I was doing? Nothing?"

"Maybe he just wanted you to be as happy as he was. He wanted something better for his daughter—can't really blame the guy for that."

"Can't blame him for anything anymore, can I?" she said mournfully.

"So there you go—all that's left is to decide what's best for you. What do you want?" All the sudden I was channeling Oprah and Dr. Phil—I was so *not* the best person for her to have this conversation with. Look at my life—total screwup, slinking home in shame.

"I wish I knew." She drummed her manicured nails against her teeth, eyes crossing as she looked down at them in dismay. Firmly lowering her hand, she restrained it by wrapping it around her empty coffee mug. "I don't really have any reason to stay." She sounded wistful, as if she wanted to stay—maybe to make her father proud even though he was gone? "I guess I'll have to close the office."

"So Masterson wins." I didn't edit the bitterness from my tone. I wasn't surprised. Masterson always won. It was enough to make me wonder if the note was right and Hardy's death wasn't natural. After all, the Masterson family had had no difficulty covering up my grandfather's murder.

"You really have it in for him. And the son, Cole."

No. I didn't. I didn't want Cole as an enemy, didn't want to fight him at all. He wasn't even supposed to be here. He was supposed to be in Madagascar or someplace far away and magical, living his dreams.

Everything I had done ten years ago, I'd done to protect the people I loved. Cole included.

Now it was all falling apart.

At least people weren't trying to run me out of town. Or maybe kill me. Not yet, anyway.

"Maybe it would be safer if you did go home," I told Elizabeth.

Silence followed. But it wasn't the polite silence where the other person was just waiting for you to quietly slink away and leave them alone. From the expressions crossing Elizabeth's face, it was a silence filled with many voices in her head, arguing.

I wasn't sure who'd won when she said, "Do you have any idea how hard I fought to keep my job? When Hunter and I split, one of us had to leave the firm, and I had seniority. He expected me to just roll over and walk away, to not fight. To let that lying, cheating bastard take everything from me. And I couldn't do that. I couldn't sit there and let him screw me. Again. I pulled rank, and he left to open his own practice."

"So you won. Right?"

She shook her head, her gaze looking way past me, way past Scotia. "I lost everything. I hate my job. The only thing waiting for me at the end of the day is an empty apartment. If I leave now, what am I going home to? Dividing assets and custody of a Chihuahua?" She jerked her chin up, her eyes focused with resolve. "Maybe helping to save a mountain or two might help me figure my life out." Her gaze narrowed, challenging me. "I'll stay and fight Masterson if you will."

SIX

David knew he was just a kid. Which meant he had no say in anything important. Like his life. But that didn't mean he had to like it.

Damn, damn, damn, he thought, scratching out a wrong answer in his Sudoku book. It would be so much easier on his computer, but his mom made him do it by hand so he could practice his fine motor skills. When he was younger, he'd heard it as "motor scooter," which sounded a lot more fun than strapping on his splint and using a pencil. But he couldn't complain too much. If Mom hadn't made him do everything he could by hand, he'd never have taught himself to draw and created Captain Awesome.

Still. It sucked, being stuck here while she was out meeting cool people like his gramma and grampa and maybe even his dad. He didn't even know his dad's name, had given up on meeting him a long, long time ago, back when he was only eight, but now that they were here where Mom grew up, he kept thinking maybe. . . .

Damn. He furiously crossed out another wrong number. *Damn, damn, damn.* It was all so unfair.

"Darn," he muttered.

"Table's scratched up enough, boy. It don't need no more gouges," his great-grandmother said—he had no idea what to call her, he'd never had a gramma, much less a great, before—from the rocking chair beside the fire where she was listening to a book and knitting or crocheting or something that had to do with a bunch of yarn and a big hook.

He'd never been in a house with a kitchen big enough to have its own fireplace along with a seating area beside it. If this was his house, he'd never leave this room—the wood floors were polished just right for his chair to spin real tight doughnuts.

"What you frettin' about, anyway?"

"Nothing." He tried to erase the mess he'd made and ended up ripping a hole in the page.

"Nothing, my sweet Aunt Bonnie. You're stewing so hard I can hear the steam rattling around your head. Sounds like you're getting ready to blow louder than a teakettle."

He smiled at that, even though she couldn't see him. Or maybe because she couldn't see him. After all, he was prepared to be mad at the entire grown-up world all day long. Maybe even longer. But he liked the way she talked—singsong, kinda like hip-hop but without the hard edges and bleeps where the swear words should be.

She took out her earbuds and set her iPod down on the table beside her along with her yarn. "Come over here—sit alongside me."

"Yes, ma'am." He rolled over, placing his back to the fire, facing her.

"You call me Flora. Or Gram if you want. Most everyone does." She rocked back, her head cocking at an angle as if she could see him—more like see right through him. "I'll bet you have a lot of questions."

He nodded, forgot she couldn't see him, but she continued anyway. "Your mom ever tell you how you were born?"

"Just said I was real sick, and they had to cut me out of her, and now she can't wear a bikini no more." The last part had to be a joke—the only girls he'd ever seen wear bikinis were the teenagers flirting with the lifeguard at the Y and girls on TV. Moms wouldn't ever wear bikinis—that'd be too gross.

"Way I hear it, you were almost borned three times," Flora said, rocking in time with her words. "Twice too early and once almost too late."

Wow, that sounded a lot more interesting than what his mom had told him—probably one of those things he wasn't supposed to know about until he grew up. He was almost ten, how much more grown up did he need to be? He rolled closer, close enough that he smelled the cinnamony scent that reminded him of one of his first-grade teachers. But Flora was way, way older, he was sure. "What happened?"

"Well, now," Flora began. "It all started on a dark and rainy night. Your mom was in a car wreck, about drowned. Came out of the old Masterson tailings pond half-dead, she did. But she's too damn stubborn to die, so she lived—and so did you."

"She was pregnant with me?" Mom never told him about any car accident or almost dying.

"Sure was. They had to call the helicopter to come save her, take her down to Smithfield and the hospital. Then they flew her again out to Baltimore. She was in a coma, barely hanging on."

"Wow." The word escaped with his breath. He'd always figured his mom had lived a boring life before he came along—she never talked about growing up or being young. He'd never really thought of her that way, about her ever being a kid like him. She was always just Mom.

Flora nodded her head, her blind eyes on him, reading his mind. "She was just a young'un herself, you know. Only seventeen—had her whole life ahead of her. But God had other things in mind. She was in a coma most of two months, you growing along inside her. A couple times she almost died, twice you wanted to come early, too early, and we thought we'd lose you both. But finally she woke. Had to stay on bed rest, give you time to finish growing. Then you decided you didn't want to come out after all. Not until your heart almost gave up and the doctors had to cut you out, just in time." She rocked her chair down hard for emphasis. "Guessin' you're just as stubborn as your ma that way."

David couldn't stop his grin—but was glad Flora couldn't see it. He *was* just as stubborn as his mother, something she never let him forget and the cause of most of their arguments. "So she almost died . . . was it because of me?"

He hadn't really wanted to ask and wasn't at all sure if he wanted the answer. But there'd always been something about his mom, a sad little rain cloud that hung over her everywhere she went. He'd blamed himself, that he needed more than other kids, took more from her. Sounded like he'd been taking from her even before he was born.

Flora's hand found his cheek, caressing it. Her palm was calloused, almost as much as his own, which surprised him—he'd expected her skin to be soft, like his mom's. "No, child. No. Don't you ever think like that. You're what saved your ma. Without you, she'd be lost for sure."

David squared his shoulders against the weight of that responsibility, and Flora dropped her hand.

He sucked in his breath and popped a wheelie. As long as she was talking, might as well ask the Big Question. "My dad. Do you know who he is?"

Flora was still for a long moment. Her blind eyes stared at him without blinking, and all the sudden he felt sweaty like he had a fever.

He was about to roll away, forget about it, when she said, "I do. He's a good man, but there's been a lot of pain for everyone these past years. You need to give your mom time to work things out. Trust her."

He rocked his chair back again, this time letting it bang down hard. There he was, being treated like a child again, like he didn't count. "Yeah, right."

He wheeled away, knocking one of the kitchen chairs out of his way, blinded by tears.

"So, I'll talk with Yancey and you'll organize the others?" Elizabeth asked.

We'd gone over her father's notes, planning our attack, and had moved into the kitchen, where I'd chewed and swallowed a ham salad sandwich without tasting it and she'd gotten another cup of coffee. I liked how she didn't dither around. She made her mind up and began to plan accordingly.

I couldn't help Elizabeth with the legal strategy involved in arguing her father's case before the State Supreme Court, but I thought I could help her win public support, especially among the local protesters. And I could investigate Masterson's operation, make sure it was staying within the boundaries of its permits.

It was no guarantee of any permanent job—she talked like she was only doing her dad one last favor before returning to the city—but it was something.

"I'll get right on it, figure out a way to check out the mining site. I just have to see to my son first."

"A son? I didn't know you had a son. How old? Is day care going to be an issue?"

I shook my head, laughing at the thought. "David. He's nine. And he's more self-sufficient than I am. Besides, he starts school here tomorrow."

"Oh good." She had the grace to look chagrined when she realized how un-PC her tone of relief was, especially for a female employer. "Sorry. It's just that, if I'm going to do this, I want to do it right. And I don't think I can do it without your help. You know the area, most of the players."

"Not for a long time."

She frowned, doing that teeth-tapping exercise again before catching herself. "Which brings us to the subject we keep skirting around. Cole Masterson. There's obviously something personal going on between you two. Is that going to be a problem?"

I wanted to tell her that it was none of her business. But it was—she was counting on me to do a job without letting my personal feelings get in the way. And my track record in that regard was less than stellar.

"I have no idea," I admitted. "The Cole I once knew—he'd never get involved in mountaintop removal, he loved this land more than anything. But ten years is a long time, and people can change."

"He seemed so angry with you when he saw you at the cemetery. Really, really angry—even more than Hunter was when I served him with divorce papers."

"If anyone has a right to be angry, it's me." I swallowed, trying to push a decade's worth of emotion back. "Cole's upset because I came home and he thinks that's going to mess up his life."

Elizabeth leaned forward, curiosity drawing her eyebrows together, punctuating her unspoken *why?*

"It's no secret—at least it's nothing I'm ashamed of or tried to keep hidden. Cole is David's father."

I scraped back my chair and cleared the table. Not because I enjoy cleaning, but I had to do something, move. Otherwise, my anger and frustration would keep boiling inside of me and I wasn't sure what I'd do. Not only anger, but also pain—that my bringing David home could inspire such hatred in Cole.

"Why is that a reason for him to feel threatened?" Elizabeth asked. Lawyers. They never have any qualms about meddling in other people's business.

But her expression wasn't one of simple curiosity—rather, she looked concerned. As if in the past few hours of dealing with her father's burial, a death threat on her life, and formulating a plan to finish her father's work, we'd become friends.

Was this what "normal" moms did? Expose their deepest secrets over coffee and ham salad? I was carpool acquaintances with a few of the parents from David's old school and on a waving, first-name basis with some of our neighbors, but between taking care of David and working, I'd never had time for a coffee-klatch friend. Confiding in Elizabeth left me feeling both stronger and more vulnerable.

But there was nothing to lose, so I told her the entire story. How Old Man Masterson found out I was pregnant and threatened to fire my folks from his company, tried to buy me off and send me away before I could tell Cole. About my car accident and the weeks in the coma, the months in the hospital, the phone calls to Cole that he wouldn't answer. I tried my best to make it sound not-so-pathetic, but I guess it wasn't good enough because by the time I'd finished she was looking away, dabbing at her eyes with her napkin.

Last thing I wanted was anyone's pity. Especially about things so long past. "David's the best thing that ever happened to me. So don't go feeling sorry about the way things worked out. If Cole Masterson is too stupid and blind to want to acknowledge his son, that's his own damn problem."

"You must be seriously pissed at my father, bringing you here to help him fight Cole's mountaintop removal plans."

"A little. I'm more pissed at Cole—and my family for not warning me he was back in town. I don't want anything from Cole or his father, and I certainly have no intention of wrecking his marriage. But David deserves better."

"You know, there are legal options. He owes you, big time."

I didn't like the glint that had entered her eyes—why was it that when you talked with lawyers everything always boiled down to winners and losers? Even when talking about her own failed marriage,

Elizabeth acted as if she was the loser, although she'd been the one to end things.

"I don't want his damn money." The dishes I was stacking in the sink rattled together. David and I had done just fine on our own. Of course, I'd thought about how much easier it could be for David if I went after Cole for child support, but until now I'd always been able to give David everything he needed. I was proud of the life we'd built.

"Think what it might mean for David. You could put it in a trust fund for him."

My spine tightened so fast, I thought I'd give myself whiplash. Was I letting my stupid pride get in the way of David's future?

Shame burned my cheeks. "I'll think about it." The warm coffee-klatch feeling had vanished. "I'd better get going."

I grabbed my jacket. She opened the front door for me, then stepped out onto the porch and glanced up and down the street. Once upon a time, around ninety or more years ago, this had been the rich part of town. Coal had been king and business was booming, supporting not only the Mastersons but merchants and professionals as well.

But that was a long time ago. Somewhere during my grandparents' generation, people had drifted away, over the mountain to Smithfield, the county seat, or to Beckley, which even had a Wal-Mart.

Now the once-graceful Queen Anne and Victorian houses that lined Chestnut Street boasted more broken and boarded-up windows than gingerbread. Other than the Hardy house, the few still inhabited wore a uniform dingy gray tint from decades of coal dust, their roofs and siding stained by acid rain. The prosperity and pride the architects had built into their craftsmanship had been replaced by an air of desolation and despair.

Somehow I'd missed that as a child—Scotia was home to me then, and I'd never analyzed why I felt so claustrophobic here. But now, coming back as an adult and seeing it in the light of day, I understood that I had grown while Scotia remained frozen in amber.

Elizabeth spotted it as well. "Doesn't look like anything around here has changed in a long, long time."

Before I could answer, an unmarked police car pulled up to the curb and a sheriff's detective got out.

"Are you okay staying here tonight?" I asked as he walked up the path.

"I'm fine. Go, take care of your son." She leaned against the porch railing, her posture sagging. "I'll call you after I talk with Yancey." Then she looked up. "Thanks, AJ. Thanks for everything."

I barely noticed my surroundings as I started walking the two miles back to Gram's. There were empty storefronts on Main Street, empty houses on Applewood Road, a few of them collapsed, knocked off their foundation. It was like walking through a ghost town, which matched my mood. I was wrestling with a few ghosts of my own.

Telling David about his father was something I'd been dreading for years, and his disability made the subject all the trickier to approach. I didn't want him to think his father had abandoned him. It would be so easy for David to assume Cole didn't want him because he was "damaged goods." Which of course he wasn't.

But if Cole was back in Scotia, there was no more luxury of time. David needed to know. What would he think when he met Cole? Would he be angry that I had deprived him of the advantages that Cole's money could have brought him?

Before Elizabeth brought it up, I'd seriously never considered the issue. I'd always thought of the money as Old Man Masterson's. Tainted by his greed.

Cole had never cared about money. He'd wanted to travel the world, study exotic places and animals, try to save them. What had happened to the idealistic boy who had pored over *National Geographic* and papered his room with pictures and topographical maps of places like Abyssinia and Madagascar and Sulawesi?

Thanks to Elizabeth, I had options. She'd be paying me more for this one consulting job than I'd been able to make in the past two months waitressing. It was a chance for David and me to start over. But how could I tell him about Cole and then take him away again?

My footstep faltered, slipping, gravel grating, the stones as rattled as my nerves. What if Cole tried to take David away from me? Fought for custody?

I shoved my fists deeper into my pockets—I'd forgotten gloves, as usual—and bent hard into the wind off the mountain. Coming home had been a mistake. I should forget about Elizabeth, forget about the job, take David, cut and run. If Cole really wanted to know about his child, he would have answered my calls ten years ago, could have come to see me in the hospital, should have—

Shaking my head hard, I stomped away those thoughts. Who the hell cared what Cole Masterson thought? David was my main concern. He deserved to know his father. Telling him was the right thing to do.

Even if it might shred my heart worse than a buzzard pecking at roadkill.

A truck skidded to a stop beside me, kicking up dust.

"Want a lift?" Jeremy called from the driver's seat of the Ford Ranger.

Walking around the truck bed, I noticed it was filled with bags of sand and pea gravel; saw a few bullet holes in the tailgate as well, two rusted, three fresh; then climbed into the passenger seat.

"Had to go to the Tractor Supply and into Smithfield to the grocery," Jeremy said, nodding to the bags nestled behind our seat. "Forgot how much a growing boy can eat."

Guilt shotgunned through me. Flora was on a fixed income—I couldn't expect her to stretch it far enough to feed us. "Let me pay you." I calculated the cash I had left—around $60 give or take. "How much is it?"

Definitely more than $60, but as soon as Elizabeth paid me, I'd make up the difference.

"Don't worry about it." He spun the wheel around a switchback. "This one's on me."

That didn't settle well, but I didn't know him well enough to argue the point without running the risk of insulting him.

"David's a great kid," he continued. "You must be very proud of him."

"I am." I waited. It was plain there was more on his mind.

"You sure it's a good idea, bringing him here? Especially if you're going to take up Zach Hardy's work."

"How'd you know that?" News traveled fast in Scotia, but unless there was a new psychic in town, Elizabeth was the only one who . . . oh, of course. "George McCoy."

"Said you and Ms. Hardy were real friendly at the funeral service. Said he dropped you off at her place so you all could talk business. He also said someone was making threats."

"You think I shouldn't help her stop Masterson and the mountaintop removal?"

"I'm from a small town myself. Rankin, just south of Pittsburgh. It's not like this—not pretty, kinda gray and dingy, only thing of note is the gang graffiti and the abandoned steel mill. Got out of there as soon as I could—folks didn't care for my lifestyle choices. Came here on a temp job, and, well, there's just something about this place."

His voice dropped as he downshifted and slowed the truck, craning his head to admire the view. We were just below the farm where a clearing in the evergreens opened up to a spectacular vista across the valley. "It gets into you, you know? Like, all my life I've been searching for something and didn't even know it until I left the city and came out here, and suddenly everything makes sense."

I knew what he meant. I hadn't realized how dead inside I'd been, living confined by concrete and exhaust fumes in D.C., until this morning when I'd walked outside and felt the wind scour my soul clean. It was a hard feeling to explain—either someone understood or they didn't. I was glad Jeremy understood—that explained a lot about why he and Flora got along so well.

Since he was being so open, I went ahead and voiced my curiosity. "How do you find someone to date? Scotia doesn't exactly have any gay bars."

"It isn't easy, that's for sure." He jerked his thumb over his shoulder to the rear of the truck. "See those bullet holes? First few came right after I first moved in with your gram, when this was still just a temp job for me. Folks didn't like the idea of a black man living in the same house as a white woman, especially if that black man was gay. Yeah, go figure the logic out on that."

"But you stayed."

He nudged the accelerator, leaving the view behind. "I stayed. Folks got to know me, stopped worrying about the color of my skin. The gay part they'll never forgive, but I can ignore that for the most part, it's not that much different back home. And believe it or not, I've made a few friends. But when Hardy began fighting Masterson, I couldn't sit back and do nothing. I joined in on a few protest marches, helped him distribute some pamphlets, and out came the guns again. Might even be the same folks, I have no idea. But I'd hate to see a kid like David caught in the crossfire."

"You think I'd put my son at risk for a job?" I didn't bother to mask my indignation. Mostly because he had a point. Protecting David was always my top priority—one of the reasons why I rarely dated and, when I did, almost never let him meet the man. Too dangerous if he became attached, especially when any relationship I had seemed doomed to die an early death.

But there was danger in any job and anywhere we could live—even if I settled for waitressing at Denny's. I couldn't live hiding from "what-ifs"—and that's not how I wanted David to live either. "I don't think you know us well enough to—"

"No, no, I'm sorry." He raised one hand from the steering wheel, palm out. "I just wanted you to know how serious folks are taking this. Even though more than half the miners lost their jobs when Masterson shut down the underground mine and switched to surface mining, the rest have families to support. And the ones out of work are hoping that if Masterson expands, he'll hire them back on, reward them for their loyalty."

"King Coal rules," I said bitterly, thinking of my grandfather and his fatal "accident" when he dared to oppose a Masterson. "Believe me, I know it."

We pulled into Flora's drive, and Jeremy parked the truck. "I meant no offense. I thought you should know that things around here haven't changed much."

I nodded, accepting his apology, wondering if I should turn down the job. But I couldn't just quit. Elizabeth was clearly out of her depth and deserved to have at least one person standing with her. Plus, I couldn't stomach the thought of letting Masterson win. Again. How could I face David if I didn't stand up for what was right?

I helped Jeremy carry the groceries in. As I thought, there was a heck of a lot of food, way more than I could afford until Elizabeth paid me. "What's all the stuff in the back of the truck for?"

"Jeremy built a path up to the wishing stone for me," Flora said as she joined us.

"I thought if the weather stays dry, I could tamp it down, add sand and pea gravel so David could use it—in good weather at least," Jeremy said. "It's steep, but no one should miss that view."

"It's my favorite." The wishing stone was where David had been conceived, way back when the future seemed written in the stars, as certain as their courses across the night sky. Back when Cole had been someone who cared about things like stars and poetry and a special rock anchored to a mountain by generations of memories.

Jeremy handed Flora a bag of fruits and vegetables, things she could put away without needing to read labels. I marveled at how in sync the two of them were. Despite the fact that she was fifty years his elder and his employer, they acted like equals.

It was David and me who were the strangers here. My stomach bottomed out at the thought, leaving behind a dull ache. I wanted so desperately to build David a place where he felt at home, a safe haven.

It seemed such a small thing, something easy for any parent to do, yet I'd failed. D.C. had never felt like home, not in the ten years we lived there. For me, Scotia was still home. Maybe, despite everything, this was our chance.

I was opening cabinet doors, trying in vain to find the place for the cornmeal, but Jeremy slid it from my hand and put it away for me. Nothing was where I remembered it from when I had been here last, and again I felt that hollowness inside, like I didn't belong here.

"Where's David?" I asked, remembering the even bigger reason why I shouldn't start to feel too much at home here—Cole.

"In the front parlor, working on his coloring," Flora said.

Good thing David hadn't heard her. His "coloring" was a lot more than that. In an effort to encourage him to practice drawing and writing with his hands rather than relying on the computer, I'd gotten him some do-it-yourself comic book kits. That had quickly blossomed into an obsession with Manga, *Calvin and Hobbes*, DC Comics, and, lately, Berkeley Breathed's *Bloom County*, especially the story lines that featured Cutter John, the wheelchair-bound veteran. Which led to David's creation of Captain Awesome, a superhero in a wheelchair with more gadgets than

Batman's utility belt. Captain Awesome was a normal, kind of nerdy student by day and an avenging guardian of the innocent by night.

The Chronicles of Captain Awesome was David's diary—off-limits to mere mortals like Mom. But occasionally he'd leave his work lying out where I could sneak a peek and see what his mind was up to. Most of the time it was potty humor, blowing things up, and beating up bad guys. Once or twice I'd discovered that David was having troubles with bullies as evidenced by Captain Awesome's trials and tribulations, and we'd worked our way through that—not as easy in real life as in the comics, but then, nothing was.

I found him in the front parlor, which used to be off-limits to kids, reserved solely for special company. With the southern exposure, large fieldstone fireplace, and inviting camelback sofa, it was the perfect room to spend the winter months when the weather made it hard to get outside.

David had his lap desk angled across the arms of his wheelchair, his hair falling into his eyes as he furiously juggled two hands filled with markers, a half-dozen shades of red. His cheeks puffed in and out as he shaded an area, reminding me of when he was younger and trying to learn to whistle. The squeak of the markers and the scent of their ink surrounded him like a halo.

I stepped closer, ready to begin the awkward conversation, when dread rooted my feet. My stomach clenched tight as if someone had suddenly jerked me by my belt, pulling me back from an abyss.

What if I told David about Cole and Cole rejected him?

Nonsense—who could possibly not love my gorgeous, intelligent, perfect little boy? Certainly not the Cole I'd fallen in love with, the Cole I remembered.

But the Cole Masterson who was blasting the tops off mountains in the name of profit? That was a man I no longer knew, a man I couldn't trust.

David looked up, registering my presence. "What?"

I arched an eyebrow at his tone. He softened his glare, blinking as if emerging from another world. Which in a sense, I guess, he had. "Did you have lunch?"

"Yep. Did you know you can make fried chicken from scratch? Flora showed me how. It's pretty easy and tasted better than that frozen stuff you buy."

I knew Flora would be a corrupting influence. I hated cooking—all that touching squishy meat and standing chopping and squinting at measuring cups and spoons and stuff. "Good, then you're promoted to chief chef."

His face lit up. "Really?"

I was fending for myself in the kitchen when I wasn't much older than him. "Sure, why not." I hesitated, remembering why I'd come to talk to him. "You remember how I told you that we'd talk about your dad when you were old enough?"

He slanted his gaze down to his sketchpad, as if drawing inspiration from Captain Awesome. His shoulders hunched, protecting himself from an unseen blow. "Uh-huh."

"I think maybe you're old enough." I couldn't stand still. My hands had a life of their own, going from balled fists in the too-long arms of the jacket I still wore, to fluttering in front of me uselessly, to jammed into the back pockets of my jeans. "How about if we talk tonight?"

That would give me time to feel out Cole, get a better idea about what was going on with him. "That okay with you?"

His shrug was calculated and way too casual. He returned to his work. "Sure."

My breath escaped in a short puff. "Okay. Good. Great."

I wanted to say something more, but had no idea what. The doorbell rang, saving me from further mom-humiliation.

David didn't know what to say. He'd always thought he wanted to know about his dad, but after hearing Flora's story about how sick his mom had been, he wasn't sure. What kind of guy would leave his mom all alone, in a hospital, sick like that?

He ground the red marker into the paper, producing a puddle of ink that looked like blood. Maybe he didn't need a dad after all.

Maybe he didn't need anyone—all grown-ups did was to screw things up. Yanking him out of school after he'd finally made some cool friends and no one thought of him as "the spaz in the wheelchair" any-more. Dragging him here where he didn't know anyone but everyone seemed to think they knew all about him.

And now his dad. His hand spasmed in anger, color lancing beyond the lines of the carefully inked panel. *Damn, damn, damn,* he'd worked all week on getting this panel right, and now it was ruined.

"I don't have time right now." His mom's voice carried through from the front hall, where she'd gone to answer the door.

"It's important. It won't take long." Another woman was arguing with her.

As long as the page was already ruined, David kept adding layers of blood red. What kind of dad would want a kid like him, anyway? No wonder he'd stayed away all this time.

Worse, what if his dad was like that crazy guy who'd shot himself during Mom's talk show? He sure as hell wasn't thinking about his kids.

Scrunching up the paper into a ball, he hurled it across the room, striking a man who stood there watching him. He was short, wore khakis and a brown leather jacket like pilots wore.

"Hey, kid, good arm there," the man said, picking up the ball of paper and chucking it back at David. It landed on David's lap desk, rolled down, and was lost below his chair.

David was no good at telling grown-ups' ages. Like his mom. When she was worried, like when all those bill collectors kept calling her, she looked older than any of his friends' moms, older even than his teachers. But most of the time she looked tons younger, like she was a kid herself. It was confusing.

This guy looked like he was trying to look younger but really was pretty old. He didn't have any old-folks' wrinkles, but his face looked too smooth to be trusted. And his eyes, they were weird, looking right through David, then suddenly sparking to life, meeting David's as if the two of them were best friends.

"I'm Yancey. Want to go for a ride in a plane?" he said. "Your mom too, if she wants to come along."

David's heart screeched to a stop, did a back flip, and lurched into overdrive. Could this guy be his dad?

SEVEN

I wasn't too pleased to see Elizabeth and Yancey at the front door. Not because I didn't want to get to work on the case against Masterson, but because now that I'd promised David, I really wanted to get this confrontation with Cole over and done with.

Elizabeth didn't understand the problem. I wasn't about to explain it to her with Yancey standing right there. "I thought you wanted to check out the site," she said. "Yancey made all the arrangements, and he's footing the bill, so what's the big deal?"

"I have things I need to deal with here," I insisted.

Yancey quickly grew bored with our discussion and moved past me into the front parlor. I shook my head at his rudeness—people said I was oblivious about social graces, but I was Queen Victoria compared to Yancey—and ushered Elizabeth inside as well.

We followed Yancey. I wasn't about to let him out of my sight; client or not, I still didn't like the man. Something about him jangled my nerves, setting off a subliminal alarm. I didn't like him playing catch with David, but also couldn't see any harm in it. Until he invited David to come along on the flight.

"Excuse me. What do you think you're doing?" I demanded.

Elizabeth touched my arm, reminding me who our client was. Yancey straightened and smiled—he seemed to have a smile for every occasion. This one exuded charm and innocence.

I wasn't buying any of it.

"I thought your son might want to come with us," he said. "After all, what kid wouldn't like a plane ride?"

Right. And what mother could refuse once the offer had been made? I tried to hide my anger from David and still let Yancey know I wasn't fooled—or amused.

He was. Amused. Meeting my glare effortlessly and raising an eyebrow as he grinned back.

"Please, Mom." David gave me an Oliver Twist look that was well rehearsed. It was more for the company than for me—he knew I didn't put up with whining. But I was cornered, and he knew that as well. That's the problem with having a kid smarter than you are.

Then he gave me a real smile, one full of excitement and anticipation. How could I resist? "Okay."

"Great." David popped a wheelie with his chair. "Can I use my crutches? It will be easier."

"Sure. Grab your coat. I'll get them from the van."

Elizabeth followed me to the van. David went to tell Flora and Jeremy all about the flight, while Yancey meandered out to the porch, taking a seat in one of Flora's rocking chairs.

"Don't you bring him here again." I didn't bother to turn and look at Elizabeth as I yanked open the door to the van. "Nobody uses my son like that."

"I'm sure he honestly thought David would enjoy the chance to go up in a plane."

"Of course he would—he's a nine-year-old boy. That doesn't make it right."

"I'm sorry. I'll deal with Yancey myself from now on." She paused, and I knew she thought I was overreacting. Maybe I was. But I'd trusted my gut instincts too many years to ignore them now. "Why don't you like him?"

"I don't know. Just a feeling."

Elizabeth nodded, but it was obvious that she didn't take me or my feelings seriously. "I'm glad I got you alone for a few minutes. I found my father's strategy for his appeal to the State Supreme Court."

"That's good news, right?" When I'd spoken to him, Hardy had sounded confident the appeal was as good as won.

"No. The legal argument he was basing everything on was overturned by another ruling a few months ago. He had no case."

"Which means *we* have no case."

"Unless you can find me some new evidence, Masterson's won."

It wasn't my job to understand all the lawyer mumbo-jumbo—the way they argued both sides of everything gave me a headache. And they always seemed to find a new angle to argue, so I doubted things were as bad as she was making them out to be.

I glanced beyond her, back up to Yancey, who appeared to be asleep as he lounged in the chair. "Maybe that's why your father hooked up with Yancey's group."

"All the money and publicity in the world isn't going to help unless we find something I can argue in court."

Maybe things were bad, after all. "Guess that's my job, then."

As impossible as the task sounded—after all, Hardy had been fighting Masterson for years and failed to stop him—I felt a ripple of anticipation flood my system. It felt good to be back getting my hands dirty, fighting for something important, instead of just talking about it.

Diving into the chaos that filled the back of the van, I spotted one wayward aluminum crutch wedged between a duffle bag and a box of David's books.

"So, your son—" Elizabeth's voice sounded hesitant, like she had earlier when she broached the topic of my relationship with Cole.

"I already told you. He's very independent. He shouldn't be a problem."

"I wasn't asking that," she said softly. "I was wondering if there was anything I could do to help. It can't be easy, moving back home and dealing with a child and a new job all at once."

I regretted my sharp tone. Reminded myself about jumping to conclusions—again.

"Thanks." The single word was clipped so short it scratched my throat. I wasn't used to saying it very often, I guess. So much easier to tackle things alone. I breathed in and tried again. "I mean it, thanks."

Elizabeth leaned against the van door. I snagged the crutch, tugged it from beneath the duffle bag, and handed it to Elizabeth before diving back in.

"Hunter and I talked about having kids."

"Why didn't you?"

"He decided it wasn't a good idea. Said the time wasn't right." Bitterness tainted her words.

"Guess maybe there never really is a right time. Kids change your life." I twisted around to glance up at the farmhouse, smiling as the door opened and David appeared, flanked by Flora and Jeremy. "But, believe me, it's worth it." I paused. "How'd it go with the police?"

"They're pretty certain the threat was a hoax. Probably some disgruntled miner. They went through my father's house again and still didn't find any evidence of foul play. The medical examiner says the cause of death is definitely a seizure—but he's waiting on test results before he can rule on what triggered it." She fiddled with the crutch. I had the feeling that if her hands weren't occupied, she'd be tapping at her teeth again. "They put his body back in cold storage—in case the medical examiner needs more samples. He and the police made it perfectly clear that they are only going the 'extra mile' because I'm a lawyer."

"Covering their collective asses."

"And not too happy about it."

"Anything I can do to help?" The second crutch was hiding in plain sight, lodged beneath David's seat, partially covered by one of his sweatshirts. I grabbed it and climbed back out of the van.

"I wish there was something more *I* could do. But thanks."

"Where are you staying tonight? Want me to ask Gram—"

"Yancey said he has room. He's rented a church camp outside of town for his group."

I rolled my eyes. "Better you than me."

"Hey, never knock a client who's paying the bills."

"Yes, boss."

Forty-five minutes later, I glanced into the backseat of Yancey's single-prop Cessna where David and Elizabeth were chatting. Of course Yancey was a certified pilot. From the way he talked on the ride to the airstrip in Smithfield, there wasn't anything Yancey hadn't done: climbed Everest and K-2 both with and without oxygen, swam with great white sharks off the coast of South Africa, crewed an America's Cup yacht, dove the Great Barrier Reef. He'd explained that was the reason why he'd founded First Earth, to protect the planet from "us dumbass humans and our innate stupidity."

David gave me a smile and a thumbs-up as he pulled his seat belt tight. I still couldn't believe I'd let Yancey talk me into this, but David was so excited, how could I say no?

Yancey finished his preflight inspection and climbed into the pilot's seat. He handed me a set of headphones and started the engine.

The roar vibrated through me, much louder than a commercial aircraft. I was thankful for the headset, which muffled some of the noise. Twisting in my seat, I looked back at David again. He and Elizabeth didn't have any headsets, but from David's excited expression as he pressed his face against his window, I doubted they would have been talking anyway. Elizabeth had settled into her seat and gave me a little wave as if to say, "Relax, Mom."

It made me feel like a worrywart—one thing I tried never to show David. I forced a smile and turned back as the small plane bumped down the runway. The wheels left the ground, the wings bucking with their newfound freedom.

The Cessna's engine was a musical instrument, its pitch varying as Yancey adjusted the throttle. I scanned the gauges, wishing I knew what they were for, just in case something happened to Yancey and I had to take over—at least that was the fantasy my control-freak brain conjured up to soothe my nerves, rattled by the vibrations and the feeling that there was only a thin sheet of insubstantial Plexiglas between us and . . . everything. Sitting up front, the view was overwhelming, so much more intense than looking out a tiny window in a commercial plane.

"Look down." Yancey's voice came over my headset.

He banked the plane to the right, and suddenly the view out my window changed from blue skies to green-brown forest. I spied Gram's red tin roof and our van parked in front of her house. I twisted around to gesture to David, but he'd already spotted the house and was waving hard, as if Flora and Jeremy might spot him.

We circled over the farm and rode the ridgeline up the mountain. Then Yancey turned east, over the valley, toward the mine and Masterson's land.

I tried to mask my gasp, but failed. I'd spent half my life walking these mountains—but someone had stolen them.

Where there had once been a mountaintop was now raw earth, gouged and flattened, the exposed rock naked. Barren. Layers and layers of bedrock had been carved into man-made straight lines, erasing all hint of nature's randomness. No trees remained, nothing moving, only dirt and rocks and desolation.

The blinding difference from the mountains I'd known made me wince. I wanted sunglasses to block the ugly, ravaged view. Worse than a moonscape, it was as if I was suddenly flying over a desert. A landscape poisoned, beyond help. Dead.

Once, when David was a toddler, before I was earning any real money and we lived in a bad part of Alexandria, I'd come home from picking him up at the Easter Seals to find our apartment broken into. We didn't have much, so nothing had been taken other than some cheap jewelry and my winter coat, but I remember feeling violated.

I'd wanted to vomit—and would have if it hadn't been for David. For weeks after, every time I turned my key in the lock, I fought a surge of panic: Was there someone inside? Could I protect David? What would they do to us?

Not only panic, but anger—they had no right to do this to us. I hated those anonymous junkies who had stolen my peace of mind, shattering my complacency, replacing it with fear.

Those feelings finally vanished once we moved. Now, as I looked down on the devastation below, I felt the same anger and violation. Along with an immense sorrow, as if I was attending my second funeral of the day.

No, not a funeral. A crime scene.

What had happened to Black Mountain was as brutal and violent.

Tears came unbidden, as hot as my anger and bitter as my disgust. Turning my head so there'd be no chance of David seeing me cry, I wiped them away with a knuckle, only to have them return as the plane continued to circle over the desolate landscape.

So many feelings tumbled together that I felt as if I was in free fall. Every time I blinked I saw the mountain as it had been, vibrant and filled with life. Then I opened my eyes and the reality smacked me hard, sending me off balance.

At one edge of the wasteland was a machine, taller than any crane I'd ever seen. The bucket on it was large enough to hold several city buses, and its gantry extended up and out, over the distance of a football field. It was parked beside a glistening black void on the far side of the mining operation.

"What's that?" I pointed down.

"The dragline?" Yancey took us lower to examine the expanse of the huge machine. Motionless, it resembled the skeleton of a misshapen prehistoric beast. A dump truck sat nearby, and several men stood outside, revealing its scale. The tires on the dump truck were at least twice as tall as the men. And the body of the dragline was more than three times taller than the entire dump truck. "Big, isn't it?" said Yancey. "It's what digs out the rubble after the blasting. Scoops the mountaintop off one huge bite at a time. Can dig three hundred feet in any direction. But that's not the worst of it. Look there."

He gestured to the black void the dragline sat beside. Something about it made me feel queasy. It wasn't water—on a clear day like this, water would reflect blue. Instead, it had a strange sheen to it, fragments of color colliding, as if it had swallowed the sun and the sky and they fought to get free.

"That's two hundred million gallons of coal slurry," Yancey told us as he circled down lower.

Now I knew why the sight of the liquid—I couldn't call it a lake, not when what it contained was so deadly—made my stomach rebel. I'd almost died in a similar impoundment pond ten years ago. A pond also owned by Masterson. A place where they dumped the waste from the mine—and that night ten years ago Masterson had made it very clear that he considered me and the baby I was carrying to be just as disposable.

Yancey continued. "Look at the building on the other side of the dam."

I forced myself to look down again. There was a wall of earth holding millions of gallons of toxic sludge in place—from up here it appeared to be a very thin wall. Maybe twenty feet thick. Yet, below it, nestled in a patch of green was a single-story brick building. A parking lot stood on one side and a soccer field and baseball diamond lay on the other side, a playground in between.

"That's where they built the new school?" There was a group of kids playing football on the soccer field, their colorful forms zigzagging with abandon. They didn't seem to mind the toxic waste pond that sat behind the hill above them.

"Not so new anymore—it's been there eight years now. Masterson donated the land. About the same time as his permits for the impoundment pond were approved, go figure. And here are my Ladies, trying to protect what little is left of the mountain."

He steered the plane over the school, past the playing fields, to a thin rim of uncut forest that covered what remained of the ridgeline— a ridge that led nowhere now that the mountaintop was gone. Compared to the devastation behind it, the forest seemed a meager last line of defense.

At the edge of the forest a road had been cut, and bright yellow machinery stood waiting to mow down more trees. From above, it was impossible to see the women perched in the trees, but their bright-colored banners were readily visible, waving in the wind like Rapunzel's hair released from her lofty prison.

"Masterson needs a new coal-washing facility to keep up with what he's digging out," Yancey explained. "He wants to build it near the impoundment above the school. Once he cuts the road through those trees, trucks will be running twenty-four hours a day, carrying eighty tons of coal each from his new MTR site—his new mountaintop removal site."

My mind was still spinning from seeing one of my mountains . . . well, the only word that described the betrayal and anger and revulsion I felt was "raped"—my mountain had been raped. "New site?"

"Yeah. He just got the permit to start another MTR site." Yancey banked the plane once more, flying us over the valley, rooftops sprouting among the leafless trees, and took us back over Gram's house and up Hightower Mountain. "There. Yellowroot Mountain."

He angled the plane across to the next ridge—another mountain that I'd spent half my life climbing and hunting and walking and thinking and where I'd had my first kiss with Cole, sitting on a rock outcropping under the light of a new moon. When I was young, Randy and I had learned to search out morels there, and we'd harvested ramps, ginseng, and goldenseal with Gram Flora before she'd gone totally blind. This was the next place Masterson intended to rape and pillage?

Over my dead body.

Then I remembered. It wasn't Old Man Masterson responsible for this devastation. It was Cole.

How could a man change that much in ten years' time?

Whatever the answer, I would find a way to stop him. I had to. Because if Masterson was willing to destroy a botanical treasure like Yellowroot to get to the coal buried inside it, it wouldn't be long before he set his sights on the real bonanza: Hightower Mountain, sitting on top of fourteen separate coal seams.

My mountain.

EIGHT

After we dropped Elizabeth off so she could pack an overnight bag, David couldn't stop asking Yancey questions during the drive home. How hard was it to get a pilot's license? Did they have hand controls available like with cars? How old did you have to be?

I massaged the knot between my eyebrows, trying to erase the vision of Black Mountain from my mind. They were still talking—something about instrument ratings—when we climbed the steps to Flora's house.

Yancey held the door open as David maneuvered through it on his crutches.

"Thanks again," I told him, suddenly awkward now that it was just the two of us. I still hadn't forgiven him for manipulating David to get me to come along, but I was glad I had gone.

"No problem. Hey," he said, as if just thinking of it. "I'll bet you're lonely up here, no one your age around. How about dinner?"

I blinked. Like he was anywhere near my age? He was at least forty. "Uh, no thanks. Not tonight, anyway."

"Sure, we'll make it tomorrow. Give you time to settle in. We can discuss the case." He strode down the porch steps to the Yukon before I could get a word in. "I'll pick you up at seven."

With that, he drove away. Great. Yancey as a client was bad enough, but Yancey as a date? Definitely not my type: too old, too cocky, too smooth. I'd send Elizabeth in my place—she didn't seem to mind him.

Thinking of the mining site and the devastation it had wreaked, I trudged inside and found David back in his chair with Flora in the kitchen.

"Sounds like you had a grand time," Flora said as I hung up my jacket.

"Let's just say it was eye-opening." I didn't want to say more, not in front of David.

"Gee," he said, looking at his watch as if there wasn't a clock on the wall not three feet away. "Look at the time, it's already after five. What time's dinner?"

"Six," Flora answered. "There's fruit and cheese in the fridge if you're hungry."

"No thanks. I'm fine. I'll see you to*night*, at dinner." He wheeled himself out, heading toward the front room, glancing back at me over his shoulder.

"Am I supposed to understand what the tarnation he's going on about?" Flora asked, a snip in her voice.

"No. He was talking to me. Don't worry about it." Facing Cole was going to be doubly hard after what I'd just seen. I held my breath long enough for my anger to scorch my ears with heat, then held it some more before exhaling.

"I'll bet that wasn't a pretty sight, what you saw from up there," Flora said.

My exhalation became a sigh. "It was horrid. We need to stop it."

"How? It's all perfectly legal, going on all over the state. It's our patriotic duty, the governor says. Our coal is vital to national security, and anyone talking against King Coal is talking treason."

"You don't believe that horse crap."

"No. But lots of folks do—folks who need a reason to believe so they can blind themselves to what they're sacrificing just to keep a paycheck and a roof over their heads. Can't much blame them for that. Mining's all most of them know."

I sank into a chair, my face in my hands. "If you could have seen—"

"Makes me glad I'm blind and old and soon headed away from this earth." She patted my head like I was a little girl again. "When I was growing up, we heard stories of what the Great War had done to Europe, how it had leveled forests, turned countries into barren landscapes of mud and barbed wire and blood and trenches. Then came the next war and the horrors it brought. I never thought we'd be fighting a war in our own backyards. Or that nobody even knows about it or cares. We're just a bunch of disposable hillbillies to the rest of the world."

"Maybe I can change that."

Silence as she appraised me with her hawklike gaze. Didn't matter that she couldn't see me—she could see inside me. "Maybe you can. But you're a mama now, don't you go risking too much that you'll be regretting later. Remember why you left home to begin with."

"Masterson."

"He's even more powerful now. He could hurt you again, hurt the entire family."

"Mom and Dad."

"They could lose everything."

Same old song. Ten years ago, I'd given up everything for my parents, sacrificed my future. Masterson had used my family to blackmail me, threatening my parents' jobs, their home. It had worked then, when I was a seventeen-year-old scared kid. Was I going to let him get away with it again?

"Surely not everything," I argued. "The house must be paid off by now. It's not like they had to worry about saving for a college education or supporting me." Bitterness rang through my voice, and I hated it. I detest self-pity, especially when it's coming from me.

Flora squinted at me, a hard look that made me wince.

"I'm sorry," I said, anxious to fill the silence between us, to erase the disappointment from her face.

She surprised me by finding my hand and patting it. "You have no idea what's going on in that house."

Her words surprised me. "What are you talking about?" I remembered the way my father had blocked me at the door last night. I hadn't even been able to see beyond the foyer and the staircase. "Is something wrong?"

"I wish I knew. I haven't stepped foot in that house since the day you left." Her shoulders slumped, and suddenly she seemed much smaller, less a force of nature and more worn down by her seventy-three years. "That's one of the reasons I wanted you to come back home. Your parents need you."

"For what?" I thought back on a decade's worth of strained conversations during birthdays and holidays. Neither of my parents had given any hint that there was trouble—but then again, we didn't talk about much more than the weather.

"Whatever is going on, it's getting worse. Your ma isn't even coming out to go to church no more."

"Dad would never let anything happen to her." I stood and began pacing, wishing I could be as certain as I sounded. Ever since Randy died, my mom had been my dad's entire life.

"Plus, you've got other problems," Flora continued. I sagged my butt against the counter. Somehow she knew, because she jerked her head, staring at me until I straightened my posture. "What are you going to do about David? Boy deserves to know the truth. Deserves a father."

"I'll tell him. Just as soon as I make sure Cole won't do anything stupid."

She twisted her mouth, considering my words, then nodded in satisfaction. "Best do it soon." She smiled and looked in the direction David had taken. "Before *tonight*. Or that boy's gonna have himself a conniption."

Chuckling, I yanked my jacket off the hook beside the door in answer. Jeremy's truck keys hung beside it, so I took them as well. "Tell Jeremy I'm taking his truck. You've got the van keys."

"Will you be home for dinner?"

"Don't count on it." After facing Cole and stopping by my folks' house to check on them, I doubted very much that I'd still have an appetite. "And don't say anything to David. Not until I get things straightened out."

Her expression was skeptical, but she nodded. "You take care now, Angie." Then she looked up. "Anything the boy doesn't eat? Jeremy mainly cooks vegetarian, says it's good for me."

I rolled my eyes. Whatever happened to meat and potatoes? Never did me any harm. "He'll eat anything you put in front of him, he's good that way. Oh, and just in case I'm late, no more than one hour of video games, and his watch alarm will go off when it's time for his medicine. He'll take it himself, but I like to watch just to make sure he doesn't forget."

"We'll be fine. You go take care of business."

She made it sound so easy.

David pumped his fist in the air when he heard his mom leave. She was going to talk to his dad—it had to be Yancey, it just had to be.

The trip today had been a test. To see if David liked Yancey before they sprung the news on him, told him the truth. How cool was that, that his mom did that for him? And even more cool to have a dad like Yancey—his own plane, tons of money, stories from stuff he'd done all over the world.

David sketched a rough outline of a plane flying over the mining site with the big machines, imagining all the places Yancey could take him, the adventures they could have as a family . . . a family. A real live family. With a mom, dad, gramma, grampa, even a great. Wow.

The thought was scary. And exciting. And really, really scary.

What if the test wasn't *for* David but *of* David? What if Yancey hadn't liked him?

Damn, he'd talked too much, jabbering like an idiot. Yancey would think he was some dumb kid. Should have talked to him more about Mom's work, trying to save the environment, that's the kind of stuff a guy like Yancey would think was cool.

David's hand spasmed, and the pencil flew free and bounced across the hardwood floor. What if Yancey didn't want David?

It was still light up the mountain at Gram's place, but as I entered the valley below, the sun disappeared, cut off by the mountains and their shadows.

Switching the truck's headlights on, I realized that I had no idea where Cole lived now, and there was no way in hell I was going to Old Man Masterson's place—last time I was there, I'd almost died.

Part of me wanted to take the excuse and run with it—as if returning to Scotia had also taken me back in time to when I was a teenager and had the freedom of thinking only of myself.

I steered Jeremy's truck down the mountain, memories calling to me from every direction. The creek where Randy had taught me how to fish. Our swimming hole—a gnarled length of rope still twisting in the wind, hanging from a thick oak limb. The trestle bridge I used to ride my bike across, hating the way the metal grating rattled my bones.

All this would be gone if Cole destroyed Yellowroot.

Tears fought with anger, and my anger won out, warming me better than the truck's heater. From the air, all the Masterson personnel had seemed concentrated at the tree-sitters' protest site. I jerked the wheel and took the left-hand fork, bypassing town and heading toward the school, then bouncing off the paved road and over the ruts left by heavy machinery up the hill to the site.

For their protest site the tree-sitters had chosen the thin line of forest above the school's playing fields and beside Masterson's coal slurry impoundment. Four of Yancey's Ladies perched on small platforms suspended sixty feet up. Below them, Masterson workers blared air horns and aimed spotlights at them in a campaign designed to give them no rest.

The Ladies took it all in stride. They had their own Wi-Fi hot spot and video cameras to broadcast their story to the world. Of course, Yancey had chosen the most photogenic young women to go up into the trees. The media lapped it up—much to Old Man Masterson's chagrin, I was certain.

The news folks must have shut down for the night. There was no sign of them or Yancey and his other Ladies. A group of local protesters held vigil, sitting in front of the bulldozers, holding candles and lanterns, their backs to the Ladies. In front of them, they'd spread a large banner that read: GOD WAS WRONG! SUPPORT MOUNTAINTOP REMOVAL.

That got a chuckle from me, and I wondered whose idea it was—and if any of Masterson's men even understood the sarcasm behind the words. Probably too clever for most of them.

I parked alongside the road and hiked past the protesters, scanning the crowd of men gathered around fires blazing in oilcans, warming their hands. Garth Brooks crooned between blasts of the air horn. The night was filled with the smell of pine needles, wood smoke, and diesel fuel. As I wove past the men, I didn't see Cole, but murmurs followed in my wake—angry murmurs, as if I'd committed some kind of terrible sin, coming home.

"Angela, what in hell you doing here?" a weary voice asked, snapping at me sharp enough to break kindling in two. I whirled around and saw, leaning against the back of a Masterson pickup truck, holding a can of Schlitz, my father.

Several of the men sniggered at his words. Made me feel like a kid getting called out to the toolshed for a strapping. My cheeks rushed hot, but I didn't hang my head as I picked my way over the tire ruts in the mud to reach him. Instead, I looped my thumbs in the belt loops of my jeans and hitched my shoulders back so I wouldn't have to tilt my head up to look him in the face.

"Looking for Cole. You seen him?"

He stared at me. No, past me, to the men standing behind us. Shook his head. "You leave that boy alone."

Arguing was no good. Never was. He wasn't about to change my mind, and I wasn't about to change his. So I changed the subject instead. "What are you doing up here?"

He yanked his chin over past the trees to where the mining site lay. "Work the dragline. Until it starts moving again, I'm here on security duty."

Security duty? A bunch of bored miners getting drunk and tormenting a few innocent college students was more like it.

"You run the dragline?" I thought about the monster machine I'd seen from the air, about the devastation it left in its wake. My father was the human force behind that destruction?

He pushed off the back of the truck, tilted his beer to finish it, then flung the empty into the dark, not looking to see where it landed. "That's right," he said proudly. "Most men only get to drive the haul trucks or bulldozers. There's six of us chosen to run the drag."

"You must be honored." My sarcasm wasn't lost on him.

"You got no call," he said, shaking his head with each word. "No call at all. Didn't we, your mom and I, give you your freedom? You were the luckiest child in the hollow. Got to do what you wanted, when you wanted. We never set no curfew, never made you sit and do no homework, never—"

"Never cared enough to," I flared back, incensed that he could spin my childhood into fantasies of happily-ever-after land. "You never cared at all after Randy was gone."

"That's not true." He stepped away as if the anger blazing through me had singed him. "You've no right to say that—and no right to come here and add hurt to your mother."

His words twisted in my gut. Suddenly I was twelve again, the child who caused pain to her folks just by her existence—and reminding them of what they'd lost. I tried to defend myself. "You know that's not why I'm here."

"She's not a well woman. Can't handle this stress. You need to pack your things and leave again. There's nothing for you here. Nothing at all." He shook his head again, hard. Final. "We got nothing left for you to take."

"I thought I had something you wanted. A chance to get to know your only grandchild."

He hesitated. For a moment, I thought he was going to relent, maybe even ask about David like he had the night before. A yell went up from the Masterson men on the other side of the truck, and his scowl deepened. "That's your gram stirring up hornets, putting ideas in your head. You need to leave. Now. 'Fore you send your mom to an early grave."

As if I were to blame for everything wrong with my mother. My parents never blamed Randy or his death for what had gone wrong in our house. Instead, they silently accused me of the one sin none of us could forgive: living.

Whatever hopes I'd had for starting over with them crashed and burned with his words, as carelessly thrown out as the beer can he'd just discarded.

I wanted to find a voice for my anger and hurt, to lash out, to hurt him as badly as he'd hurt me. But the words eluded me, stolen from my

breath as he turned away, the truck lights catching his face and silhou-
etting his features twisted with pain.

He was no longer the man who'd encouraged me to climb higher,
who had caught me when I flew from the rope swing into the swimming hole. That man had been gone for a long, long time—only I
didn't realize it until now when I was left face to face with his empty
corpse.

I stood silent, forcing my fists to open, releasing the emptiness
they'd been clutching so hard for so very long, and I let him walk away
into the dark.

Finding Cole seemed less urgent now. Why destroy his life when it
was clear I no longer had a life here in Scotia? But I'd promised David.
And it was the right thing to do—even if Cole didn't want to have anything to do with David, he deserved to know the chance was there.

Especially since it felt like we wouldn't be here very long. No sense
staying in Scotia if all I'd accomplish would be to hurt the people I love.

I'd finish Elizabeth's job, help her win her case, collect my money,
and move on, start over again.

The thought made me sad, the way it encapsulated my entire life—
other than David, of course. I wanted to build a home for him, give him
a place he could build his own memories around, a touchstone, an anchor. I wanted him to have someplace he loved as much as I loved these
mountains.

People say I'm a cynic. Wish I was—then I would have never opened
myself and David up to getting hurt by coming back home.

Anger propelled my feet as I stomped through the site looking for
Cole. Most of the Masterson employees had congregated in a group beneath the tree-sitters. They were laughing and jeering, heads tilted back,
many holding beer cans aloft. A twanging sound followed by a loud
thump echoed through the air above.

Dead leaves rained down. A woman's scream pierced the sound of
the men's laughter.

Someone aimed a spotlight up into the air. One of the tree limbs
near a Lady's platform shook violently, as if it had been struck by something. The catcalls from the men grew louder as I pushed my way
through the crowd.

They'd gotten a rope around the top of a sapling, had bent it close to the ground, and were taking turns aiming it at the Ladies' platforms, little boys shooting blue jays with their slingshots.

A burly man about my age hauled the still-vibrating tulip tree sapling down and guided the rope, changing the angle it would spring back up at. He turned into the light, and despite the full beard and the potbelly, I recognized him—Dickie Ellings. He'd been a bully in school, a year ahead of me until he dropped out when he was sixteen to go to work in the mine. Looked like he was still a bully.

He took a swig from a Mason jar someone handed him and released the sapling. It shot through the air, springing up and striking the underside of one of the platforms. Cheering erupted from the crowd.

"Bull's-eye!"

The platform jumped, and two five-gallon buckets slid off, plummeting through the air. They broke open against the ground a few yards away, releasing water and food packets. Yancey's Lady shrieked. She waved her arms, fighting for balance. For a moment, it looked like she might win.

Then the sapling rebounded. The platform lurched, wood scraping against wood. The girl tumbled and fell through the air, spinning head-first into space.

Now everyone was shouting, heads thrown back, watching the girl. Her climbing harness and safety rope caught her ten feet down, jerking her hard. She spun on the rope, still head down, arms flailing to catch the line and pull herself upright.

"Looks like we got ourselves a piñata!" Ellings tugged on the rope that controlled the sapling, bending the tree back down. "Who wants to take a whack?"

Although his coworkers laughed, pointing at the hapless Lady, her skirts tangling over her head, no one took Ellings up on his offer, restoring some of my faith in humanity.

The protesters shouted encouragement to the Lady while others jeered at Ellings for his reckless action. The Lady finally hoisted herself upright, still dangling ten feet below her platform. To my dismay, Ellings took this as a challenge. He paced backwards, yanking the rope that held the sapling with him, measuring the best angle to strike her.

A black SUV drove up and parked at the edge of the crowd. Old Man Masterson and the woman who'd been with Cole at the cemetery emerged.

The sight of Old Man Masterson rooted me to the ground. My boots felt filled with ice so thick I couldn't even twitch my toes. I was as frozen as I'd been in that pond, ten years ago, drowning. Sucked in air, but got nothing.

Ten years ago, he'd held my fate in his grubby little hands. All that time, and he hadn't changed. He was still short, only a few inches taller than me, broad-shouldered, thick-chested, with small but strong hands. His hair maybe had a few more streaks of gray—hard to tell in the dim light—and his eyes were as sharp and deadly as ever.

He and the woman stood beside their Escalade, watching in silence, neither condemning nor condoning. Except for the smirk that tweaked Masterson's lips.

Ellings crouched down, ready to launch his next attack. I strode forward, grabbed the rope, and pulled the length that hung free into a loose loop. "Why don't you pick on someone who has both feet on the ground?"

He stood, towering a good eight inches over me. His eyes were beady, made smaller by the flush that swelled his cheeks. His nose was littered with the broken blood vessels of a man who did more than enjoy his drink, and his neck veins jumped like bowstrings.

"You got no call to interfere. Not if you know what's good for you." Releasing the rope, he sneered as I fought to anchor it, my feet yanked from the ground for one stomach-lurching moment. I heaved my weight back against it, planting my feet, the heels of my boots digging into the red clay. Gathering up the slack in the rope, I held it in a loop in my free hand.

Ellings drew a knife. He was smart enough not to aim it at me but instead lay it against the rope. "Coming back here was a big mistake, AJ."

"The mistake is a man ugly as you thinking he's smarter than he looks, Ellings." Before he could react, I looped the free end of the rope over his head and torso, in effect lassoing him to the tree. Then I shoved him hard enough to rock him off balance. The tree sprang up a few feet, tightening his bonds, the rope cutting hard against his arms. The knife fell from his hand as he struggled to stay on his feet, the tree dragging him as it fought just as hard to get free.

Before I could reach for the knife, sirens filled the air. A man's voice shouted from behind me, "Stand where you are. Nobody move!"

A spotlight targeted us, accompanied by a dog's barking.

Men in sheriff's uniforms swarmed through the crowd. I looked over to where Old Man Masterson's Escalade had been idling, but it had disappeared. No sign of my father either.

One deputy untangled Ellings, taking care to slowly release the tree so that it wouldn't spring up anywhere near the Ladies. Then he turned to me, yanking his handcuffs from his belt.

"Welcome home, AJ," my former best friend, Ty Stillwater, said. "You're under arrest."

——— NINE ———

Things got a little crazy after that. Ellings kept jeering at me—right up to the point where he got hauled off in cuffs himself. The media returned, alerted by the Ladies no doubt, bringing with them large spotlights that danced through the trees. The Ladies took turns diving off their platforms and spinning upside down, re-creating the incident.

Local protesters competed for their chance in the media spotlight, demanding to be arrested as well, joining arms and singing anti-mining hymns as they surrounded the sheriff's department SUV I sat in.

Suddenly I was a hero. Which was probably the craziest thing of all.

Ty had a dog with him, a gorgeous shepherd with a dark brown coat and black face, and together they easily worked the crowd, disbanding the protesters, helping other deputies as they put a few of the rowdier ones from both sides under arrest, generally bringing calm to the chaos.

I couldn't help but smile. So very typical. I'd known Tyrone Stillwater most of my life. He and Cole were two years younger than Randy and two years older than me. Like me, they adored Randy. They'd followed in his cleats ever since their first Pop Warner squad. Ty was the peacemaker. He always knew the right thing to say—either to make you laugh or to diffuse a situation or to bring back a smile when you thought everything was lost.

As surprised as I'd been to see Cole here in Scotia, it was no surprise at all to see that Ty was still around. He's the smartest person I've ever met, probably could have done anything he wanted, but unlike me and Cole, he's never wanted anything more than to stay here, close to his mom and brothers and sisters and the mountains he loves.

He'd kept growing since the last time I saw him—he was now at least six-two, nicely muscled but lean, his skin the same shade as pine bark after a soaking rain, his cheekbones sharp, proclaiming his mixed heritage. He passed my window on his way to put his dog into the back of the SUV and smiled—how could I have forgotten that smile? It wasn't bright and shiny like Cole's or Randy's; instead, it was tempered with strength and knowledge and understanding and truth. A smile that said: Might as well enjoy today because tomorrow everything changes.

Told you he was smart.

"In you go, Nikki," he said as the dog bounded into the back of the Tahoe. She was clearly interested in me, nosing her snout as far through the grate as possible, drinking in my scent. I noticed her tail wasn't wagging but her ears were cocked at a friendly angle, interested rather than aggressive.

"Don't worry, she won't bite unless I tell her to," he joked, then closed the hatch and walked around to my door and opened it. I perked up, hoping he was about to release me.

No such luck. Instead, he tugged the seat belt down and leaned across me to fasten it. He smelled good—Ivory soap and hardworking male sweat, an irresistible combo. As he straightened, he flashed me a grin. "Mama always said you'd end up behind bars."

"No. Chantelle said *we'd* end up behind bars."

When Randy died, a part of us—me, Ty, and Cole—died as well. We went a little crazy, feral even. Running around the woods, stealing Cole's dad's truck, breaking into the mine to steal blasting caps and bits of explosives.

Then we'd blow things up. Not trying to destroy anything, just trying to find a bang loud enough to blast our grief away. We were lucky we didn't kill ourselves, but that was part of the thrill. For twelve-year-old me, it was the unconscious thought that dying might be the only way I'd ever get my parents' attention again. For the boys, it was testosterone and adrenaline—a dangerous combination when mixed with grief.

"Guessin' she was right."

"As always."

Long pause as he climbed into the driver's seat, started the engine, and we bumped down the hill and onto the paved road. "Heard you saw Cole today."

"More like he saw me. I came out here tonight looking for him."

"He never comes out here. Hates the mining site."

"Way I hear, he's in charge of it. Fixing to uproot your family next when he does the same to Yellowroot."

He squirmed, caught my gaze in the rearview, and looked away. Very unlike the Ty I remembered. "You've missed a lot since you went away."

"You make it sound like I had any choice in the matter." Ty used to be my best friend. Suddenly he was treating me like a suspect he was interrogating. And I couldn't understand why.

"Didn't you?" He blew out his breath so loud the dog alerted, immediately pressing her face against the grate, staring at me accusingly. "Relax, Nikki. She's a friend. At least she used to be."

Elizabeth parked her Subaru Impreza in front of the two-story log cabin standing on the edge of a mountain meadow. The sun slid behind the ridgetop, leaving in its wake a broad ribbon of ruby and amethyst twisting through the indigo sky. Yancey and several of his Ladies sat in rocking chairs on the wide wraparound porch, watching the sunset while sipping cocktails.

Yancey rose to greet her; the Ladies did not. There were five of them, and sounds of giggling revealed there were more inside. They'd changed out of their flowing gowns, their "work" clothes, and wore an assortment of jeans, sweats, and fleece. Elizabeth was certain not all of them were of drinking age, but as an officer of the court, she wasn't about to ask. There is a good reason lawyers never ask any question they don't already know the answer to.

"Elizabeth." Yancey made her name sound like he'd found her after searching for years. "I'm so happy you could join us."

As she approached the porch and realized just how far she skewed the average female age of the group, she felt the same trepidation she'd felt back at Penn when her mother convinced her to pledge Tri-Delta. She'd failed miserably, hadn't even made it to Wednesday of rush week.

Without asking, one of the Ladies, indistinguishable from the others with her wholesome, fresh-scrubbed good looks, glided to the makeshift bar set up on a windowsill, poured her a martini, and handed it to her.

"You all," Yancey commanded lazily as he lounged in his chair, "go inside, make sure dinner is ready. I have a few things to discuss with our guest."

The girls rose, almost as one, and floated past, as ephemeral as a flock of butterflies. Except one with sharp eyes who hung back and tilted her head in a question to Yancey. He nodded, and she remained behind, taking the seat beside his. They both stared up at Elizabeth expectantly until she finally took the hint and sat down as well, pulling the Adirondack chair close to theirs.

Now that the sun had set, she was glad for her winter coat. Yancey and the girl weren't dressed for the cold, but neither seemed to notice it. "I wanted you to meet Caridad," he said. "She's a reporter with *Rolling Stone*, embedded with us."

The woman, dark hair, dark eyes, just as young and fresh-appearing as the other Ladies, extended her hand. Elizabeth put down her untouched martini and took the young woman's hand, shaking it with a businesslike grip.

"Please, call me Charity—that's my name as a Lady."

"Do the others know you're a reporter?"

"No, no one else knows. Except your father did. I'm very sorry for your loss. I'd love to talk to you about his work sometime. In fact," Charity's face fell, "I was the one who found him."

"You did? Why were you at my father's house?"

"We were supposed to meet in Charleston the night before. But he never showed up at the restaurant, so I went by his house the next morning. I'm so sorry. Maybe if I'd gone that night instead—"

"You were having dinner with my father?"

"I was going to interview him for my feature. The legalities and ethics of eco-activism, that kind of thing. He called to say he was going to be late, but I guess—" Again her words hung in midsentence.

Elizabeth wasn't sure if it was some kind of journalistic technique, inviting subjects to fill in missing information, or if Charity was just flustered about talking about her father and his death. As if the reporter was more moved by his death than his own daughter. Either way it was annoying.

"Why was he running late?"

Charity shrugged. "I don't know exactly. But he was excited. Said he'd finally found the smoking gun he needed to stop Masterson for good."

She looked at Elizabeth with cunning expectation in her eyes. Ah, so Charity wasn't so naive or flustered after all. She was waiting for Elizabeth to provide her with answers.

Too bad Elizabeth had no idea what she was talking about.

"David, dinner," Flora called.

David ignored her, eyes fixed on the clock. Six-eleven and his mother wasn't back yet. She'd said they'd talk tonight. She'd promised.

Mom never, ever forgot her promises.

But she wasn't here. Visions of her and Yancey laughing, driving off in Yancey's fancy SUV, leaving him behind, battered his mind. No, no. Mom promised.

"Did you hear me, boy? Time for dinner. Go wash up." Flora sounded just like Mom, except for her accent. It made David feel a little better.

"Yes'm." He put away his computer and wheeled himself into the kitchen. The table was too tall, but not by much. Better than most restaurant tables. Jeremy was at the sink, straining something green. Broccoli. Ugh. He hated broccoli.

"Aren't we going to wait for Mom?" he asked when they were all seated.

"She said not to wait," Flora answered, reaching for his hand. He pulled away, wondering what she was doing. "Around here we give thanks for our bounty."

"You mean pray?"

"She does," Jeremy said with a grin. "Don't worry, it doesn't hurt." He took David's other hand and reached across the table for Flora's, completing the circle.

Flora began praying, her words a singsong cadence punctuated with an occasional uptick with every "Thank you, Jesus." It was kinda nice, but also weird—especially the holding-hands part. But when they finished with a chorus of "Amen" and let go, David realized that he felt special being included in the circle, like it was them against the world.

He felt like that a lot with his mom—like when she got one of her headaches from trying to read too much, so he'd read her legal and research stuff for her out loud. Or when she came home all excited about some new cause and he'd help her research it on the computer. She always said he was her silent partner. Called him her little genius, indispensable.

He thought he heard a car outside. Stopped to listen. No, it was just the wind. How indispensable could he be if she couldn't even bother to come home in time for their first dinner in Scotia? Or keep her promise about telling him about his dad?

"You're not eating," Flora said.

"Is there something wrong?" Jeremy asked. "I can fix you something else."

"No. The boy can eat what we're all eating." Flora's voice was firm. Just like his mom's would get when he tried to worm out of something. He shifted in his chair and poked at the food with his fork, still not bringing it to his mouth.

Finally he pushed it away. "I'm not hungry."

"You'll not get any dessert then."

"That's okay."

Flora and Jeremy exchanged one of their near-collision glances. "You worried about school tomorrow?"

He nodded, even though school was only a tiny part of the problem.

"You'll be fine," Jeremy said. He was always so chipper and happy. It was annoying. Reminded David of his old best friend, Evan, back in D.C. Evan was like that, always smiling and laughing, even when big kids picked on him for being a "dork" and hanging out with "the spaz."

He wished Evan were here now.

"When's my mom coming back?"

"She didn't say."

"Can I be excused?"

"Can you *please* be excused," Flora corrected him. She nodded. "Take your plate to the counter, we'll use the leftovers in the compost."

He pushed back from the table and cleared his plate, then wheeled into the parlor while Jeremy and Flora finished eating. He had his cell phone—it was only for emergencies, but this counted, didn't it? His mom was missing. That was an emergency. He dialed her number. She always had her cell with her, always answered when he called.

She didn't answer. It went to voice mail after five rings, but he didn't know what to say and hung up.

He stared at the phone. He wasn't supposed to use it to call friends, but he needed to talk to someone from back home. Someone who knew him—Flora and Jeremy were nice and all, but they were strangers, they didn't really know him. He called Evan's house.

"Hi, Mrs. Bedard. Is Evan home?"

"Yes, David, he's right here. How are you and your mom getting along? I'll bet the mountains are pretty."

"I guess so."

"Here's Evan."

"Hey" came a familiar voice. Suddenly David didn't feel so scared or all alone.

"Hey."

"So, how's it going?"

"Okay. I start my new school tomorrow."

"Cool, so you had the day off today? We finished the science module, the one on geology. And Jerry Hansen did his world cultures presentation on Italy today, and you know what he brought for his home-made project?"

Jerry Hansen was a well-known idiot. He picked his nose, never showered, and was always trying to get David in trouble. "What?"

"Pizza. Still in the Domino's box!" Evan's laughter sang through the phone, and David felt like maybe he wasn't so far away after all.

"What an idiot."

"Well, I gotta go. Bye."

"Bye." The phone went silent, but David still hung on to it. The display on the front said 7:08.

Where the heck was his mom?

TEN

Believe it or not, I'd never been arrested before. Wouldn't recommend the experience. It's not like the movies. They don't use fingerprint ink anymore; instead, they roll your fingers and press your palm against this copy-machine thing that scans them, messes them up, and ten minutes later they're doing it again, until the machine is happy with the results. Then they take your picture, bright flash, no warning, barking at you to turn right, turn left, until you forget which is which.

For most of the protesters that was it—they were handed a ticket for trespassing and disturbing the peace and set free.

Even Ellings got to go free since the Lady he'd assaulted refused to come down from her tree to press charges. He leered at me as I sat handcuffed to a steel bench and said, "Can't wait till we meet again, AJ."

When no one was looking, he snapped his finger hard against my cheekbone, then left.

"Don't I get a phone call?" I asked. In the movies, everyone gets a phone call.

"I told you," the deputy manning the desk said, not even bothering to look up as he typed on his computer. "After we finish processing you."

"What's left? De-lousing?"

He quirked an eyebrow that said he was seriously considering the possibility if I didn't shut up. So I shut up. Went back to reading an old

Sports Illustrated I'd found on the bench beside me. He finished typing. "Okay. They're ready for you."

I didn't like the sound of that. "Ready for what?"

"Strip search and then detention in a holding cell."

"You're kidding me. Don't I get a desk appearance ticket like the others?"

"Not when Ellings is pressing assault charges against you, you don't. You're staying the night, courtesy of the Smithfield County taxpayers. Then court in the morning."

I sat up so fast the handcuff clanked against the steel. "No. You can't do that. I got a kid at home—c'mon. . . . "

A female deputy emerged from behind him. "Palladino, let's get this over with."

Which was how, fifteen minutes later, I ended up in stocking feet and without my belt in a cell with cement-block walls, a stainless steel toilet/sink combo built into the wall, and two steel bunks. A thin mattress encased in a plastic cover and a blanket were spread across the bottom bunk. No pillow, but they'd let me keep the worn-out, two-year-old *Sports Illustrated* that I'd been looking at while I waited. It was better company than my thoughts, which were focused on how upset David would be and colorful images of Ellings hanging upside down and being lashed by his own sapling.

"My phone call?" I asked the deputy. You'd think we'd be on a first-name basis by now, but she hadn't introduced herself.

"I'll bring a phone for you to use, but you've got a visitor first."

I craned my face through the bars, hoping it was Elizabeth come to spring me. It wasn't.

It was the woman I'd seen with Cole at Hardy's funeral and with Old Man Masterson at the tree-sitter site. She was a skinny-assed thing, taller than me by a few inches, sleek hair styled by no hairdresser around here—I'd reckon she drove all the way over to Beckley or maybe even Charleston to have it done—and a designer pantsuit that would have been at home in any powerbroker's conference room on the Hill.

"I'm Waverly Masterson," she said through the bars that separated us once she dismissed the deputy. "That's Mrs. Cole Masterson to you."

I'd overheard the deputy offer to bring me out to a visitation area, but Waverly had refused. Not because she was afraid of me—that much was clear from her posture and haughty expression—but to remind me where my place in the scheme of things lay. She was the one holding the key to freedom. I was the prisoner.

Yeah, right. I stifled an impulse to curtsy and say, "Yes'm."

Instead, I lounged back on my uncomfortable bunk and crossed my ankles. Trying for a combination of insolence and frankly-my-dear-I-don't-give-a-damn, I lowered my eyelids as if suffering from terminal boredom. It was an expression I'd copied from David, who had it nailed. "Funny, Cole never used to like women with no asses."

Ouch. Even I surprised myself with the depth of my bitchiness. But this woman was the reason why David didn't have a father. Even though all that was more Cole's fault than Waverly's, it didn't stop me from hating her.

Of course I hated her—had ever since that night in the hospital when, despite my brain being muddled with trauma and fear, I'd dared to pick up the phone and call Cole to tell him that I was having his baby. And *she'd* answered.

"I think there are surgeons who can do something about that, you know." I continued my female James Dean impersonation. Rebel with a cause. I liked it.

Her smile pulled wider, revealing her teeth—gleaming, white, and sharp, as if she got them filed every time she went in a for a mani-pedi.

"I wasn't expecting to like you," she replied. "That's good. Makes this easier."

True to James Dean, I merely grunted that I'd heard her.

"It was a mistake for you to return to Scotia. It will be a bigger mistake for you and your son to remain. If you agree to leave now, tonight, and never return, I will have the charges dropped and give you five thousand dollars for your trouble."

Wow. She said it just like that—barely took her two breaths to plot out my entire future. And David's. She probably spent more time and effort telling her hairdresser how to get her highlights right.

Now I was mad. Madder than I'd been up in Yancey's plane looking over the ravaged wasteland Cole had turned Black Mountain into. Just about as mad as when I'd seen that poor girl topple from that tree stand and Ellings taking aim to hit her.

When I get mad, I don't get loud—words from people like me are worthless to people like Waverly and Old Man Masterson. No, I get quiet. Searching for soft spots to strike.

I opened my eyes to let her know I'd heard her offer and was thinking about it. Swinging my feet from the bunk, I stood, my back to her, and stretched as if I'd been in solitary confinement too long. Breathing deep, palms reaching toward the caged-in light fixture over my head, bouncing on my toes, trying to look a lot taller than I actually was.

"I need your answer now," she continued.

The hint of uncertainty that had crept into her voice pleased me. She'd chosen the figure—$5,000—well. It was the same amount Old Man Masterson had offered me ten years ago, along with the same deal: leave and never return, never contact his son again. What I did with the baby was up to me; as long as we were out of Cole's life, he didn't care if I kept it or got rid of it.

Wishing they'd let me keep my boots—I am so much more intimidating with my boots on—I tapped my foot against the cold concrete floor. I needed to let her know what my answer was and exactly how far I'd go to protect what was mine. Hard to do standing behind bars in my socks.

The ragged *Sports Illustrated* I'd been reading earlier was peeking out from beneath the blanket I'd wadded up to use as a pillow. I rolled the magazine as tight as I could, my back hiding my movements from Waverly.

"I'm waiting," she said, her designer-clad toe dancing out an impervious rhythm. "You've got ten seconds or the deal is off the table. Forever."

Ten—nine—eight—seven— . . . I gathered my strength, harnessing my fury, reining it all in, focusing. Then I whirled, leaping to the bars, striking out with the magazine so hard that it sounded like a sledgehammer, rattling the steel.

Not just the steel. Waverly jumped back, skidding on her heels, arms waving wildly as she worked to catch her balance, a squeal of fright escaping her.

Her breath came ragged and loud as she stared at me, eyes so wide their whites showed. Then she hauled in a breath and dared to come close to the bars once more. Her gaze never left me, as if I was some kind of terrible, dangerous wild beast, not to be trusted.

But what tied the knot in my stomach and made me regret my childish actions were the tears shining in her eyes.

"Please," she said, her voice coming close to breaking. She tightened her posture, one hand patting her cheek, hiding the tear that had slid free. "You almost destroyed Cole once. Please. Don't hurt him again."

I stared at her, stunned. Shame burned through me. She was here to protect Cole—just like I was trying to protect Cole's son.

Footsteps came running. It was Ty. By the time he was in sight of the cell, I'd tossed the magazine and it lay innocent, unfurled, on the floor.

"What's wrong?" he asked, one hand on his empty holster. No weapons allowed back here with us dangerous felons.

Waverly stepped back, as far away from me as she could. She didn't look at me anymore. Instead, she seemed to pull into herself, replacing the fear that had shocked me a few moments ago with a rock-solid calmness. "Nothing," she said, in command of her voice once more. "I thought I saw a cockroach."

"I think you should go now, Mrs. Masterson." Ty glanced from me to her, clearly not liking what he saw.

"Fine. I got my answer." Waverly turned to follow him out, then spun back. "Just remember—whatever happens, you had a choice. It's on your head."

Ty opened the door at the end of the hall for her, and she strutted through as he held it. He stood there a moment longer, looking back at me, shaking his head as if sorry for me. The same "how could you be so dumb?" look he used to give me in high school when I talked back to the principal, earning extra detention when I could have kept my mouth shut and gotten away clean.

I had the feeling that, just like ten years ago when I'd turned down Old Man Masterson's offer, I'd made a big, big mistake. But damn, it had felt so good. Irresistibly good.

Right up until the moment when Waverly reminded me that my actions had hurt Cole as well. Even though he played a role in that pain, I couldn't shake the feeling that I was being selfish. Like somehow I was the bad guy in all of this.

It wasn't a feeling that I liked. Not at all.

Then the door at the end of the hall clanged shut. The noise thundered against the concrete walls with the finality of a coffin slamming. I was alone. In jail. My baby with people he'd only known for a matter of hours, without me.

Hugging myself against a sudden chill, I sank onto the bunk, the mattress too thin to protect my butt from the hard steel surface.

James Dean would have been proud. I didn't cry.

Not much, anyway.

After dinner, Yancey took Elizabeth aside, leading her to a comfortable den where he poured them both a glass of cognac. Elizabeth held hers, admiring the color as it swathed over the crystal, but not drinking—she didn't like cognac. Not that Yancey had asked.

"So. Now that we're alone, I wanted to give you an update," he said, lounging in his leather Mission-style recliner. "I saw the footage of you at the cemetery on the evening news. You were magnificent. I doubt we could have gotten anything like that if I'd consulted with you first."

Elizabeth drew herself in, holding very still, the cognac a sudden mirror, reflecting the mask her face had become. Her courtroom face. She'd copied it from her father. "Excuse me?"

He waved a hand and took another drink. "Don't worry, you'll get the hang of things soon. Like forgetting to introduce Angela Joy Palladino to the reporters—I took care of that, made certain they knew exactly who the new player in town was. Such a coup, your father getting her here." Then he suddenly leaned forward, his face stern. "But really, we need to coordinate better. Her stunt at the protests tonight? I could have had the media there ready and waiting if you'd given me a heads-up. The way scandal follows that girl around—she could be a star if she just learned to capitalize on it. Like that shooting on the air a few months ago? Oh, the things I could have done with that!"

Elizabeth blinked, found herself still in the same reality when her eyes opened again, and leaned forward, matching his posture. So many questions she wanted answered, but sometimes the best way to ask a question is to shut up and listen. So she did. She listened hard.

Yancey continued. "I'll try to bring her up to speed. Oh, and I have to remember to get her to sign a release. The video of her getting off the plane today—such raw fury and passion. It's certain to go viral."

"I didn't see any reporters filming when we were at the airport."

"Of course not." He appeared offended. "That would be too self-serving, they'd see right through it. Please, dear, you're working with a pro. Leave it all to me."

"And that reporter—"

"Caridad? She's putty in my hands. The piece she's writing will be amazing—you know I'm currently in talks with the networks, right?" He spread his hands wide, palms out, Hollywood-style. "*Charlie's Angels* meets *The A-Team*, Yancey's Eco-Mercenaries." He frowned. "The title still doesn't work for me, but we'll think of something." He glanced at his watch, stood, and gave her a wink. "Remember, not a word to Caridad. We need to maintain the illusion."

Elizabeth stood and followed him, her mind reeling. Yancey spoke as if they were partners in some kind of collusion—surely her father would have never agreed to such a thing. Was Yancey playing her? Taking advantage of her father's death?

Or was her father somehow involved?

Before she could ask, the quiet of the house was shattered by the sound of tires squealing and a truck horn sounding a rebel yell. Then came the sound of gunfire.

The sidelights on either side of the front door blew in, glass flying. Bullets thudded against the front door, shaking it.

From outside the laughter of men cut through the night. Inside was the sound of women screaming.

ELEVEN

For what seemed like days, I lay alone on that bunk. I'd never been any good at solitary confinement. I need people around me—otherwise I get tangled in my thoughts.

Footsteps sounded in the hallway, and I looked up. Ty appeared, rolling a telephone on a stand with one hand and carrying one of those plastic porch chairs that blow away with the slightest wind. He pushed the phone close enough to the bars that I could reach it, then plopped down in the chair so hard the legs bowed and quivered.

I wanted to jump up and grab the phone, call David, and make sure he was okay, but the look on Ty's face stopped me. He reached into his breast pocket and pulled out a handful of wallet-sized photos.

Sitting up, I slid to the edge of the bunk near the door. "Can I have those back?"

I tried to keep the need from my voice and failed. He nodded, but didn't hand them through the bars. Instead, he kept his head bowed, shuffling through the pictures of David. He leaned his elbows on his knees, the front legs of the chair moaning as they scraped forward. Finally, he raised his face and looked right at me.

"Why didn't you tell us?"

I blinked. Why should I tell anyone about David's disability? I wasn't looking for charity, didn't need their pity. "It wasn't anyone's business but mine."

Anger buffeted his face, rocking his body as if he'd taken a hard punch. "Don't you think Cole deserved to know?"

Now it was my turn to be angry. First, Waverly acting like I was to blame, and now Ty. Ten years of pent-up fury pounded against my rib cage, demanding release. "Cole didn't want to know. I tried to call him, tell him about David, but he wouldn't talk to me."

Ty stood. The chair flew back, hitting the opposite wall, and fell to the ground feet up, surrendering. "You tried to kill yourself, AJ! He thought you'd killed your baby—his baby. He was a nineteen-year-old kid who'd just lost everyone in this world he loved—first his mom, then you and his son."

"What the hell are you talking about?" I got to my feet and lunged for the bars. He stepped back, still holding David's pictures in one hand, the other dropping to his empty holster. From the look on his face, it was a good thing he wasn't allowed to bring a gun back here. "I never tried to kill myself. Who told you that?"

"But—" He paced to the far wall, spun on his toe, and whirled back. Confusion wrestled his anger and won. He dared to come close, leaning against the bars. "They lied. Why would they lie?"

He handed me my pictures. Straightened as if to leave, but I clutched at his arm. "Wait. Who lied? No one would believe Masterson, certainly not Cole. Not about something like that."

"You know, we came to see you, Cole and me. They turned us away. Told us not to come back, that even if you woke up from the coma— they said *if*, not *when*—it would be too disturbing. Then later, when I heard you were going to make it, I hitchhiked back, tried to see you again, but security caught me, and they had me thrown out."

I shook my head, understanding his words but not wanting to know the meaning behind them.

No. It couldn't be.

In an effort to deny his version of the truth, I filled the air between us with the few facts I knew. I gave Ty everything I had to offer, hoping he could make sense of it.

"I was in the coma for two months. I had swelling on the brain, hy-poxia they called it. Lack of oxygen from almost drowning. For a long while after I woke, I didn't remember much of anything except Cole. And you. I kept asking to see you. I was worried about you, thought you were hurt in the accident too—but you weren't there."

I'd painfully reconstructed most of that night—could remember my argument with Old Man Masterson clearly, but things got jumbled after that. It had been raining, roads slick, there was a coal truck speeding, headed right at me, and then I was in the water—oily, foul-tasting water that burned as I gagged and swallowed and breathed it in, panicked, knowing I was dying. . . . A fresh memory intruded. A face. "You *were* there."

He turned his face away, staring at the exit as he nodded. "I'm the one who pulled you out."

"You saved my life. Why didn't anyone tell me?"

"Why did everyone tell us that you drove into that pond on purpose? That you were trying to kill yourself and your unborn child?"

He looked back at me, forcing me to meet his dark, dark stare. We both knew who "everyone" had to be. Frank and Edna. My ever-loving parents.

"After I woke up, I overheard my dad arguing with the doctors. Telling them to take my baby if it meant saving me. I hated him for that, sent them both away once I could put the words together. Everything was so jumbled, confused. . . . " Surely that wasn't enough for them to hurt Cole that way, tell him I'd killed his child? My parents were lacking in the home and hearth department, but they weren't cruel—at least never on purpose.

"They left you there? All alone like that?" His fingers tightened on the bar until his knuckles popped out as if he was getting ready to hit someone.

I nodded, not wanting to put the truth into words—it would make it all too awful, too much to face.

"When they came home and told everyone you'd lost the baby, Cole took it—he took it hard. Especially after his dad told him how crazy you'd acted that night, that you'd said you were going to kill yourself because Cole was getting serious about Waverly."

"That's stupid—I'd never—you guys believed that?"

"We were away at school. All we knew was what we heard. Plus, well, everyone around here said you started acting real strange. Picking fights, almost thrown out of school. Not just your folks said that."

"I was seventeen and found out I was pregnant. Of course I was acting strange."

I needed a moment to think. For ten years I'd tried to block out memories of those horrible weeks of uncertainty and the months in the hospital that had followed. I'd wanted to only remember the joy I'd had when I finally held David in my arms.

But I'd lost more than a few memories, I realized. And so had Cole. No wonder he'd never answered my calls. No wonder he'd looked at me with such hatred this morning at Hardy's funeral. Not just hatred. Disgust. He thought I'd killed his child.

My knees trembled, and I sank back onto the bunk, clutching my pictures of David, hanging on to them as the truth. Because suddenly, everything else I'd once believed seemed to be a lie.

"I need to talk to him." I couldn't manage anything louder than a whisper. Not without my voice failing me. "He has to know the truth."

Ty hesitated. I knew he was considering telling Cole himself—he was that kind of guy, one who'd do the hard things to save his friends pain.

"Please, Ty. I want it to come from me."

He nodded, still uncertain. Finally said, "Okay. I'll make it happen."

He walked away, leaving me alone with my life of lies.

Yancey pushed Elizabeth against the study door, shielding her with his body. The sound of gunshots, big booms, louder than what she'd thought they'd sound like, thundered through her, repeating and echoing, stampeding her pulse.

She pulled at the doorknob, again and again, trying to open it, to put a thick piece of wood between her and the gunfire, but the door refused to budge.

Yancey was saying something, his mouth open wide enough to be shouting, but all she heard was the sound of gunshots. Until, with the suddenness of a thunderclap, his voice penetrated the noise of her pounding heartbeat.

"Are you okay?" Yancey reached past her, turned the doorknob she still gripped, and pushed the door open.

She tried to swallow, couldn't force anything past the knot in her throat, and tried again. Beyond him glass sparkled on the wood floors, but otherwise there seemed to be no damage. In the vague distance she heard the sound of the car horn with its rebel yell.

"Why don't you sit down?" he suggested, guiding her to the couch. "You look panicked."

Nonsense. Hardys didn't panic.

She thought she'd spoken the words, they sounded so clear, but then she realized it was her father's voice in her head saying them. A stray memory caught in her mind. She'd been eight or nine, and she and her father were walking at night from a children's concert to their car parked several blocks away. With darkness falling, the city had transformed itself into a claustrophobic maze filled with looming towers and strange, frightening denizens calling to them from doorways and alleys.

"Daddy, I'm scared," she'd whispered, gripping his hand as tight as she could and scrambling to keep up with his longer stride.

"There's nothing to be frightened of. You're a Hardy. Hardys never panic. Remember that, young lady."

She remembered how his words only made the night seem colder, as if she was surrounded by darkness, despite holding his hand. Almost as scared as she was now, with the crack of gunshots still rattling her brain.

But she didn't succumb to panic. Instead, she sat silently, listening as Yancey calmed the Ladies down and ushered them into a backroom, then returned to the study and called the police. She marveled at the way he took it all in stride—of course, he wasn't the one they'd come to kill, was he?

The shakes hit her hard. Nausea washed over her, blackening her vision until she had to bend forward and lower her head between her knees. Good God, someone really was trying to kill her.

It was absurd. Nonsense. She'd done nothing wrong.

It just wasn't fair, goddamn it!

She sat up, alone now in the room. Men's voices came from the front hall. Yancey dealing with the police. Good. One less thing for her to worry about.

She stood. Goose bumps lined her arms, but she felt feverish, not cold.

Hardys didn't panic. And they didn't run away.

Her father didn't. Neither would she.

Earlier, when she'd decided to stay, she thought she had something to prove to her father and needed to finish his work. Now she had something to prove to herself.

This was about more than a law case or her father's lifework. This was about her—for once in her life she wasn't going to back down and sit quietly in the corner, following the decisions others made for her. Like Hunter deciding to walk out on their marriage because she dared to protest his infidelities.

For the first time since Hunter left her she felt . . . something, anything. As if she'd been numbed, encased in ice by the coldness of his betrayal, by her mourning of their life together, by her loss of identity—if she wasn't Hunter's wife, her parents' child, a lawyer at Martin and Stein, then who was she?

Now the ice had cracked, was crashing all around her louder than the glass shattered by the shotgun blasts.

"I'm as mad as hell, and I'm not going to take this anymore!" *Network*, one of her father's favorite movies. The affirmation felt good, so she tried it again. A little louder this time. "I'm as mad as hell, and I'm *not* going to take this anymore!"

The door opened, and Yancey stood there smiling. "Glad to hear it. Because neither are we." He beckoned to her to join him.

"Did the police think they were here trying to kill me?" she asked. The thought no longer came with only fear but also a new thrill of adrenaline.

Never before in her life had she been important enough that someone would want to kill her.

"They weren't sure. Those boys have been here before, shooting their guns—just never actually hit anything before tonight." He led her into the large community room in the back, a room set up for prayer meetings with a large cross hanging on the front wall and chairs gathered into a circle.

Now it was filled with Yancey's Ladies. She counted nine of them, including Charity, who stood aside, filming the activity. In a scene surreal enough to have been directed by Bergman, the Ladies were methodically unpacking large plastic crates, removing body armor, pistols, and machine guns.

"Are those legal?" Elizabeth asked before realizing she didn't really want to know the answer.

"This is West Virginia. Home of swap meets where you can buy anything from an AK-47 to a bazooka."

She took that as a yes. Beside her, a Lady wearing a Duke sweatshirt began loading a pump-action shotgun, her freshly manicured pomegranate red nails color-coordinated with the shells as if she'd planned it that way. She handled the weapon confidently, and instead of showing concern or worry, her expression was one of excitement.

"I thought you guys didn't believe in violence."

"We don't, but we won't be victims to it either. We protect our own. That includes you now." He smiled down at her and winked again. "Don't worry. It doesn't cost extra."

TWELVE

The phone Ty had left me was older than David. Black desk model, the receiver chipped and cracked in spots. The grip felt grimy, coated with a decade's worth of sweat, and smelled like disinfectant that had valiantly tried to kill all the leftover germs but had given up in defeat.

I was tempted to call my folks and let them have it—my mind stuttered over angry words, words that I couldn't begin to force out of my throat, choked with fury. Why, why, why?

It had to be Masterson. He would have threatened them the same way he'd threatened me, by threatening to take away everything—their jobs, their home, their futures.

My father's family had always been Masterson men. Four generations worth of loyalty was hard to fight. It was why he'd stayed with Masterson even after my Grandfather Absalom was killed. Flora didn't talk to him for over a year after that, but she had finally relented, understanding that there was little choice for a miner with a four-year-old son and another child just born.

But this? Destroying my life and Cole's, playing God with their grandson's future? I couldn't find words to fathom the depth of their betrayal.

Instead, I called Flora—besides, she was the only one who I was certain would take my collect call. Elizabeth had given me her cell-phone number, but it was long-distance, and with cell coverage spotty at best around here, odds were I wouldn't reach her anyway. I didn't have Yancey's number, but he'd given David his card, so I hoped Flora could track down Elizabeth, have her work some legal magic, and get me the heck out of here and back home in time to make sure David would be ready for school in the morning.

I hadn't counted on Flora's phone being busy the first three times I tried it. Finally she picked up, sounding exasperated. "Hello?"

The mechanical operator did the whole collect call thing, and to my relief Flora accepted the charges.

"What the tarnation you got yourself into now?" she snapped before I could say anything. "I heard you tried to strangle Ellings, and he almost stabbed you. You even think about your boy? What would happen if—"

No chance of getting a word sliced through her jumped-up speech, so I waited for her to take a breath. "I'm fine. And I don't need lessons on raising my son from you, thank you very much."

Her sigh rattled through the phone line. "You might rethink that if you could see him moping around here, watching the clock. We were worried about you, Angie."

"I need to talk to David—and then I need your help getting me out of here."

"Ty says you're being charged with assault."

"It's a long story. Can you put David on?"

"Here's David."

From the *swish* that carried through the handset, it sounded as if David had yanked the phone from her hand. "Mom?" His voice carried an unfamiliar waver. "When are you coming home?"

The cord didn't reach far enough for me to sit on the bunk when his question knocked my knees out from under me, sinking me to the floor. I clenched the phone like a lifeline. "As soon as I can, sweetheart."

"So you're not going away with that guy Yancey?"

What the heck did Yancey have to do with anything? And how did he go from being the next anointed saint of aviation and all things "guy" to earning such scorn from David? "No, of course not." I didn't have time to ask David to explain—sometimes the minds of nine-year-olds are a mystery best left untouched. "Actually," I tried to sound light and airy, like I was on an adventure, "I'm in jail."

"Jail?" He drew the word out to two syllables. "How come? Did you kill someone?"

I could see him prepping for show-and-tell: my mother, the ax murderer. He'd be the most popular kid in school. Unfortunately, the truth was bound to make him less than popular with the kids in Scotia. "No, of course not. It's all a misunderstanding. There was a man, and he was trying to hurt a girl who couldn't defend herself—"

"A bully." David understood all about bullies. "So you protected the girl? Stopped him?"

His voice ached with a need for his mom to be a hero. Guess it'd been way too long—with men killing themselves and blaming me and all—since that was true.

I knuckled tears back behind closed eyelids. "Yes. Yes, I did."

"So why are you in jail? Shouldn't he be instead?"

"He might be someday. But right now I'm in trouble because instead of finding a way to use my words to stop him, I kind of, well, shoved him." Great example of maturity I was setting for my kid. Maybe they should keep me in jail.

"Wow, Mom, that's awesome. Way to go." And I knew he meant "awesome" with a capital "A," as in Captain Awesome.

"It's not the right way to handle a bully. We've talked about that."

"Yeah, right, sure." Patronized by a nine-year-old. Worse thing was, I couldn't help but feel a glow of satisfaction at the way he sounded so proud of what I'd done. "So did you get to take care of that other thing we talked about?"

"No. I'm sorry. I tried."

His sigh practically rattled the handset. "Okay."

"Are you ready for school tomorrow? You have your clothes laid out and your backpack ready to go?"

"Yeah." His voice changed, a hint of trepidation sneaking in under the too-cool-to-care veneer. "You are still gonna be able to take me, right? Maybe I should stay home. Wait until next week."

"I'll be there." Damn, I hated making promises I wasn't sure I could keep. "You know where the big binder I keep all the school stuff in is, right? I want you to get that out and have it ready for Jeremy to take with you tomorrow. You guys can pick me up here."

"You're not coming home all night?"

"Doesn't look like it, but I'm trying. You can bunk there with Gram and Jeremy, sleep on the couch. You're okay with the downstairs bathroom, right?"

"Yeah, but there's no shower—"

"Jeremy can carry you upstairs or take you down to the summerhouse when you go to get your stuff for tomorrow and you can shower tonight."

"But, Mom—" No one messed with his morning routine, not even a jail-bound mother.

"David, please. Cut me a break here." Silence, which I decided was agreement. "Do you still have the card Yancey gave you?"

"Yeah, why?"

"Give it to Jeremy. I need the phone number on it. Can you go find it now while I talk to Gram again?"

"Okay." He didn't sound very happy.

"Hey, David."

"Yeah."

"Love you."

"Whatever."

The phone clattered, and there was the distant sound of voices. Finally, Flora came back on the line. "Boy's not too happy."

"I'll make it up to him." How, I had no idea. "Did he find that card?"

"He's looking for it. What do you need us to do?"

"Call Yancey. Elizabeth Hardy is staying there. Tell her I need her to bail me out in time for me to get David to school tomorrow." I really hoped there was some option that would get me home tonight, but I wasn't counting on it. "Are you guys okay with David staying there?"

"Of course we are. You've been gone too long if you need to even ask." Her tone was pointed, putting me in my place.

"I wasn't sure after hearing that you let my folks tell everyone he was dead and I killed him." The words snapped out, hard and sharp enough to draw blood.

Silence followed. I couldn't even hear her breathe. For a second I thought maybe she'd had a heart attack or something. "Flora?"

When her voice came, it was heavy, dragging itself through the distance between us. "There are some mistakes you just can't fix, no matter how you regret them and want to."

My anger dulled down to a low simmer. I heard the regret in her voice, but she still hadn't explained herself. "Why? Why'd you let them do that to me and Cole?"

"Who was I to say what was and wasn't true? You were in a coma. I was just an old blind lady left on her own to worry about her family."

"Don't play the sympathy card with me. I never should have let you talk me into coming home. Looks like we're not going to be able to stay long, not with this mess you and my folks have created."

"Maybe it's for the best. David's been telling me about his school in the city and the great things you guys do, going to museums and parks and concerts, and all his friends. I was wrong to try to patch things up between you and your folks before I'm gone. I thought enough time had passed, but maybe it hasn't. Maybe you two should just go on back to the city."

For a moment I wished we could.

I remembered waking up this morning feeling free and refreshed and alive for the first time in so very long. The view from Flora's back porch. The turkey buzzard that soared between the mountains. The way my heart flew with it. This place was still in my bones, a part of me in ways the city could never be. Roots. Home. Whatever you call it, I wanted David to have that gift.

Not to mention the chance of having a father. I couldn't take that from him, even if we could afford to pack up and leave again. My son deserved better.

"Maybe you should mind your own business and let me decide what's best for my son."

Before, talking like that to her would have earned me a verbal slap. Now, all she answered with was a muffled sigh and wounded pride. "You're right. I'm hanging up so we can find you that lawyer."

I didn't want to hang up with this rift between us. Even if I was still mad at her for her part in this mess that was my life. "Thanks, Flora."

Time is funny when you're all alone in a room with no windows or clock. I'd about worn a hole in my sock, pacing from one end of the cell to the other, trying hard to unravel the snarl of memories and confusion that Ty's revelation had left me with. And failing.

Footsteps sounded. Heavy, uncertain. But familiar. I lay on the bunk, half-considered closing my eyes and pretending to be asleep. No, that wouldn't do anyone any good.

I climbed back to my feet and waited for Cole.

He wasn't dressed in a fancy suit and uptight tie like he'd been at the funeral. Now he looked like he should, like *my* Cole. Mud-caked hiking boots, jeans, untucked T-shirt beneath a ragged flannel shirt that might have been the same one he'd worn ten years ago. The gaunt cheeks and creases bracketing his eyes were new—to me, at least. Could be they were there because of me.

Ty waited down the hall, watching. Not sure who he was there to protect—me from Cole or Cole from me.

Cole lumbered to a halt in front of my cell. The silence between us was harder to break than the concrete walls surrounding us. He stared at me, his eyes cold. Blinked once, slowly. Weight on both feet, ready to run—or to attack.

"Ty says we've both been lied to," he said, his voice flat, sounding like a stranger's. "Says we need to talk."

Talking was the last thing I had the strength for. It took everything I had to creep close to the bars and hand him the pictures of David. He didn't take them at first, still staring straight at me—above and beyond me, really. As if I were a man the same size he was, as if he didn't already know every pore of my skin, every inch of my flesh. As if I wasn't me.

My hand hung there, trembling, clutching those pictures like they were worth my life.

Finally, he snatched them from me and stepped back, away from the bars. His face crumpled as he fought the urge to look down at them, and I had a feeling he knew what they were—that he, like me, was trying hard to deny the source and extent of our betrayal.

Curiosity got the best of him, and he glanced down. Then he lowered his head, shuffling from one photo to the next, his shoulders bowed as if beneath a great weight. His entire body shook, and he made the noise of a large animal smothering its grief.

"His name is David," I said, surprised my voice had the strength it needed to travel far enough to reach him.

His chin jerked up, his hair falling into his eyes from his cowlick just like David's. Now it was my turn to stifle tears. His jaw quivered, the muscles clenching so tight I thought he might break a tooth.

Ty walked down the hall, stopping between us. "I can see if there's an interview room free if you like."

Cole shook his head, his gaze locked onto the photos in his hand. Ty unlocked my cell door, swinging it wide open, ushered Cole inside, and sat him down on the bunk before he collapsed.

"You're the only prisoner," he said when I glanced at him, worried he'd get in trouble. "I don't think you're going to make a break for it."

"Thanks."

He turned to go, but I was suddenly afraid to be alone with Cole. The worst was yet to come. "Stay," I told Ty. "You're part of this too."

He hesitated, then settled for leaning against the wall of bars. The differences between him and Cole had never been more pronounced—Cole who wore his emotions open for anyone to see, Ty who had learned with time to keep feelings under guard. Both were tall, over six feet, in good shape, but Cole's build was more muscular—the kind of man you'd ask to help you push your car out of a ditch or chop a cord of wood—while Ty was lean, graceful, a man who could move silently in the forest or run a mile without getting winded. On the football field they'd made an unstoppable team, Cole's quarterback to Ty's wideout.

Cole held out the picture of David playing basketball. "What's wrong with him?" he blurted out, but his tone was one of concern, not derision.

"He has cerebral palsy."

He looked up at that, his face filled with anguish. "Does it hurt?"

"No."

"How'd he get it?"

"When I almost drowned, the lack of oxygen affected David's nervous system, so some of his nerves didn't develop quite right. He was born that way."

"Is it going to get worse?" His unspoken question was clear: Will it kill him?

"No. He's had a few operations to release tight tendons in his ankles and hips. Takes medicine. But he's smarter than anyone in this room."

That made him smile, and I knew he'd been thinking David might be retarded—so many people assumed that about kids with CP, just like they thought it was a fatal disease. I sat down on the bunk beside him, lay a hand flat on his thigh, felt his muscles bunch with tension. "He's a great kid, Cole. Really."

Still he looked worried. "The other kids, they don't tease him? I mean—being different and all?"

"Sure they do—that's how kids are." I shrugged. "We deal with it."

"I could maybe help with that," Ty volunteered. "Teach him a few things."

"He's nine, Ty. I don't need him turning into a ninja assassin."

He smiled, and I caught a glimpse of my best friend again. "I meant things your brother taught me. How to talk, deal with bullies."

Being part Cherokee and part African American with some Scotch-Irish thrown in for good measure had made Ty a target his whole life. "That'd be nice, thanks."

"So," Cole tore his gaze away from the photos clenched in his hand, "how the hell did this happen?"

We all looked at each other, silent. Ty heaved in a breath and pushed off the bars. "I think that's pretty obvious. All that stuff about pregnancy-induced psychosis—"

"Psychosis?" I asked. "You're kidding me."

Ty shrugged. "That's what your folks and Mr. Masterson told everyone. Said that's why you—"

"Tried to kill myself and my unborn baby." I leapt off the bunk, stalking the truth, my unseen prey. "That's not what happened." I turned and stared down at Cole. "You were supposed to be home that weekend. I went to tell you about the baby, so we could decide together what to do. But you weren't there."

He scuffed his boot, a clod of mud plopping to the floor. "My frat had a party the night before, and I was too hungover to drive home."

"Your dad was waiting for me. Somehow he knew I was pregnant. He laid into me, said he'd fire my folks, take their house away—my mom would die before she'd ever leave that house. It was Randy's home, she'll never give it up. And what kind of work would they be able to find around here if they were fired from the mine? He offered me money to leave, just disappear and never see you again."

"He was just trying to protect me, Angel. You know how my dad gets—only heir and all that. Sometimes he goes overboard, but he'd never make good on his threats. All you had to do was wait and talk with me." Now he stood, his body inches from mine. "I'll bet you got mad, egged him on. You always knew how to push his buttons."

I bit my lip before I really pushed something. Hard.

Cole always defended his father—always. I should have remembered that. Just like Old Man Masterson always defended what he thought was best for Cole. The two of them were a strange mix—neither understanding or even much liking the other, but welded together like a shiny new hood ornament on an ancient Cadillac.

"Maybe I did. He was talking about ruining my life and taking away everything my parents had. Anyway, I told him to go to hell and ran out, drove home." I paused. Cole stepped back, giving me space. "It gets kind of foggy after that. I remember a coal truck coming around the bend, right down the middle of both lanes. I swerved to miss him, and everything's blank after that."

"That's when I came along," Ty put in. "I didn't see the truck, but I saw your car in the pond just as it was about to go under. I jumped in, pulled you out, but you weren't breathing."

"It wasn't just my dad who said you tried to kill yourself," Cole argued. "Your folks did too, when they came home from the hospital. You were still in a coma, and they said you'd lost the baby. How was I to know different?"

I had no words to answer him. I kept my face hidden from the men, ashamed of what my parents had done. "I tried calling you—after I woke. But you wouldn't talk to me."

He slumped back onto the mattress, hands hanging between his knees.

"You must have hated me. Thinking that I—" I couldn't even put the thought into words. "—That I could have done something like that."

He nodded, still not making eye contact.

"Then, the last time I called, after David was born, a woman answered. Said you were getting married. So I stopped calling."

He looked up, his lips pursed so tight that they held back his sigh, but still I felt it in the way his chest heaved out and then collapsed. He was blinking faster than normal, as if that could mask the emotions warring on his face.

"It was no one's fault," Ty said, playing his role of peacemaker just like we were teenagers again. "What's important is that the truth is out now."

"Can I see him?" Cole's tone was tentative.

"He'd like that. Maybe after school tomorrow." I tried to lighten the tension that filled the small cell. "He'll probably want you to take him to see the big equipment on the MTR site—we flew over it today, and he was fascinated by the haul trucks and dragline."

He winced. "He saw that? It's not something I'm proud of."

Relief soared through me. "I heard your dad put you in charge of it."

"Only after he'd already begun it. Made both me and Waverly—my wife—VPs and told us he wanted to step back from the day-to-day operations, go into politics. Waverly does most of the work, she's an engineer, understands all about it. I just sign off on any forms she gives me." He shook his head. "I hate that damn site—did you see the fill they put in Jacob's Hollow? Used to be the best fishing in the county, now you won't even find any newts left alive down there."

"But I heard you're working on permits for Yellowroot."

"Dad promised that he'd only do one site, said it was quick money, would get us back on track until we could upgrade the underground mining operation. But now we have a mortgage on all that surface equipment, and the price of coal is soaring, and it's so much easier and faster and cheaper."

"So you're just going to sit back and let him get away with it?" I put my hands on my hips, looking down at him with my best "what kind of jerk are you?" glare.

He had the grace to look sheepish. Then he gave me a small smile. "Maybe not. I'm working on a few projects of my own." He stood. "Now that I have a son to leave a legacy for, I might have to work harder."

His words hit me hard. This was the Cole I remembered. The man I'd fallen in love with. But we still had big problems. "What will Waverly and your father say? About David?"

"Who cares? He's my son. Nothing they say can change that."

"You don't understand, Cole. This can't be about you and how you feel. You have to protect David—or at least don't stop me from protecting him. I'm not about to let him get hurt by anyone, not even your family."

He nodded slowly at that, taking it all in. I'd had ten years to learn how to fight for my son. I guess it was only fair that I give him more than ten minutes.

"Can I keep these?" he asked, holding the pictures.

"Of course. I have plenty at home."

"Maybe we can talk more tomorrow? I want to hear everything about him."

I looked to Ty. "What time can I spring this place?" Then I remembered. "Wait. I have to get David to school in the morning so I can go over his Individualized Educational Plan with his teachers and the school officials. I'm not about to let him face a new school by himself."

Ty shrugged. "Depends on the judge. And how fast you can post the bond."

"I'll make sure the charges are dropped," Cole volunteered. "That way she can get out first thing as soon as the paperwork is done, right?"

"If you can convince Ellings to withdraw the complaint."

"Ellings is a jerk. He'll never drop the charges."

"He will if he wants to keep his job," said Cole—the new Cole, hardened and sounding more like his father than I cared for. "I'll see you tomorrow."

He strode out of the cell and down the hall. Ty and I exchanged looks. "That went better than I thought it would," he said.

"Yeah." I wasn't so certain. There was still a lot of fallout from what happened ten years ago to deal with—starting with Flora and my folks. "Do I have to stay here tonight?"

His gaze softened. "Sorry. Can't release you until the complaint is withdrawn. I'll let you know as soon as I hear from Ellings. In the meantime, why don't you get some rest? The deputy on duty will be right down the hall if you need anything."

I gestured to my palatial surroundings. "What could I possibly need?"

Elizabeth's father had told her about protesters who had their tires slashed, houses shot at, dogs poisoned. He'd even hinted that his own life was threatened once or twice, but he didn't seem to take it seriously. The "new" Zachariah Hardy didn't believe in getting too stressed out about anything—so different from the corporate barracuda she'd grown up with.

Still, she never dreamed she'd find herself caught between trigger-happy mine workers and an equally gleeful eco-faction made up of coeds bent on saving the world while fast-tracking their acting and modeling careers.

She remembered AJ's tears when she witnessed the devastation created by the mountaintop removal mining and had the sudden feeling that those tears were the only truth in this farce.

How the hell had her father gotten involved with someone like Yancey? And what had Yancey meant about "charging extra"? He didn't talk or act like a client—more like a publicist.

The sound of a phone ringing broke through the Ladies' chatter. The door opened, and a Lady dressed in camo, carrying a machine gun across her chest, beckoned to Elizabeth. Yancey followed Elizabeth out to the foyer, where she picked up the house phone. The Lady went back to guarding the front door, blowing Yancey a kiss instead of saluting.

"Is this Zach Hardy's girl?" an old lady's voice came through the line.

"Yes. I'm Elizabeth Hardy. Who is this?"

"Flora Hightower. Angie's gram. She's in jail, needs your help to get her out. 'Fore morning—she's gotta take her young'un to school, get him started there." The woman's words weren't rushed, despite her undercurrent of urgency.

"AJ's in jail?"

"Dinna I just say so?"

"What'd she do?"

"That don't matter. You go do your job now—get her out of there so's she can come home, be with her son."

Elizabeth fought to translate the hills and valleys of the mountain accent. "I'm not sure—"

"You're a lawyer, ain't ya?"

"Yes, but—"

"Your father could. You saying you can't?" The old lady's words were spat out like a gauntlet being thrown.

Technically, she wasn't allowed to practice law in West Virginia until she made a personal appearance at the Supreme Court of Appeals, took their oath, and signed the West Virginia roll of attorneys. Plus, there was so much more to it. What kind of charges, felony or misdemeanor? Elizabeth wasn't even sure of the bail process here in Smithfield County—did she have to wait until morning for a judge or magistrate or could an official at the sheriff's department set bail? Her mind spun with unanswered questions, the biggest being—what the hell had AJ done?

Flora took her silence as acquiescence. "Good. Here's my number. You call when Angie's ready to come home."

She hung up before Elizabeth could protest.

"What is it?" Yancey asked.

"AJ is in jail."

"Of course she is." He looked surprised. "You didn't send her to the protest site to get arrested?"

"Why would I do that? I didn't even know she was going to the protest site."

He shook his head, eyes creased in annoyance. "Come with me."

She followed him back into the study. He opened a laptop and brought it over to the coffee table, clicking on a video. Elizabeth watched as one of Yancey's Ladies fell from her tree stand, followed by AJ confronting the man responsible—some big miner who looked half-stoned. And who had a very big knife. Jesus Christ, what had AJ been thinking, taking him on?

"It's not edited yet. We'll have it ready for the morning news shows, though. You'll probably want to leave her in jail overnight so we can arrange for media coverage of her bail hearing." He sighed. "I wish I had time to coach her beforehand. The right word at the right time and she could have the judge raising a ruckus, throwing contempt charges around. It'd make for a nice cap to the story."

"Cap to the story? AJ's sitting in jail—that means David is at her grandmother's, alone, without his own mother."

"I'm sure she thought of that." His eyes widened. "Can we bring David to court? What a great human-interest angle: single mom separated from disabled son as she fights to save mountains for him and his generation." He spread his hands again, Hollywood-style, as if framing a movie.

"No. We can't use David like that." She stared at Yancey. "This is getting totally out of hand. I'm not sure why my father took you on as a client, but—"

"You've got it backwards."

"But—what?"

"Your father didn't work for me. I worked for him. Well, he signed the checks, but I'm sure there's someone else behind things."

"What are you talking about?"

"Honey, I don't pay people to fight *my* causes. I get paid by them to bring more media attention to *their* causes."

She blinked, forced her tone back to courtroom-neutral. "So you're not an environmental activist?"

"I am this week. Next week, who knows?" He shrugged. "Call me a media activist. I activate them to cover whatever cause hires me."

"That's what my father hired you to do?"

"He wanted me to turn mountaintop removal mining into a national disgrace, one that would force Masterson and the other mining companies to stop the practice permanently. Made it sound like he couldn't count on the law, so he was courting public opinion instead."

Exactly opposite of the man—the lawyer, the father—she thought she'd known. "I need time to think about all this."

"Fine, I'm already paid. Just do me a favor and don't out me to the public. I've got a good feeling about 'Yancey and His All-Girl Eco-Militia.' Don't want to ruin my chances with the networks."

THIRTEEN

David woke more tired than he'd been when he finally fell asleep—which felt like maybe four minutes before Jeremy shook him awake.

"Hey there," Jeremy said. "We gotta get a move on. You okay getting dressed and everything?"

David grunted and pulled the covers up. "I'm not going without my mom."

"I just got off the phone with Elizabeth. We're picking your mom up on the way. Which means we need to leave early."

David peeked above the blanket. "Really? My mom's getting out of jail?"

"Yep. They're springing her as we speak." Jeremy looked like he was about to laugh. He seemed to always look that way, either smiling or grinning or outright laughing. David didn't understand how being happy all the time didn't just wear him out. "You get dressed. I'll fix you some breakfast."

Mom was okay, she wasn't going to be stuck in jail. The thought energized David as he crawled out from under the pile of quilts and blankets and transferred into his chair. Then he remembered. He was still mad at her.

Dumping him on people he barely knew (forget the fact that Jeremy let him stay up way past his bedtime and play all the video games he wanted and Flora made fudge and let him lick the bowl) just because it was convenient for her. The only time he ever got to stay over with friends back home he'd have to beg and beg and his mom would practically interrogate them before saying yes, and she'd still call every twenty minutes to check on him like he was a baby.

Plus, she'd broken her promise to him. He strapped on his AFOs with quick snapping motions, tugging the Velcro too tight the first time and having to readjust the ankle splints. He was never gonna meet his dad.

And now he had to go to school. He liked school—loved it, in fact—but that was his school back in D.C., the one with Mrs. Carleton and his friends like Evan and the cool library and . . .

"David, breakfast," Jeremy called.

"Yeah, I'm coming." He finished dressing, thought once about folding the sheets and blankets strewn across Flora's couch—she called it a "Chesterton"—but he didn't know where anything went anyway, so he left them and wheeled into the kitchen.

"You sleep okay, boy?" Flora asked as she stirred sausage links in a frying pan.

"Yes, ma'am." David still marveled at the idea of a blind woman cooking, but Flora hadn't thought twice about showing him how to fry chicken or make biscuits yesterday, and so far nothing had caught on fire, so he guessed it was okay.

Jeremy was busy slicing an apple into a bowl of something that looked like thick, brown oatmeal. "Muesli?"

"No thanks." David hated having to remember his manners first thing in the morning—he hadn't even had his shower to help him wake up, since he'd had to take it last night.

"You'll have some sausage and eggs," Flora declared. "Proper start for a growing boy."

He really wished she'd stop calling him "boy" and missed his Frosted Mini-Wheats. But the eggs smelled good, and a few minutes later his plate was clean except for some honey that he'd run out of biscuit to sop up.

Jeremy finished a big glass of milk, wiped his face, and pushed back his chair. "We gotta go. Brush your teeth and grab your stuff."

His mom wasn't a morning person—she always overslept—and she talked like that too, like it was his fault they were always running late for school. But Jeremy wasn't his mom, and neither was Flora.

He sat there, feeling his face pull down and his eyes slit shut, fingers gripping the arms of his chair, ready for the anger to burst right up and out of him, spewing all over everyone and everything in sight.

Before it could, Flora came over and gave him a hug from behind, her lips brushing the top of his head just like his mom's did. "Everything will be okay," she whispered. "You're gonna go make your mom proud, I just know it."

He was still mad at his mom, the last thing he wanted was to make her proud, and yet. . . . Flora's words squeezed the anger from him, made his chest empty out enough to allow a fresh breath in. His shoulders relaxed, and his face surrendered to a smile.

"Go on now, boys," she said, lumping Jeremy in with David. "I'll take care of cleaning up."

David showed Jeremy how to unstick the van's emergency brake and the trick with wiggling the defrost knob until it came on. They drove down the mountain and then took the highway—two lanes, but they still called it a highway, which seemed weird since the highways in D.C. were like six or eight lanes—over a few more mountains to Smithfield, where the county courthouse and jail was.

Along the way Jeremy asked polite questions about David's old school and friends, but David stopped answering them, pretending to be interested in the scenery, which was just a bunch of boring trees without even any leaves yet, alternating with pine trees and valley views that made him kinda dizzy, interrupted by the occasional small, saggy house or trailer. Talking about his school and friends back home made him sad. He knew he was missing out on all sorts of good stuff and everyone's life would just go on without him, without them even thinking about him, and here he'd be, stuck out in the woods where no one even knew him.

Jeremy finally shut up. The quiet in the van wasn't the good kind of quiet like when he and Mom were headed somewhere fun and were busy thinking about what it was going to be like. This quiet was more an awkward, fill-in-the-blank quiet, like taking one of those achievement tests where you had to color the bubbles without going out of the lines.

He hated those tests. His teacher said he could take his on the computer, but his mom always said he should try first with a pencil like the other kids, and since he always scored really good, the teacher let him. But he knew he could do better on the computer. And his hand and shoulder and teeth always ached after filling in all those little bubbles. He hated those bubbles.

Maybe this new school wouldn't have them. That would be cool.

They pulled up in front of a two-story brick building with big white columns out in the front. Elizabeth and his mom were waiting, his mom running down the steps to them before the van even stopped. She flung the side door open, reaching in to hug him.

"How are you?" She rumpled his hair, squeezing him hard. She stank, her clothes were all rumpled, and her hair was hanging like it had given up trying to stay in place. "I missed you so much."

"Mom." She didn't get the hint, kept on kissing him. "We're gonna be late."

That got her. She let go and backed out of the van. It wasn't until she exchanged keys with Jeremy, pointing him to a fenced-in parking lot where the police had left his truck, and getting money for him from Elizabeth, that he realized she was expecting to take him to school looking—and smelling—like that. Bad enough being the new kid in the wheelchair, but to roll in, meet everyone, with his mom looking like, well, like she'd just got out of jail?

He slumped, his head rocking against the window. Doomed. There was no way he'd ever live this down.

She jumped into the van, and they took off with a squeal, her steering with one hand and checking the thick binder that sat on the seat beside her with the other. "We may be a few minutes late, but we'll have all our paperwork."

"Think there's time for you to brush your teeth?" Or hair?

They pulled up to a stop sign, and she examined her reflection in the rearview, dragging her fingers through her hair. "Got any gum?"

Sometimes he wished she carried a purse instead of relying on him for everything. "Here." He handed her a pack of his Big Red. She took a stick, jammed it in, and began chewing. "Maybe some perfume?"

"Don't have any—next time I go to jail, remind me to bring deodorant and toothpaste."

"How about this?" He unbuckled and reached under the seat for the spray bottle of fabric cleaner she kept there. Without slowing down, she spritzed it inside her jacket on her T-shirt like it was perfume. Now she smelled like a sweaty flower. Great. Then he noticed her shirt. "Not the Godsmack shirt. Mom."

"I'll zip my jacket, they'll never know." She tried fluffing her hair again, but it kept falling limp like day-old ramen noodles. "Did you have fun with Flora and Jeremy?"

He rolled his eyes, safely out of her line of sight. "Yeah. I guess." He sighed. "I saw the video of you shoving that guy. It was online. He had a knife." Fear stretched his voice until it sounded thin and tight like a wire ready to snap. "He could have hurt you."

"No. I'd never let that happen, and you know it." She took her eyes off the road for a quick second, meeting his in the rearview so he'd know she was serious. "He's just a bully, wouldn't ever really hurt anyone. At least not anyone who stood up to him. But I was wrong to shove him. I should have found a better way."

"I liked how you lassoed him with that rope."

She laughed, not her usual gut-buster laugh, more like an inside joke laugh. "He walked right into that. Idiot."

"That's not a nice thing to call someone," he mimicked her own voice.

"Yes, *Mom*." Now they both laughed. She watched the road, glancing at the clock and frowning. "I talked with your dad."

He leaned forward, as far as the seat belt would let him. "Yeah?"

"Yeah. Told you I would, didn't I?"

Had to admit, she'd kept her promise—despite being in jail.

"He wants to meet you today. After school. What do you think?"

"Yeah, that'd be cool." He kept his tone casual, but inside his stomach was getting ready to spew the eggs and sausage right out of him. A few deep breaths later he'd calmed it back down, but his voice was still unsteady with excitement. "What's he like?"

"His name is Cole. Cole Masterson. He's a good man, a few years older than me. Was one of my best friends before, well, before things between us changed. He left Scotia before you were born, never knew about you. So it's not like he abandoned you or anything. When I told him about you, he was real excited to meet you—said it'd be a privilege."

"How come no one told him about me?" Meaning: How come she didn't tell this Cole guy he had a kid? Back home in D.C., lots of his friends didn't have a dad, it was no real big deal, but usually they at least knew who their dad was.

"I tried, but he wasn't—available. And then he got married, and, well, let's just say that there were other grown-ups involved and they made some mistakes. But Cole wants to fix all that, and so do I. He's really hoping that you like him." She looked for David in the mirror again, and he knew that what she really meant was that *she* really hoped he liked Cole.

Hmmm. That was different—he got to decide if he wanted this Cole guy around, if he wanted a father. After all this time of only having Mom, he wasn't too sure what he wanted. "We'll see."

They pulled up in front of the school, and just as he'd feared, they were late. There were no kids hanging out in the parking lot or the playground beside it. She jumped out and helped him into his chair, the big binder sitting on his lap as she pushed him up the handicapped ramp to save time.

They got inside. There were no metal detectors, no guards at the door. The hallways were empty. Dark and dingy, the only color some limp paper banners talking about not using drugs and hailing the Scotia Miners. Gray vinyl floor, gray walls, gray lockers, kinda white but really more like gray ceiling tiles. David was glad for his racing red wheels; otherwise he might have faded into the background in his jeans and gray sweatshirt.

The place was only a few years old, but it smelled musty, like someone had left a wet towel lying around for a long, long time. And the floor was uneven in spots, hard to see, but he felt the bumps as he rolled over them.

Mom ran ahead to the office, but even with him pausing to look around, he still flew past her and got there first. She smiled as he held the door for her. "Such a gentleman."

He joined her inside. Couldn't see above the counter she leaned on, but she was talking to someone. Then a door in the counter opened, and a fat lady with dark hair and pink lipstick came out, stopping short when she almost walked right into David. Like she hadn't expected to see him there—what did she think? That Mom wouldn't bring him with her?

Knowing that good manners were the fastest way to charm adults, he pushed off and got to the door before either of the women did, hauled it open, and held it for them. It was harder in this direction, like the door had been hung so it was easier to come in than to leave.

"Thank you, David," his mother said. "This is Mrs. Nowicki, your new principal."

Mrs. Nowicki paused just inside the doorway, forcing David to keep holding the glass door so it didn't smack her on the ass. His arm muscles bunched and twitched, and he had the feeling she knew exactly how heavy the damn door was. He refused to let her see the effort it took to keep it open. "Pleased to meet you, Mrs. Nowicki."

She looked back over her shoulder, giving him a look that said she was surprised he wasn't a retard and could talk. Followed by an arch of her eyebrow that told him children were expected to be seen and not heard. Great. One of those.

His mom wasn't a retard either. She grabbed the door from David right before his arm was ready to get pulled off. He pushed out into the hall, and she let the door bang shut behind them. Mrs. Nowicki jumped and glared—this time at his mom, not him.

"I'm sure you had a chance to review David's records and his IEP," his mom said, striding down the hall as if she owned the joint, her boot heels clicking against the floor, stomping out the dainty flip-flopping of Mrs. Nowicki's slingbacks.

"After reviewing David's Individual Education Plan, we've placed him in our Support Unit," Mrs. Nowicki said. They reached a door at the end of the hall. No decorations on this one, not even the colored paper that had adorned the other classrooms. It felt sad and lonely. David had a sinking feeling he knew what lay inside. "I'm sure he'll be very happy there."

"Support Unit?" his mother stopped, glancing into the small window in the door. She didn't like the sound of it either. Back home, David had been in the advanced track, taking some fifth- and sixth-grade classes. There they'd called it the Individualized Learning Unit. Maybe Support Unit was the Scotia name for their advanced placement program.

Right. And Captain Awesome was going to spring out of David's notebooks and fly him away from here any second now.

Mrs. Nowicki ignored her, opened the door, and gestured for David to enter. "Mrs. Hansen, this is David Palladino. He'll be joining you."

David wheeled himself over the threshold. There were seven other kids in the classroom, not just kids David's age. A few looked like they belonged in kindergarten or first grade, and two were big enough to be eighth-graders. Two of the boys and one of the girls had the features of Down's syndrome and looked up at David with smiles. Another boy was too busy banging his head against the corner of a table and tearing at his hair to notice David's arrival. And the rest just kind of stared—one of them wore a bib to catch the drool slipping out of his open mouth.

"Mom—"

She jerked her chin in a nod. Her lips were pressed tight, and her jaw muscles were working as if she was still chewing the gum she had spit out before they came inside. "Wait for us here, David. Mrs. Nowicki and I have a few things to clear up."

"David's placement is unsatisfactory," I began as soon as we'd made it to Nowicki's office and had the door shut behind us. She marched her fat ass around her desk, plopping down into a leather chair that squeaked like a whoopie cushion in protest.

"Well, Miss Palladino"—she put the emphasis on the "Miss"— "you're always welcome to home-school your son if our facilities don't agree with you."

Ah, now I knew what the problem was. Had nothing to do with David or his needs and everything to do with me and my past. She thought I was a dumb slut who'd dropped out of school, run away to have a baby, and now had the audacity to flaunt my sins by coming back again. Damn small-town gossip mill. I was certain the tongue-waggers had been working overtime ever since I arrived home.

I reached across the desk and picked up the receiver to her phone. "What are you doing?"

"Calling my attorney. Hello, Miss Hardy?"

Elizabeth sounded like she was in the car. "Don't tell me you got arrested again already."

"It's Angela Palladino. I'm here with Mrs. Nowicki, the principal of my son's school, and she tells me that they simply won't be able to accommodate David's special needs. As you know, Part C of the ADA—"

"You mean Part B of the 1997 Individuals with Disabilities Education Act," Elizabeth corrected me.

"And of course, Part B, which guarantees my son's free, appropriate public education."

"Quit messing around and let me talk to her."

I handed the phone to Nowicki, who took it with a disdainful scowl. The scowl soon fled, replaced with a frown. Then Nowicki grew pale, bit her lower lip, and finally nodded and said, "Of course, I understand, Miss Hardy. Thank you."

She hung up the phone. I sat back and smiled at her. "I take it you'll be able to accommodate David after all?"

"Yes."

"You're lucky we don't just sue the pants off you and the school district."

Her glare returned, and I realized I'd gone too far—as usual. It's one thing for a city lawyer to put the fear of God into a principal, quite another for a single unwed mom with a history of being a troublemaker. Well, she'd just see how much of a troublemaker I could be. Wait until I talked to the parents of the other students in the so-called Support Unit and explained to them what their legal rights were and forced the school to supply the services their children needed instead of warehousing them for the day.

"You don't remember me, do you?" Mrs. Nowicki said.

"No. Should I?"

"My maiden name is Dorman. Letta Dorman."

Oh boy. She'd tried to go out with my brother, had pined for him in fact, but he'd dumped her after she'd said something nasty to me—I couldn't even remember what it was, something about being a pest.

Which I probably had coming, because I'd hated all of Randy's girlfriends and was always trying to sabotage their efforts to get close to him.

I forced my smile wider and stood. "Nice to meet you again, Letta." I offered her my hand, but she ignored it, leaving it hanging there in the air. "I'm sure we'll be seeing each other again." I turned to leave.

"A word of advice, Miss Palladino." Her voice cracked like a whip, reeling me back. "An attorney isn't always the best way to solve your son's problems—especially around here where people have long memories."

She looked down at her papers, not bothering to meet my gaze, dismissing me. Like I was going to let a fat harpy like her threaten my son.

I stepped back to the desk, my shadow blocking her light. Stood there for a solid half-minute before she finally deigned to glance back up. "Let me give you some advice, Principal Nowicki. My son is in your care eight hours out of every day. Which means I hold you personally responsible for his well-being. And I have a longer memory than anyone else in this town."

I spun on my heel and left. Figured she got the message.

FOURTEEN

After dealing with AJ's release, Elizabeth had returned to Yancey's house and gathered her things. The Ladies were taking turns patrolling the grounds and providing additional security for their sisters up in the trees at the protest site. Yancey was nowhere to be seen, which was good, because Elizabeth was having second thoughts about him.

She drove back to her father's house and decided it was time to learn more about Yancey from someone other than Yancey. She called a PI her father had referred her to during her divorce.

"Lowenstein here."

"Hal? It's Elizabeth Hardy. I need a favor."

"Sure, what is it?"

"I want you to do a background check on a man named Yancey. Not sure if that's his first, last, or only name. Could even be an alias. He's an environ—"

"Already done. Well, most of it. I was waiting to hear back from your dad, see if he wanted me to dig deeper into Yancey's financials."

"My father asked you to check out Yancey?"

"Sure, around two weeks ago. Sent him my preliminary report five days ago, but haven't heard from him since. Everything okay?"

It was the first time Elizabeth had to tell anyone that Zach was dead, and she had no idea how to say the words. Not without making them real. Too real, that was. Something she couldn't ignore by immersing herself in the case.

"He died four days ago," she said, her voice coming out a strangled whisper that she covered by clearing her throat. "I'll look for your report in his things, but in the meantime could you summarize it for me?"

There was an awkward silence. "Jeez, Elizabeth, I'm sorry, I had no idea. What happened?"

"They're calling it a seizure."

"You don't sound so sure about that."

"I was, but not now. I've been getting death threats since I decided to take over his case." It sounded so melodramatic when said out loud like that, she half-expected him to laugh.

He didn't laugh. "You got protection? Want me to make some calls, get you a list of good men?"

"No, no. I'm fine. Just tell me about Yancey."

"Well, in technical terms, I'd call him a shady character."

"Want to be more specific?"

"Never arrested or even charged with any crime, but tons of suspicion. His name has appeared linked to everything from counterfeit vodka to pornography to SEC insider trading."

"So he's not legit."

"No. He is. Kinda. Made a fortune in Silicon Valley in the nineties but lost it in the dot-com bust. Poured what he had left into real estate speculation, then the bubble burst, and so on. He's been rich more times than I can count, but still doesn't have enough cash to leave a tip at Starbucks. But at least those deals were legit."

"And the other stuff? Counterfeit vodka and porn?"

"When I was a cop, we used to see these repeat offenders—stupid stuff, taking risks that were sure to get them caught. Most of them were criminals because they had no other means of support—it was an easy way out.

"But there were others, ones who could have made a legitimate living. People who see other people only as a means to an end. The shrinks labeled them sociopaths. One thing I noticed all these guys had in common, aside from total denial that any rules applied to them, was risk-taking. They were all adrenaline junkies, needing more and more stimulation."

"And you think that's Yancey? A sociopathic adrenaline junkie?"

"Feels like it to me. Remember, the crooks I dealt with were the ones dumb enough to get caught. Your Yancey is a smart dude. He's not in it just for the money, he's in it for the thrill."

"A risk-taker. Wanting the limelight." She thought about that. Yancey had been close to her father—and he'd been around her when she'd received the death threat yesterday. Would he go that far, just for publicity? "I see where you're going. But is he someone who would use violence to get what he wants?"

Lowenstein paused. "He's never been associated with any violent crimes. But . . . a guy like Yancey, he might not think the rules applied to him. If someone stood in the way of something he wanted, yeah, I guess he'd do what he needed to remove the obstacle."

"Including murder."

"Could be. This is all speculation. I don't have any facts, just thirty years of gut instinct."

"Thanks, Hal." She hung up, wondering.

David was glad his mom had left. Otherwise, he had the feeling some-one might have gotten hurt. Because Mrs. Nowicki, after hearing that David's old school was only K thru six, had decided that he needed "mentors" to help him get oriented and introduced him to two eighth-graders: Lenny and Walter.

Lenny and Walt just happened to be Neanderthals. Maybe they were even further down the evolutionary food chain, Cro-Magnons. They were big enough and hairy enough and ugly enough.

And they thought it was hilarious that a little fourth-grader in a wheelchair was placed in their care.

"I'm going to take David to his homeroom now," Mrs. Nowicki chirped, obviously pleased with herself. "But I expect you two to make him feel welcome during recess and lunch."

Recess and lunch, the two most dreaded periods for a new kid in a new school. The times when you were outnumbered, with no idea which cliques held which territory or who ruled.

The Cro-Magnons smiled, zits popping like clusters of tiny red vol-canoes, nodding to the principal. "Of course, Mrs. Nowicki. We'd love to help out, Mrs. Nowicki," they said together, eyes gleaming with antici-pation. "See you at recess, David."

After making sure David was situated—although I could tell he was still pretty steamed about initially being dumped in Scotia's so-called Support Unit—I went back to the summerhouse and finally got a few hours' sleep. When I woke up, I treated myself to a long shower, washed my hair twice until it no longer stank of jail, and changed into jeans and a flannel shirt. With my stomach growling, I wandered up to Flora's and was delighted to walk into her kitchen and smell fried chicken.

"Was just heating up leftovers from yesterday," she said, although it was Jeremy standing at the stove, while she sat at the table. "I know it's your favorite. Figured you'd be hungry." A peace offering for our argu-ment last night. I was happy to take it—I had enough to worry about without Flora adding to the mix.

"Figured right." I looked over Jeremy's shoulder. In addition to the chicken there were some brown hockey puck–like things in the skillet. "What else you got there?"

"Falafel. Want some?"

"We rented a room above a Lebanese restaurant for a while, way back when David was little. I used to love their food until I had to smell it day in and day out for a year and a half. But David still loves it," I added quickly when Jeremy looked disappointed. I redeemed myself by throw-ing together a salad for all of us, and we sat and ate. Neither asked me about my experiences last night, which I was grateful for, but that made conversation a bit limited.

"Heard Elizabeth almost got herself killed last night," Flora said, by way of small talk.

I dropped my drumstick. "She didn't say anything when I talked with her. What happened?"

"Some punks shot up Yancey's house."

"The police think they were aiming at Elizabeth?" Maybe I shouldn't have left her on her own today. She said she'd be working on the legal arguments and didn't need me to help, but now it sounded like she should have someone around to watch out for her.

"Yancey's house has been targeted before," Jeremy put in. "And anyone around here really aiming to hurt Elizabeth—"

"—Would have gotten the job done," I finished for him. Folks who rely on the game they bring in during hunting season to get their families through the winter have to be good shots. "Why are they working so hard to drive Elizabeth off? Masterson probably has the court bought and paid for already."

"Maybe it's a judge he can't bribe."

Flora snorted at that. "Ain't no judge around here you can't bribe. Maybe there's something more than the court case they're trying to stop."

"Like what?"

"How would I know? That's what always happens in the movies."

I finished my meal and cleaned my plate. "I've got to go. Thanks for lunch." It was weird depending on someone else to provide my meals. About time I began helping out. "Do you need anything at the store? I can stop on my way."

Flora saw right through my offer. "Don't worry about it. It's nice to have a good eater like David to cook for. And we like having you up here for dinner—livens the place up."

Still. I hadn't come home to live off Flora's goodwill. But this wasn't the time to argue. "I'll see you later."

I drove down the mountain. Figuring on two birds, I headed toward the protest site. I needed to talk to the local protesters, make sure there wasn't something they knew that might help Elizabeth, and I was long past due for another chat with my dad.

The van's undercarriage made a scraping noise as I pulled off the road to the school and turned up the dirt road to the protest site. The mud from yesterday had baked into hard ridges dug into the clay. I held my breath, waiting for the van to drop something—with my luck, it'd be something expensive—but the poor thing gave a shudder and soldiered on. Instead of forcing it all the way to the top of the hill, I parked it alongside the edge of the school's playing field and got out there.

The field was set up for soccer, with two goal nets at the ends, but it was a muddy quagmire. Sparse grass sprouted in tiny soul patches, forgotten brown stubble in between puddles, slick with a greasy orangish tint. The wind shifted, and a whiff of something that smelled like turpentine drifted across the field. Below the field, kids appeared on the playground, specks of vibrant energy in a stagnant landscape. Their cries of joy punctuated the air like the calls of an eagle tasting the wind. Recess. Shading my eyes from the sun, I looked for David, but didn't see him.

I turned and trudged up the hill to the stalled worksite, my boot heels sinking into rust-colored clay. I was surprised to find my dad perched in the cab of the dozer, high above the rest of us—except the Ladies in the trees, of course—his lunch pail beside him as he used a spotting scope to watch the kids down the hill.

"Thought you were supposed to be watching Yancey's Ladies." I used the handholds to swing up onto the tread and join him.

"I'm on my lunch break. No law says I can't keep an eye out for my grandson. Seeing as you don't want me to meet him."

So typical of my dad to rewrite reality to suit his needs. "It was you who turned us away."

"What do you want, Angela?" He said it with a resigned sigh, as if all I ever did was make demands on him and Edna.

A burning sensation simmered from my gut up to the back of my throat. When I swallowed, I tasted acid and anger.

"Cole and Ty told me what you did—lying about my accident, lying about David. Did you really think you could get away with it?"

He shrugged, still looking past me with the scope. The feeling was so very familiar—the feeling of being invisible even when I was standing right in front of my parents. All they could see was Randy, their pride and joy, their beloved ghost. "You shouldn't meddle in what you don't know nothing about."

"It's my life! And you were the one who meddled—you and Masterson. How much did he pay you to spread those lies, to bury the truth?"

"We did what was best for you," Frank said. "You'd do the same for your child."

Back to that old song-and-dance. "I heard what you told the doctors when I was in the hospital. You told them to take David if it meant saving me. You were willing to kill my baby."

"To save you. Everything we did we did for you."

"Including lying to Cole and everyone here? How was that good for me? Or for your grandson?"

"I'd like the answer to that as well." Cole walked out from behind the bulldozer. He was dressed a lot like I was: boots, jeans, flannel shirt, leather jacket. Looked like he was ready to go for a hike or hop on a Harley. Except his eyes. They'd gone cold again, like they had yesterday at the cemetery.

His face was a mask, but his hands bunched into fists at his sides told a story. He wasn't out here hiking.

Growing up, I had a crush on Cole—I think just about every woman who's ever met him has had those feelings. He's one of those guys who do that to women. Doesn't even try. But then Randy died, and we grew to be friends, best friends. And then later, things changed and we grew even closer . . . for a while. Until he went away to college.

When he came home for his mother's funeral, those old feelings resurfaced—not only the like and lust and love, but also the confusion of grief, the need to explode, to feel, to prove you're alive. But instead of stealing blasting caps and blowing up tree stumps like we did when we were kids and lost Randy, this grief took a more physical form, and David was the result.

For something so wonderful and beautiful to come from something so dark was an affirmation that the world isn't always a bad place—at least not as bad as I imagine it to be most of the time. But having David also meant losing Cole.

First, I cut my parents out of my life, putting David ahead of them, and then when Cole didn't want to have anything to do with us—or so I thought—I sacrificed him as well. Dug a hole in my psyche and filled it with all those old feelings, buried them down deep.

Until now. Last night, I'd been too numb, overwhelmed with everything happening, to feel much. But now old feelings, new feelings swamped me, spinning me off balance. I had to hold tight to the steel grip on the side of the dozer cab, so tight the paint flakes ground into my palm. All I wanted to do was to let go, jump down, and throw my arms around Cole, loving the way he'd come to fight for a son he hadn't even met yet. Ten years I'd been fighting that fight alone. The glimmer of hope that I might have help, that David had someone else in his life who cared, washed over me like sunshine.

For about a microsecond. Then all that sunshine fled—but not before bouncing off Cole's wedding ring, slapping me in the face with the fact that he was off-limits, out of bounds, and still miles beyond my reach.

"You got an answer for me, Frank?" he said, standing below the cab, looking up at us.

My dad frowned. Instead of lowering the scope and addressing Cole and me, he squinted and pushed it up closer to his eye as if that would help him make sense of what he saw. "What the hell those boys up to?"

FIFTEEN

Recess came, and David resigned himself to an hour of unimaginative torture. It was the price any new kid paid, and the best thing was to just smile and get through it, not be a wuss or, worse, a whiner.

He wasn't too worried when Walt and Lenny got the brilliant idea of carrying him onto the soccer field and ditching him there. One thing these two junior Einsteins didn't seem to have figured out was that they were halfway up a hill. Gravity rules, whether you are on wheels or slip-sliding on your feet through the mud.

Under most conditions, he could move faster in his chair than "normal" people could on foot. He pictured himself gliding down the hill as soon as they released him, soaring into class just as the bell rang—and leaving these two yee-haws in his wake to straggle in late, wet, and covered in mud. Captain Awesome would love it.

His fantasy image faltered when Walt stumbled, letting his side of the wheelchair lurch. It wasn't far to the ground, maybe six, eight inches, but if they dropped him, David had to make sure his chair landed on its wheels. Otherwise he'd have to belly crawl in the mud, push it upright, and haul himself back into it.

Not a pretty picture. So very un-Awesomey.

Walt was making a wheezy noise, worse than when David had gotten pneumonia after one of his surgeries. His face looked funny too—mouth wide open like a fish, neck muscles straining, eyes squinched up. Was he drooling?

"If I'm getting too heavy for you, you could set me down anytime now," David said, taking care to make it sound like a suggestion and not a plea. He knew better than to show any weakness.

"No way, you little turd," Lenny said, laughing and jostling his side of the chair extra hard.

Walt slipped again. This time he let go of the chair.

Lenny slipped as he struggled with the unexpected weight, and fell into a puddle, dropping the chair and David. They hit the ground with a thud, the mud cushioning the blow and helping to keep the chair upright. Lenny climbed to his knees and whirled on Walt. "What the hell's wrong with you?"

Lenny's face had grown bright red, and his words emerged with a stream of tobacco-colored saliva. He began shaking, his eyes rolled back, and he pitched forward, landing face down in the puddle beside David, arms and legs flailing in a full-blown seizure.

David twisted, reaching down with both hands to grab Lenny's collar and haul him up out of the water. Walt went down as well.

Then David saw his mom's van at the edge of the field. Thank God for overprotective, control-freak Mom. She'd know how to help.

"Mom!"

I shifted my weight, turning to look over my shoulder to see what my dad was looking at. Two boys, big boys, probably twelve, thirteen at least, were carrying David in his wheelchair to the center of the muddy playing field. Splashing through the puddles, their jeans soaked, mud and clay covering their boots and lower legs, they were laughing as if stranding a handicapped kid half their size in the middle of a field of mud was the most hilarious thing in the world.

Then one of them threw his head back, his mouth gaping open like he was drowning. I yanked the scope away from my dad so I could see better. With its magnification, I saw the boy's face was turning purple. He dropped his side of David's chair.

The other boy slipped and fell into a puddle. David landed between them, his chair remaining upright, thank God, the mud cushioning his fall.

The first boy stumbled blind, arms pinwheeling as he hauled in air, gasping. The second boy began having a full-blown seizure, mud and water flinging from his arms and legs. David shouted for help, caught between them.

"Call nine-one-one," I told my father. I jumped from the bulldozer and ran toward the field, Cole matching me, then outpacing me. More footsteps sounded behind us, and I realized my dad was also in the race.

The scope slipped from my fingers as I pumped my arms, trying to go faster. The first boy had now also fallen. The second lay still, too still.

But all I could see was David, his bright red chair the only spark of life in that lifeless field.

Clods of mud disintegrated beneath my pounding boot heels. Then we were in the wet section of the field, no traction, grass and mud creating a slippery nightmare. The smell returned, stronger. Acrid, burning my nostrils like turpentine, tasting sharp and oily against the back of my throat.

All this I barely registered, my attention riveted on David. He was bent over the side of his wheelchair, fists balled in the back of the jacket of one of the boys, hauling the kid out of the puddle he'd fallen face down into. Cole reached the first boy, the one not breathing, and grabbed him. Dad and I reached David pretty near simultaneously. Dad splashed into the puddle, taking the boy from David. He rolled him face up. The boy was gasping, sputters of foamy saliva filling his mouth.

David was a bit flushed but otherwise appeared unharmed. I scooped him up into my arms.

He was getting almost too heavy for me to lift—it was a point of contention between us, since I wanted to be able to help him if he needed it and he wanted to be as independent as possible—so I wasn't surprised by his first words, "Mom, don't!" Pride washed over me when his second words came, "I'm fine. Help them. They're sick."

I hugged him closer. My dad and Cole had taken the other boys off the field. I goose-stepped through the mud, slower now, so that I got as little as possible on me or David. That smell. I knew that smell. From my failed investigation of Pinehurst Chemicals. They'd been dumping an old, illegal pesticide, toxaphene, contaminating the groundwater near Hagerstown, but I could never prove it. I'd read up on everything I could about insecticides, and had gone and talked to some guys at the EPA who'd showed me examples of what toxaphene could do to a person.

In high enough concentrations, it caused trouble breathing, seizures, tremors, vomiting, coma, and eventually death.

My foot slipped into a puddle, and I glanced down at the rust-colored water. An oily sheen coated its surface. There was no rain last night. Why was the field wet and not the road?

We stumbled off the field. I wasn't taking any chances and continued to carry David to my van, setting him inside on the driver's seat so he could see everything. After patting down his clothing and making sure he was dry, that none of the water had gotten onto him, I asked, "Do you remember the chemicals I was checking out at Pinehurst, the insecticide?"

He nodded, his stare angling past me to where Cole and Dad had the boys laid out on the dry ground. "Toxaphene. But, Mom, who—"

This wasn't the time to stop and introduce him to Cole or my dad. "I think those boys were exposed. Can you use my phone to call nine-one-one and let them know? They'll need hazmat to decontaminate the field and protect the kids at school. Tell them to warn the ambulances and the hospital."

That got his attention. His hand shook a little when he took my phone, and he gulped loud enough for me to hear. "I got it. Go help Lenny and Walt."

I gave him a quick kiss on the forehead. "Love you." Then I ran over to where the boys lay. "It's absorbed through the skin," I told my dad and Cole. "We need to strip them and wash them off—and be careful not to touch anything wet."

Cole was already wearing leather gloves. I retrieved mine from the van along with my Leatherman and a tarp we could cover the boys with.

"How did they get exposed?" Cole asked as he used his knife to cut the clothing off one of the boys, who was wheezing and drooling, his color poor. I turned the boy's head to one side so he wouldn't choke. There wasn't a whole lot more we could do for him.

"I think it was sprayed on the field." I gestured to the mud and standing water.

He stopped, his gaze meeting mine. "By whom?"

"I don't know." David's bright red wheelchair stood alone out in the middle of the field. "But I'm going to find out."

We had the first boy undressed down to his T-shirt and briefs—they were dry, so we left them on and wrapped him in the tarp against the cold. I turned to help my dad with the second boy. He was wheezing now as well, but his seizures had stopped. Dad was moving slowly—he'd only managed to get the boy out of his wet coat and was now fumbling with his shoelaces.

"Just cut them," I snapped, using my Leatherman to slice through the laces.

He didn't answer. Instead, he leaned his weight onto his thighs, a strange gasping sound whistling through his lungs.

"Dad?" I dropped the shoe, stood up, and realized that he was soaked through with water from the field. "We need to get those wet clothes off you. Sit down."

He could barely raise his head to look at me. His mouth opened, but the only sound he made was a strangled whisper that I couldn't make out. I grabbed his arms to support him. "Cole, help me!"

He collapsed just as Cole reached him, his weight sagging against us.

SIXTEEN

"I'm fine, I'm fine," my dad said, his color returning as soon as he sat down and put his head between his knees. "Just got dizzy is all."

"You stay put, we'll take care of the boys," I told him, not liking how the veins in his neck were jumping like bongo drums. He said nothing, only nodded.

Cole and I stripped the second boy. By that time some of the protesters and Masterson workers had seen what was going on and ran down to help, bringing blankets for both boys. But they still weren't breathing right and their color was dusky.

Two vehicles pulled up: Elizabeth in her Subaru and Ty in his Tahoe. "Don't let Nikki out," I shouted to Ty as soon as he opened his door. "The field is contaminated."

"With what?"

"We don't know. I think it may be an insecticide called toxaphene. It can be absorbed through the skin."

"What can we do?" Elizabeth asked.

"Could you keep an eye on David? I left him in the van."

She nodded and jogged over to the van.

Sirens announced the arrival of the ambulance and fire truck. I quickly explained the problem to them. The two ambulance guys took it in stride even though they now had three patients counting my dad, who was arguing that he didn't need anything. They coordinated with the fire guys and began hosing down each of the boys to wash off any residue from their skin, then quickly bundled them into clean blankets and hustled them into the warm ambulance where the medics could work on them.

My dad was awake enough to fight the firemen who stripped his clothes off and hosed him down. By the time he was done, Cole had brought his SUV down, and they lifted Dad into the back. Some of his coworkers found a spare pair of coveralls for him to wear and stayed with him as the medic assessed him.

"How is he? Is it toxaphene poisoning? He was only exposed for a few minutes."

"No signs of toxicity," the medic said, removing his stethoscope and adjusting the oxygen mask he'd placed on my dad. "But his blood pressure is sky high, and he's doing a bit of wheezing. He should be checked out at the hospital." He looked behind him to where his partner was slamming the door to the ambulance, waving to him that it was time to go. "Your father is stable right now, and we don't have any other ALS medics, so I'm going to ask one of the firefighters to ride with you."

"No problem. You do what you need to do and we'll follow right behind."

"Go on," Dad said, his voice almost normal. "Take care of them boys."

The ambulance took off, lights and sirens going strong. A firefighter trained in Basic Life Support stayed behind to care for my dad. "Hey there, Mr. Palladino, I'm Brad," he said, shaking my dad's hand, then twisting his fingers to take his pulse.

After Cole had his turn getting hosed down, he emerged from behind the tarp the firemen had erected as a privacy wall wrapped in a silver space blanket, his teeth chattering. One of the firemen gave him a pair of boots to wear as he trudged back to his SUV and changed into jeans and a sweatshirt he had in a backpack.

"Your turn," one of the firemen said to me, raising the tarp for me to step behind and disrobe.

"No," I protested, "I'm fine. The only thing that came into contact with the mud were my boots."

He squinted, realized I was dry except for the mud caking my boots, and relented. "Those are leather. Hosing them off isn't going to be enough, we'll need to dispose of them. And those gloves."

"Whatever." I shucked the gloves, tossing them into a red biohazard bag he held, then kicked off my boots. All I wanted was to check on David. "I don't suppose there's any way we can save my son's wheelchair?"

He looked across the field, thought about it, and nodded. "Let me see what I can do. Your son okay? Does he need to be decontaminated?"

"No. The chair saved him." God, I never thought I would be saying those words. But David's disability had saved him. "How are the other two boys?"

"Don't know yet."

Ty joined us. He'd been cordoning off the area and talking to the protesters and Masterson's men, trying to see if they knew anything. "What made you think of toxaphene?"

We walked over to my van, my feet already freezing despite my socks, and I told him about the Pinehurst Chemicals case. "I ended up getting fired in the end," I finished. "We never did prove anything."

"Well, if you're right about this being insecticide poisoning, that case you lost may have just saved some lives." So typical of Ty to find the silver lining. "I'd better let the school know what's going on." He saluted David and tipped his hat to Elizabeth before heading down the hill.

I rummaged in the back of the van for a matching pair of sneakers, already mourning the loss of my favorite pair of boots. "David, those boys, what were they doing before—"

"Before they came and got me? They were tossing a ball around on the field." Ah, that explained why they'd developed symptoms so fast—their exposure was longer than we'd thought. Grabbing the shoes, I moved to the van's backseat—the one where David usually sat—to tug them on.

"And you're sure you didn't get any mud or water on you? What about when you grabbed that boy?"

"His coat collar was dry, it was just the front of him that was wet."

Still. "No headaches or flushing or blurry vision or—"

"No. I'm fine." He squirmed as I hopped out of the van and placed a hand on his forehead. I couldn't help myself. "Mom."

Ah, the all-too-familiar eye roll and three-syllable delivery. He *was* fine. I kissed the top of his head and gave him one of my patented sideways hugs—the best I could do with him in the car and me outside. Elizabeth smiled at me from the passenger seat. She seemed unusually quiet, but given the chaos raging around us, I could understand why.

"Are you okay if Elizabeth stays with you while I ride to the hospital with my dad?"

"Is he going to be all right?"

"I think so. Elizabeth is going to pick up my mom, and you guys can come to the hospital."

He nodded, then hesitated before asking, "Can I get my chair back?"

The thought of me or some stranger carrying him around until he reached stable ground where he could use his crutches was probably killing him. Poor kid. I should have realized that sooner. "The firemen are going to wash it down and bring it to you."

That brought a smile to his face. "Great."

"I have my cell if you need anything at all. Bye." I left, reluctantly, but Cole had pulled up alongside us. My dad and the firefighter were in the back of the SUV, so I ran around to the front.

There are a lot of ways to get rid of illegal chemicals. But I could only think of one reason to spray them on a school's soccer field: Someone wanted to make people sick. Not just people, they were targeting kids.

I had no idea why. But I sure as hell was going to find out who.

Elizabeth watched AJ and the others drive off. Leaving her with David.

She picked her way around the front of the van to the driver's side, streams of water from the decontamination process now flowing through the ruts left behind by heavy equipment, once again regretting her choice of footwear. She was supposed to be headed to Charleston, to take her attorney oath and be sworn in by the clerk of the Supreme Court of Appeals. She'd stopped only because she saw all the commotion and spotted AJ's van in the middle of it.

They were never going to win this case if she didn't finish getting admitted to the West Virginia bar so she could argue it. Of course, the more she looked over her father's notes—he'd eschewed the computer for his legal arguments and wrote them out instead on any random scrap of paper that had come to hand, before shoving them all into an accordion file—the more she doubted that they had any chance of winning at all.

Her father's tactic had been to sue the U.S. Army Corps of Engineers and the state Department of Environmental Protection. If he could prove that their system of granting mountaintop removal mining permits violated state and federal laws, he would gain injunctions for all the MTR permits across the state, including Masterson's.

The stakes of such an approach were high. A loss wouldn't just be a legal victory for Masterson. It would set a precedent for all the mining companies pursuing MTR permits. It would be a huge blow to the environmental community.

Not to mention losing the one case her father had poured his heart and soul into winning.

She'd never heard him so excited, so passionate about anything—or anyone, herself included—until he began fighting Masterson and mountaintop removal. Kicking a clod of dirt so hard that it exploded in the air, showering her with red clay and bits of gravel, she considered her options. With her father's arguments now made moot by the new court ruling, her legal alternatives seemed slim to none.

"Do you think Walt and Lenny will be okay?" David asked.

He didn't look so very traumatized. He watched, apparently fascinated, as the firemen donned special protective suits and lumbered across the soccer field to retrieve his wheelchair. Others were using some kind of monitoring device and scooping up samples of the mud and water from the field.

"I'm sure they'll be fine." She had no idea and hated giving the kid false assurances, so she changed the subject. "How'd your mom know about the pesticides?"

"A case we worked on a few years ago. It's really bad stuff. Can kill you." He shuddered and looked in the direction the ambulance had taken with Walt and Lenny. "I was just a kid then, but I helped her read about organophosphates."

"Helped her read?"

"Yeah. Mom doesn't read so well. She had some kind of accident back before I was born. But she's a whiz at remembering stuff she hears. That's why we make a great team."

"But a few years ago you would have been, what, six when she was working the Pinehurst Chemicals case?"

He looked at her like she was slow. "Seven. I've been reading since I was three. Besides, me and my mom are a team."

Hmmm . . . no wonder her father liked AJ's approach—unconventional hardly began to describe it. Just like his own style of doing things.

Elizabeth smoothed her skirt as the wind caught at its hem. "So you weren't scared out there?"

"Nah, those guys were just playing a joke. You know, hazing the new kid. It's nothing to get afraid of." His words were confident, but his voice betrayed him.

She wasn't talking about the bullying, but she made a mental note to mention it to AJ, just in case. "No, I meant when the other boys got sick. Sounds like you saved one kid's life with your quick thinking."

He brushed his heroics aside. "Anyone would have done that. Besides, I knew my mom was here, so there was nothing to be scared about."

Such a simple declaration. Trust, pride, confidence. Everything she wished her folks would feel about her—maybe they did, but who knew? Elizabeth felt a knot in her throat, one end tugged tight by her mother's distance and the other by her father's absence.

On paper, AJ appeared to be a self-educated, self-made failure. Seeing the pride in David's eyes, Elizabeth knew she was anything but. "Your mom's one smart woman, but you were a genuine hero out there today."

He seemed surprised by that. "Really?"

"Really."

A fireman brought David his chair, scrubbed clean and buffed dry. "Good as new," he proclaimed, helping him from the front seat to the back and folding the chair in beside him. He smiled at Elizabeth, handing her a notebook bristling with loose papers. "We even saved his homework for him, so he wouldn't get in trouble with his teachers."

Elizabeth laughed as David groaned from the back. "What do you tell the man, David?"

"Thank you."

The fireman put out his hand for David to shake. "You did good work out there today, kid. Come on by the station sometime and we'll show you around."

"Really? Cool. Thanks."

"You all take care now." The firefighter left.

Elizabeth watched for a moment as the hazmat team maneuvered a bulldozer to the field. It looked like they were going to scrape off the top layer of dirt and haul it away in one of Masterson's dump trucks. Hopefully to somewhere safe.

"David, what were the symptoms of that poisoning again?"

"Lots of stuff. Trouble breathing, drooling, blurry vision, seizures, throwing up."

She tapped her fingernail twice against her front incisor, then grabbed her phone and dialed the medical examiner's office.

The trip to the hospital was spent in silence—there was a lot that needed to be said, but not in the closed confines of the SUV, not with the firefighter in the back, not with my dad sick. Cole sped over the mountain to Smithfield, making the thirty-minute trip in a little more than twenty. He kept glancing in the rearview at my dad, his frown deepening each time.

I sat twisted in the front seat, dividing my attention between my dad and Cole, fighting to keep control of my emotions as I thought about what had just happened. It was easy to stay calm in the middle of the action, but not so much when I finally had time to realize that people could have died on that field—people I loved.

The firefighter didn't seem to have that problem. He was calm and competent, every few minutes listening to my dad's breathing, jotting notes on a piece of white tape he'd placed along his pant leg. "He's doing fine," he kept assuring me.

My dad divided his energy and glares between the firefighter, the oxygen mask clamped to his face, and me. Like somehow this was all my fault.

"Don't go worrying your mother," he finally said, pulling the oxygen away to make his words clear.

"Elizabeth won't worry her. She's gone to give her a lift to the hospital." It seemed perfectly reasonable to me, but his face grew red again—and not a healthy shade of red, but the kind of red that makes you think ugly words like "stroke" and "apoplexy."

"No. Call her off." He talked like Elizabeth was a hit man. Then he went into a coughing fit.

The monitor on Dad's finger bleeped, and the firefighter shoved the mask back up. "Deep breaths, that's it, nice and slow."

We pulled up in front of the ER. I helped the firefighter get Dad out of the truck and inside while Cole parked. The firefighter spoke with a nurse, and Dad was whisked back into the treatment area. I tried to follow, but he waved me back and the nurse shrugged. "Patient's choice," she said. "Sorry."

I turned to the receptionist. "Can you tell me how the two boys are? The ones from Scotia Elementary?"

"I'm sorry. We can't release any information."

So there I was. Lord knows what was happening to my dad, who didn't want me anywhere near, two boys almost died, my son could have been killed, and I was alone. Waiting.

I turned around in a circle, lost. The room was painted a gray-green, a color that no doubt had originally been meant to be restful but had faded into depressing. There were four lines of plastic chairs connected together, eight in a row, back to back, with more along the perimeter. A half-dozen patients waited—a blur of white and black and gray faces avoiding eye contact. A few vending machines in the corner added the only color to the place.

I headed over to the coffee machine, but the last thing I wanted was to be holding hot liquid in my hands right now. Not the way they were trembling. Placing my palm flat against the side of the machine, I turned my head, staring at the small bit of wall exposed behind it, blocking out the rest of the world.

Then I let go. Gave in to the temptation of falling apart. That was the real reason I'd asked Elizabeth to take David—no way I could let him see me like this. Fist to my mouth so the others wouldn't hear, body shaking, silent tears gushing out of control, unable to swallow or talk past the terror throttling me.

I was drowning again, only this time was worse, much worse. The fear of something happening to David trumped the fear I'd had when I almost died ten years ago. That fear had felt like a release, soft, beckoning, a dark whisper. This fear was awful, a caged tiger clawing, snarling, frenzied.

What would I have done if something had happened to David?

The thought snagged my heart, buried itself deep, refusing to let go. It was so awful, so terrifying, that I couldn't even begin to answer the question. As if by not answering, not imagining that impossible possibility, I could erase it. Delete it. Live my life without ever acknowledging its existence.

My body knew better. I wanted to vomit, to purge myself of the memory of what had just happened. Instead, I drowned it in tears.

A pair of strong hands turned me around. Cole pulled me to his chest. He squeezed me tight. "Everything's going to be all right. You're not alone in this anymore."

His words were meant to comfort, but instead they added to my fear: Did I really want more people in my life that I risked losing? I knew I should turn away from him, but I couldn't. It was intoxicating, the idea of giving in, of letting someone else carry the load, even for a few minutes. Just a little breathing space, two minutes—was that too much to ask?

He cradled my head, his fingers stroking through my hair, holding me. I finished my blubbering and pulled myself together. This couldn't happen. *We* couldn't happen.

I'd gotten my two minutes, they would need to last me a lifetime. Bracing my palms against his chest, I raised my face to his, ready to push away.

"What the hell do you think you're doing with my husband?"

SEVENTEEN

"You've got the emergency brake still on," David told Elizabeth as she steered the van down the hill.

"It's stuck."

"Push it down, let go, then push it again."

She followed his instructions and the brake released. "Thanks." When they got to the main road, she stopped and turned around. "Do you know how to get to your grandparents' house?"

AJ had given her the address, and she had a vague idea of where it was—just a few streets over from her father's—but directions would be nice. Elizabeth liked having a precise idea of where she was going, but the van didn't have GPS and her cell phone wasn't getting any reception here. She'd barely gotten it at the school. The best cell reception she'd had since she arrived in Scotia had been at the cemetery.

David seemed startled at her question. He looked away, looked back, then shrugged, a quick, angry jerk of his shoulders. "How should I know? I never met them. We went there the first night we came, were supposed to stay there, but they sent us to Flora's."

There was a story behind that, an unhappy one by the twisted look on his face, like he was trying hard not to cry, so Elizabeth dropped it. AJ had told her how she'd been forced to leave Scotia and that she hadn't come home in ten years, but she hadn't filled in all the blanks about her family. Why should she? They'd only known each other for a day. Seemed like longer somehow.

"Okay, no worries, we'll find it," she said. How hard could it be? Other than Main Street, there were only three other roads that made up "downtown" Scotia, and Maple was one of them. The houses weren't as large or as well kept as the ones on her father's street, but they were far nicer than the small company houses and trailers that dotted the outskirts of town. AJ's family home was halfway down the block, a two-story house with a wraparound porch and a well-kept lawn and garden.

Despite that, the house showed definite signs of neglect: sagging gutters, a shutter missing, curling shingles. Small things, easily glossed over or denied, but they pricked at Elizabeth. A professional who could never afford a house this size in the city, she hated to see a nice property go to waste.

She left David in the van as she walked up to the porch, wondering if the way AJ's parents treated their house was a reflection of how they had treated their daughter. Maybe they were like her own mother and father, who'd worked long, hard hours and had neither the time nor the energy to pay attention to her.

Wasn't really her business either way.

She made it to the front door and rang the bell. It echoed inside the house. Through the sidelight's lace curtains she saw that the house had a similar layout to her father's: a wide foyer with a large staircase, rooms on either side, their oak doors closed, and a hall past the stairs leading to the rear of the house. Unlike her father's place, here there was a door in the hallway. It looked new, out of place with the rest of the house.

Through this door came a woman dressed in a broomstick skirt and turtleneck. Thin, like AJ, with the same blond hair, but more ash with a little gray thrown in. The same eyes, green and spooky, unsettling. This had to be AJ's mother.

"Mrs. Palladino?" she asked when the woman opened the front door.

"Yes. What can I do for you?" The woman stood in the doorway.

"I'm Elizabeth Hardy. A friend of your daughter." Here's where it got tricky. How to explain about the accident without panicking Mrs. Palladino. "AJ sent me. It's about your husband—"

"Frank? Has something happened?"

"There was a problem at the site. He was accidentally exposed to some pesticides, and they're taking him to the hospital to be examined. He's fine," she said, hoping she wasn't lying. "It's just a precaution. But AJ thought I should come by, offer you a ride to—"

Her words were interrupted by the shrill ring of a telephone. Mrs. Palladino startled, half-turned back toward the closed door behind her, then whirled on Elizabeth as if she thought she was being tricked. Her face closed down with suspicion.

"You wait right here," she told Elizabeth. "Don't move. Don't touch anything."

She scooted through the rear doorway so quickly that Elizabeth couldn't get a glimpse into the room beyond. Don't touch anything? What was there to touch?

Despite the similar layout to her father's house, this house had none of the warm, open charm his had. Elizabeth circled around, glancing out the sidelight to check on David. He was immersed in reading something and seemed oblivious to her absence.

With all the doors shut, the narrow hallway felt claustrophobic. There was no furniture—not even a coat stand—and the only ornamentation was a photo of a teenager dressed in a football uniform. It was framed in a large and heavy black wood, a faded grosgrain black ribbon cutting across the upper left corner. AJ's brother, the one who'd died.

The lonely photo certainly set the tone for the house. All alone on a wide expanse of blank wall, as if he was the only occupant.

The murmur of voices behind the closed door ended, and Mrs. Palladino reappeared.

"That was my husband. He said the doctors said he's fine. No need to worry." She looked slantwise at Elizabeth, sizing her up. "He told me not to bother with going to the hospital, he'd be home himself soon enough. So I guess Angela Joy overreacted. She's prone to that sometimes."

Elizabeth had no idea what to say. She'd seen the sick boys and how bad Mr. Palladino looked. AJ hadn't overreacted—in fact, she'd been remarkably calm and in control. Even if AJ's father was okay, wouldn't his wife want to see him?

"Are you sure you don't want a ride to the hospital?" Elizabeth tried. She honestly didn't really want to get involved, to get tangled up in whatever was going on here, but AJ had listened patiently to her talk about her father, had been willing to champion his cause alongside Elizabeth, so she felt obligated to try to help. "Really, it's no trouble, I'm going there anyway—"

Mrs. Palladino marched past her to the front door and held it for her, as gracious and stiff as a hostess clearing out her final guest from a party. "No thank you. We'll manage just fine. Thank you for stopping by."

She made it obvious that Elizabeth wasn't needed—or wanted. It wasn't until Elizabeth stood outside on the sidewalk and glanced back at the very ordinary-appearing house that she wondered what secrets lay hidden behind the closed doors behind her.

Once the women went inside and David realized he wouldn't get even a glimpse of his grandmother until they came back out, he turned on his iPod and rummaged through his homework binder while he waited for Elizabeth. The binder held more than just a pile of catchup homework assignments—most of which he'd breeze through because it was all stuff he'd already learned back home in D.C. It also held the small sketch-book he used for doodling Captain Awesome ideas.

He pulled the book out and began flipping through the pages. It wasn't his imagination. The man who'd helped Walt looked just like Captain Awesome. Just like.

Wow.

He knew he should be worried about Lenny and Walt, and he was. He was also still kinda scared about what could have happened if his mom hadn't been there and known all about toxaphene. And kinda proud that she'd trusted him to call the firemen and explain what was happening and that they'd said he'd done a good job.

But seeing a real-life version of his imaginary hero . . . that was just . . . wow.

He pulled out a pencil and sketched a few rapid-fire panels depict-ing the rescue on the field. Only this time there was toxic smoke rising from the ground like a deadly fog and Captain Awesome was the only rescuer but there were a ton of kids and their teacher and . . . he stopped. Looked at what he'd drawn. Propped himself up on his hands and leaned over the driver's seat to look in the rearview mirror.

Holy crapola. Captain Awesome—whatever his name was—he looked like David. Or David looked like him.

Captain Awesome was his dad.

His dad was a real-life hero.

He smiled, shading in his comic version, making him even more handsome and muscled and amazing. His mom was a hero, everyone said so, except when they were mad at her and blaming her for stuff, but she'd always been that way, it was just part of being Mom—and part of her job. Which he didn't like, because she was always working and never had enough time for him or for fun or just to smile every once in a while.

But his dad . . . a flush of pride raced over him, widening his smile. His dad was really a hero, swooping in out of nowhere, risking his life when it wasn't even part of his job and no one asked him to, to save a kid who was a total stranger (not to mention a Cro-Magnon a—hole). Now *that* was a hero.

He leaned back, a thousand scenarios of father-son bonding flickering through his mind, and blew out his breath in contentment. Awesome.

Waverly stood there glaring at me, at Cole's hand—it happened to be his left, and I imagined his wedding ring burning through my jacket, Waverly's stare lighting it on fire. I jerked away from Cole, feeling guilty even though we'd done nothing wrong. He slowly slid his hand down my arm, lingering, not dropping it for a beat, as if to prove our innocence.

Stupid. He'd given me a hug. That's all. My dad was in the ER, my son could have been seriously injured—*his* son—we were old friends, more than friends . . . ah, there was the heart of it. I felt sorry for Waverly, recognized that, like last night at the jail, her anger was kindled by pain.

It couldn't be easy for her, my bringing David home to Scotia. I stepped away, leaving Cole behind. "There was an accident at the school—"

"I know all about it. From our men at the site. A real mess." Her words were clipped, run so tight together they were in danger of colliding. She dismissed me, turning her attention to Cole. "Your father is inside, getting an update from the doctors."

They wouldn't tell me anything, not even about my own father, but of course Old Man Masterson expected to waltz in and get an update? As much as I wanted information, I half-hoped the doctors would send him back out here with nothing. Petty, I know, but Masterson brought out the worst in me. Cole had been absolutely right about that.

"Are you okay?" Waverly asked Cole, her tone softer now, intimate on a level that shut out me and the rest of the world.

I moved over to the registration desk as she and Cole spoke. Now it was her shoulder Cole's hand rested on. I looked away, angered by the jealousy that washed over me. I knew the facts and would have to learn to live with them—for David's sake.

Old Man Masterson came out, beaming at Waverly and Cole. "The boys are going to be all right," he announced, clamping a hand on Cole's shoulder. "Thanks to your quick thinking."

"How's my dad?" I asked.

Masterson's scowl hit me and skipped on past, barely acknowledging me. "He's fine. Just his lungs acting up a bit."

The doctor joined us. "Miss Palladino?" he asked, looking from Waverly to me. I nodded, and he turned to address me, but obviously didn't care if the others overheard. So much for patient privacy. "Your father asked me to tell you that he'll be going home shortly. Mr. Masterson has already made arrangements for transportation and follow-up with his own physician."

"But what's wrong with him?"

The doctor looked at me in surprise. "High blood pressure and a mild flare-up of his emphysema. Brought on by exertion, no doubt."

"Emphysema?"

"It's why I moved him to the surface mine," Masterson put in, obviously happy to be more privy to the details of my father's health than I was.

"From his X-rays, it probably saved his life getting him out of the underground mine," the doctor said.

Great. Now I had Masterson to thank for saving my dad from the lung disease that he'd gotten from working Masterson's mine for the past thirty years?

"Anyway," the doctor continued, "your father said you could go on home. He'll be fine."

"How can he be fine? You just said he had high blood pressure and emphysema."

"Which we are treating." He turned to leave.

"Wait. I want to see him—"

"Young lady." No hint of bedside manner now. "We've only just gotten your father's breathing and blood pressure under control. We don't want to do anything to aggravate him further." He swished through the electronic doors.

So that was what I was to my dad? An aggravation? I remembered two nights ago, all those hopes I'd stirred up inside myself, fantasies of coming home, building a new life with my family. Idiot.

"I suggest you leave your father to me," Masterson said. "I'm sure you have other things to take care of. Like finding a job."

"I have a job. Finding out who poisoned those boys is part of it."

Cole stepped in between us. "We had nothing to do with that."

"We?"

"Yes, *we*." Waverly wrapped her arm around Cole's, standing alongside Old Man Masterson.

Three against one. I squared my hips, facing them dead on. I'd taken on bigger odds—and won.

Plus, this time it was personal. My son had been out on that field. My father too. And yes, even though Cole was siding with his father—as always—I cared about the fact that Cole could have been hurt as well.

Cole looked like he was about to say something—at least I hoped he was—when the doors opened and David and Elizabeth entered the waiting room.

Masterson stared at David for a long moment, as if appraising the purity of a seam of coal, then he turned to Waverly and Cole. "We'd better get back." He left without waiting for them, walking past David without even a second glance. Waverly hesitated, began to follow, then stopped when Cole didn't move.

"I'll catch you up," Cole said, his gaze on David, a half-hidden smile playing hide-and-seek across his face as if afraid to come out into the open.

Waverly frowned, glared at David, glared at me, then left.

I was too busy to care much, since it was all I could manage to keep my heart from galloping away from me. Suddenly I was dry-mouthed and drenched with a nervous sweat, caught between Cole and David. I turned to David. He was staring at Cole with something akin to hero-worship—smart kid, he'd already figured it out.

"David, there's someone I want you to meet," I said, crouching beside him so we were at eye level. Everyone else in the waiting room stared at us, and I had no doubt that the entire county would be privy to our little family reunion before the day was out.

David bobbed his chin, acknowledging that he'd heard my words, although his gaze never broke from Cole's. "Awesome," he sighed.

Cole was stuck, mouth half hanging open, no hint of a smile left, looking as scared as I'd ever seen him. He glanced at me, eyes wide in supplication, but all I could do was shrug. David, however, knew exactly what to do. He pushed over to Cole, sat up straight, chin high, and extended his hand.

Cole wiped his palm against his jeans, and took David's hand, shaking it formally.

"It's nice to finally meet you"—David hesitated over the last word—"sir."

Silence thudded through the room. Cole gulped, hard enough to make his Adam's apple bounce. "Sir?"

David appeared stricken, as if he'd ruined the moment with a *faux pas*. But Cole only gripped his hand harder, practically hauling David out of the chair as he flung himself to his knees and pulled David into a tight embrace. Then they were hugging and laughing and making all those grunty male-bonding noises to pretend they weren't really wanting to cry, and I could breathe again.

EIGHTEEN

We adjourned to the cafeteria. Elizabeth and David hadn't eaten lunch yet, I wanted to supervise Cole's meeting with David, and I hoped I might be able to sneak into my dad's room and check on him in person. We snagged a large table in the back corner but the food lines were a bit crowded, so I debated whether to leave David with Cole while I got his food, or take him with me, stranding Cole there alone until Elizabeth made it through the line, or . . . such a simple thing, but my brain spun with indecision, so very unlike me.

David made up his own mind—as usual. "Mom, do you have any money? I'm starving." He held out his hand, palm up, but before I could fish out a bill from my pocket, Cole opened his wallet and gave David a twenty.

"No. That's too much." I kept forgetting about the money issue—wishful thinking that it would magically vanish, I guess. Might as well get some ground rules down before Cole started throwing more money around.

"I expect change," he said, affecting a stern, fatherly voice that was totally foreign-sounding coming from him.

"Thanks." David rolled toward the food line. I took a step after him, but he glared over his shoulder at me—the equivalent of a warning shot over the bow of a pirate ship. A look that said, *Please, Mom, don't treat me like a baby and embarrass me in front of my dad.*

"Independent," Cole said.

"Stubborn," I countered.

"Guess he takes after you."

I shot him my own glare, one that didn't need translating.

"Can I still spend some time with him this afternoon?"

It was nice of him to ask, but it also felt weird. Forced. So unlike the way we used to be able to talk with each other. "Of course. Maybe you could hang out at Flora's?"

He tilted his head. "You don't trust me alone with him?"

"No. It's not that. It's just—I don't want him to feel uncomfortable. I thought familiar surroundings—"

"Sure. Flora's will be fine." He cleared his throat. "Any topics, er, off-limits? How much have you told him?"

"Nothing. I made it clear that you didn't abandon him, but that you just never had the chance because you didn't know about him. Told him there were mistakes made, but we're all trying to fix things." I shifted in my seat to keep David in view as he approached the cashier. "I kept it pretty vague."

"So he never knew anything about me? You never even told him—"

Here it came. I blew out my breath, counting to five. "No. I never told him. I never wanted him to think ill of you, and it was just too hard to try to talk about you without leaving this gaping hole. . . ." I trailed off. Cole covered my hand with his.

"I meant what I said before. You're not in this alone. We'll figure it out."

I smiled my thanks as Ty came around the corner and joined us. "The hazmat unit from Smithfield finally showed. They confirmed the presence of organophosphates—we'll need further testing to see which one, but they said the readings were off the scale."

"That field was fine yesterday," I said. "Whoever sprayed the toxaphene did it last night."

"We're checking all the chemicals and fertilizer at the school's maintenance department, but so far nothing."

"I can't believe anyone would target kids," Cole said.

"They may not have been the target. After what happened last night at the tree-sitters' site," Ty nodded at me, like I was to blame for Ellings's idiocy, "Waverly and Mr. Masterson asked the school for permission to move the protesters down to the field so that they could increase a security perimeter around the tree-sitters."

"Why? It wasn't the protesters' fault that Ellings—"

"We just want to keep everyone safe," Cole said, playing devil's advocate—defending the devil himself, his dad. As usual.

"But if the protesters were the intended victims, who would target them except for Masterson or his people?" I asked. Cole winced, realizing he was one of those "people."

"They aren't the only protesters around," he said. "Maybe Yancey was tired of sharing the spotlight."

"That's ridiculous."

David and Elizabeth rejoined us. We stopped talking about who might have poisoned the field and instead I introduced David and Elizabeth to Ty.

"I saw your dog," David said. "What kind is he?"

"She's a Belgium Malinois. Her name is Nikki."

As Ty and David discussed the use of canines in policing—David surprising me with the depth of his knowledge until I remembered how fascinated he'd been when the DARE officer brought his dog to his old school last fall—Cole chewed slowly, his gaze focused on David, a smile dancing across his face. Pure paternal pride.

I could relax. We had a lot of hurdles still—both of our families for a start—but the most important one had been cleared.

As the boys transitioned into a discussion of football—Ty and Cole were mortified to learn David was a Ravens fan—I noticed that Elizabeth only picked at her salad. She'd gather up a forkful, then lower it and spear a new selection, with never a bite making it to her mouth. "Everything all right?" I asked, my maternal instincts aroused.

She nodded, not meeting my gaze.

"Didn't my mother want to come?"

Finally actually eating a forkful, she took her time chewing. As if it was a difficult question to answer. "Your dad called while I was there, told her not to."

"Figures. Thanks, anyway."

"I really need to get over to Charleston, finish my bar admittance."

"You can keep the van. Cole can take us home to Flora's." I looked to him for confirmation, and he nodded.

David slurped the bottom of his milk carton. As usual, nothing could affect his appetite, not even almost being killed. "Mom, are Walt and Lenny okay?"

"I don't know, they wouldn't tell me anything."

"Their nurse said they were going to be fine," Ty said. "Thanks to you. You kept your cool out there. Didn't panic."

David blushed and shrugged. "Can Ty take me out to see Nikki?"

"Do you have time?" I asked Ty. "We'll be out in a minute."

"Sure, no problem."

David pushed away from the table. "Hey, take your tray to the trash," I reminded him. He rolled his eyes but grabbed the tray. He and Ty left, talking as if they'd known each other forever.

Elizabeth watched them go, tapping on her teeth in that irritating habit of hers. I wanted to grab her hand, but she stopped herself before I could. "I don't trust Yancey," she blurted out.

"Why?" I asked.

"Do you think he had anything to do with poisoning the field?" Cole added, leaning forward as if Yancey was his problem, not ours.

"If it was Yancey, then not only do we not have a legal case any longer, but we're also sunk in the court of public opinion. Hell, we might even be liable."

"What do you mean about no legal case?" Cole asked.

Elizabeth glanced at him suspiciously. He was, after all, technically the opposition. "I'm sorry, I can't discuss that."

He looked affronted, a flash of the old Cole, the little boy who always got his way, crossing his face. But then he smiled. A strange, sneaky smile. "I'm not the enemy, Elizabeth. Check your dad's computer for a file called EIS."

"EIS?" I asked. "You mean an Environmental Impact Survey? I thought the Army Corps of Engineers refused to do one. They ruled that the MTR would have minimal impact and therefore an EIS was unnecessary—isn't that why it's been so hard to stop mountaintop removal? Because without an initial EIS, there's no way to prove that the damage is secondary to the MTR."

Elizabeth arched an eyebrow. "You were paying attention yesterday."

"I'm a fast learner. But that's right, isn't it?"

"That's right." She turned to Cole. "But I have a feeling our friend here knows something we don't."

"Just check the file. Then we'll talk."

Elizabeth gave up on her food, and we left. I tried to sneak into the back of the ER, but a nurse stopped me. "My dad's here," I told her. "Frank Palladino. I just ran to the cafeteria."

"Mr. Palladino was discharged twenty minutes ago," she told me. "I'm surprised he didn't tell you. Was he waiting on you for a ride? Because I believe he left with Mr. Masterson."

"We must have gotten our wires crossed." I tried to make light of the fact that I hadn't actually talked with my dad—of course, I wasn't sure if we'd actually talked for the past ten years . . . or longer, maybe not since Randy died. "Thanks so much."

The news people had followed the boys to the hospital and were camped out in the parking lot. Yancey and his Ladies had arrived as well, decrying the "poisoning of innocents." As Cole situated David in his SUV, Ty beckoned me to the rear of his Tahoe where he was giving Nikki some water—and where we could have some privacy.

"She's beautiful," I said, offering my hand palm down for Nikki to smell. She nosed it, then licked it, wagging her tail to show her acceptance.

"I already told her you were a friend," Ty said. "But don't try to approach her while we're working—she's more focused than anyone I know."

"You talk like she's a person."

He looked offended, his hand combing through her thick coat. "She's more than a person, she's my partner. She'd take a bullet for me, and I'd take one for her. That's the way it works."

I was glad Ty had someone like Nikki at his side—but I felt a little sad that he'd never found a human companion as loyal and devoted. "So, any word from Masterson's men or the tree-sitters? Did they see who spread the insecticide on the field?"

"Why, you thinking of some vigilante justice?"

The image of David stranded in that field of toxic sludge flashed through my mind. Yes. Maybe. "No. Of course not. If I found anything, you'd be the first person I'd call."

"There were only two security guards left behind after we rounded everyone up last night. They didn't see anything—I suspect they were asleep in their truck. Yancey's Ladies refuse to cooperate with us 'government stooges,' so I've no idea what they saw."

"They'd have a perfect view of the field from that high up."

"My thought exactly. Too bad there isn't a nongovernment type, someone on their side, who they might talk to."

"Hmmm . . . too bad. Of course, it would be hard to get up to them. I doubt they'd say anything over a phone line, and Masterson won't let anyone cross onto his property."

"They've been up in those trees a few weeks now, must have some way of resupplying. Plus, I swear it isn't always the same Ladies. I think they're swapping out."

"Makes sense. A few zip-lines hidden in the trees would do the trick—as long as you could stay clear of Masterson's men."

"The forest gets pretty thick over to the east."

"And it's not all Masterson land. Not the graveyard." There was a plot of land in the middle of those trees that had been the local "slave" burial ground for almost two centuries—although the name was a misnomer. No one around these parts had ever been wealthy enough to own slaves. But it was where African American laborers had been buried for generations. A spooky spot, hidden in the woods, sacred symbols carved into the trees surrounding it, strange talismans left on the stones that marked burial spots. When the moon was full, we used to go there, just beyond the boundaries of the graveyard, and dare each other to run in and grab the small bundles of chicken bones or bird skulls or feather totems.

My brother Randy was the only one I'd ever seen take the bet. Ty's mom, Chantelle, heard about Randy stealing from the grave offerings and had practically turned him into a corpse.

Ty nodded, a smile filled with memories crossing his face as he followed my thoughts. "Too bad your brother isn't around. He was the best tree-climber I ever knew."

"Too bad." We both knew Randy had taught me everything he knew about climbing a tree—and being lighter and more flexible, I could climb higher and faster than even Randy. Only thing I ever did better than him. Of course, that had been fifteen years ago—and tree-climbing wasn't a skill I'd needed in D.C. Odds were I'd fall and break my neck.

He smiled. "So, where you off to?"

"Think I'm going to go pay my respects to a certain graveyard."

"Give me a call if you hear anything interesting."

"Yes, sir, will do."

I dropped Cole and David off at Flora's house. They were debating DC versus Marvel comics, and I doubt they even realized when I left. Jeremy was kind enough to let me use his pickup until Elizabeth returned with our van. I'd forgotten how casual folks were with swapping vehicles around here—when I was growing up, there was a constant trade-off of cars and trucks depending on your needs and sobriety. The share-and-share-alike attitude was so different from the city—but of course, people here in Scotia still took pride in never locking their doors as well.

As I drove down the mountain and around the backside of Masterson's property to the overgrown dirt track that led up to the burial ground, I remembered why I'd loved growing up here. More than the humbling beauty that filled every view, it was the people. Yes, they could be stubborn and reluctant to change their ways—though that was equally true of city folk. But here, maybe because of the mountains that insulated us from the rest of "civilization," people seemed to live life without all the harsh edges that come with the frantic, cram-every-minute-full urban lifestyle.

Not so much slower as more thoughtful. Which seemed a wonderful gift for David. With the Internet breaking down educational barriers, he could have the best of both worlds. Of all worlds.

The possibilities combined with the crisp spring air to make me giddy. Especially after seeing how Cole accepted David and the way David lit up around his father. His life would be so very different than mine. Rich and varied and filled with people who loved him, like me and Jeremy and Cole and Flora. My mom and dad would come around as well—at least in my fantasy daydream. And there'd be more new friends like Ty and his mom Chantelle and his brothers and sisters and their kids. Maybe Elizabeth would stay as well.

If I wasn't careful I was going to break out into song—something certain to scare off all wildlife within hearing distance. But each new thought tumbled into greater and bigger possibilities, like the spring melt-off cascading down the rocks beside me, and it was irresistible not to jump in and go along for the ride.

I pulled up in front of a rusted wrought-iron gate—the only marker of what lay beyond—and parked the truck, wishing I had my boots since the ground here was mushy with a layer of fallen leaves that hadn't dried enough to blow away. I slipped through the gate. The path was barely discernible—more a feeling of cleared ground, a suggestion of which way to go rather than an actual trail. On either side were tulip trees, red-buds, dogwood, oaks, a few sugar maples, along with hemlocks, spruce, and pines. The older trees were surrounded by thick rhododendron mingling with patches of fiddleheads, and the younger trees fought for space alongside wild raspberry canes. Nothing was blooming yet, but a few trees had visible buds, and the air was perfumed with the sweet scent of moss and dead leaves—a harbinger of spring.

The burial ground was demarcated only by a thicket of honeysuckle and wild roses surrounding it. The path continued past it and headed deeper into the woods. I followed it, heading west to a gulley cutting down the side of the mountain, spring runoff tumbling down its rocks. I craned my gaze up until I caught a flash of purple climbing rope strung twenty feet overhead along the branch of an oak.

I climbed the tree—grateful that my muscles remembered my old skills and that I hadn't acquired any new acrophobic tendencies—and hauled the rope in, bringing with it the guideline for a second overhead rope to form a two-strand bridge to cross the gulley. On the opposite side there appeared to be more ropes, leading higher into the tree boughs. It'd have been nice if they'd left a carabineer on the ropes or if I had a safety harness—or even a bicycle helmet—but I was on my own. I was sure Yancey's college students didn't think twice about their own mortality or the price to be paid if they slipped and fell, but they also didn't have a kid waiting for them at home.

Testing the ropes before trusting them with my weight, I sucked in my breath and stepped up. Crossing the gulley wasn't as hard as I'd feared—there was no breeze, and as long as I kept my momentum going, the ropes barely swayed. When I reached the other side, I felt flushed with satisfaction, although there was no one around to share in my accomplishment. Still, it felt good, flexing muscles, working up an honest sweat, breaking the law—kinda. Technically, I hadn't stepped foot on Masterson land, nor did I intend to.

It didn't take me long to maneuver my way across the quarter-mile of forest that stood between me and the Ladies. By the time I reached the final set of ropes, I was sixty feet off the ground and hidden by thick branches. I let out a soft whistle, and the Lady closest to me looked up from her platform, where she'd been typing on a small laptop.

"Okay if I come over and visit for a spell?" I asked.

She held up her hand, touched her Bluetooth—Yancey had provided them with their own cellular/WiFi hotspot to broadcast their story to the outside world, of course—spoke to someone, then nodded and beckoned to me. I crossed, staying as quiet as I could, although I couldn't see any of Masterson's men within hearing distance. The closest ones I spotted were leaning against their truck, smoking and laughing down near the police tape that cordoned off the soccer field.

The Lady pulled her privacy tarp around her platform, cleared a space for me, and when I arrived was sitting cross-legged, pouring me a cup of tea.

"Solar-heated, peppermint," she said, handing me the tea.

"Thank you." I sat down across from her, folding my legs under me, mirroring her posture. "I'm AJ."

"I know. I'm Lacey. Yancey said to cooperate fully and answer your questions. He said we could trust you."

Funny coming from a man I didn't trust, but I wasn't about to argue. I took a sip of tea. "You were here all last night?"

"Yes."

"Did you see any vehicles after the police left? Maybe a truck, something with a tanker?"

She gazed at me, her eyes clear and steady. "If I did, would I be a witness?"

"Maybe. Is that a problem?"

She twisted her waist-long hair over one shoulder, kneading it as if we were filming a shampoo commercial. "No, not at all. I believe in doing my civic duty. That's why I'm here."

Right. Saving the trees and launching her TV career. "Good. So, did you see anything?"

"There was one of those four-wheelers. Dark, came up with its lights off, so I can't tell you what color it was or anything. There was a container in the back of it, something light-colored, but I couldn't see what it was."

"Could you see who was on the ATV?"

"No, but there was only the driver. He was wearing a weird jumpsuit, all bulky, light-colored, I could see it in the moonlight. And he had a helmet on, something shiny that reflected the light over his face."

A protective suit. "What did he do?"

"He began driving slowly across the field, going up and down, in rows."

Spraying the poison. "What time was this?"

She shrugged. "My cell phone said a little after three. But I didn't check until I realized whoever it was, was going to be there a while, so they got here maybe ten, fifteen minutes sooner."

"Weren't you suspicious?"

"Are you kidding? All sorts of strange people come up here, doing weird things. Last week they caught two guys trying to catch us naked with night-vision goggles. And you saw that creep yesterday trying to bat Willow off her tree, like she was some kind of piñata. I was just happy to get some sleep last night without any spotlights or air horns going off all hours. Saving the world isn't easy, you know."

She finished her tea with an air of long-suffering martyrdom. I glanced around at the platform with her sleeping bag, solar charger powering her computer and phone—I bet she stayed caught up on all her favorite TV shows and blogs, no problem.

"Yeah, I see what you mean." I handed her back my empty mug and stood. "Do you think the other Ladies saw anything?"

"No, they had their tarps closed—after those pervs last week, they always shut them up for the night."

"But you don't?"

"I like the fresh air. And I'm not letting anyone tell me how to live my life. Besides," she said, stroking her hair again, "I'm very comfortable with my body. I don't mind it if anyone sees me."

I'll bet she didn't. "Thanks. Okay if I have one of the sheriff's people call you?"

"If Yancey says it's okay to talk to them. He's the boss."

She gave me a spare climbing harness to wear on my trek back, which was more enjoyable without the constant worry about falling and crash-landing. I left the harness tied to the last rope, shinnied down the tree, and headed down the path.

With no cell reception, I couldn't call Ty to let him know what little I'd found out. When I reached the old burial ground, the air around me grew hushed. The muscles along my scalp twitched as I froze, listening to the silence.

I wasn't alone.

It took everything I had not to whirl around to search for the danger that I knew was out there, lurking. Instead, I scanned with my eyes, just like Randy had taught me. I shifted my weight, ready for an attack from any direction, and forced myself not to hold my breath but to breathe slow and steady, filling my lungs from my belly.

A crack exploded the silence. Then another. Someone big and bumbling, not used to walking through the woods—or at least not used to walking through them quietly.

A man whistled. I focused on the sound. It came from behind a massive hemlock. I didn't call out, play his game. Instead, I waited, the graveyard at my back, the hemlock standing between me and escape. If need be, I could bushwhack my way to the truck—probably outrun whoever was there if I had to.

I was hoping it wouldn't come to that. A man's figure separated from the tree's shadow and emerged into the dappled sunlight.

"Saw that bright red truck, figured I'd find that freakin' faggot back here," Dickie Ellings sneered. "But looks like I hit the jackpot."

NINETEEN

Feeling unsettled and on edge, Elizabeth left the hospital behind, grateful for the peace and quiet of the van. AJ and the others seemed to revel in the prospect of chasing down a would-be killer and miring themselves in a crusade to stop Masterson. Their raw emotion and enthusiasm—not to mention the sight of David and Cole meeting for the first time—was draining.

She blew out her breath in frustration. Elizabeth was used to a well-ordered world of briefs and appeals with only an occasional confrontational deposition to spice things up—but even then, nothing was ever personal. She never got involved in her cases, not like this one.

It was plain to see why her father had found his fight against Masterson so consuming. Probably fancied himself a twenty-first-century Atticus Finch. Defending the high ground, fighting to save the world—so very unlike his decades spent in corporate litigation.

She fought the wheel, braking hard as what appeared to be a gentle curve turned hairpin on her. Something heavy in the rear of the van slid, coming to halt with a thud.

Even though it was midday, the mountains towering over her blocked the sun enough to cast the road into shadow. Definitely not like driving in Philly, that was for sure. Although she had to admit that it was nice the way the fresh air filled her lungs so effortlessly, making her feel buoyant, as if the city air had been too heavy, had weighed her down.

Another car's headlights appeared in her rearview—the first she'd seen since leaving Smithfield and turning onto Route 60. She guessed from the way it was barreling toward her that the driver knew these roads better than she did. She increased her speed, hoping to get to a straightaway where he could pass, but the road continued its serpentine winding. The car filled her rearview mirror—a dark SUV or pickup truck, something high enough off the road that its headlights blinded her so she couldn't see the driver clearly. Not only was the jerk tailgating, he had his high beams on—as if that would miraculously make the road straighter and give him room to pass.

She did what she'd do on the Schuylkill—tapped her brakes as a warning: Back off, bozo. He didn't get the message but crowded her even more, riding her bumper.

Using all her muscles, she maneuvered the van around the curves—it didn't appreciate them the way her Subaru would have. The van protested, shimmying and bucking, fighting her all the way. More boxes and bags in the back collided.

She fought to divide her attention between the idiot behind her and the twisting road before her. A sign suggesting that she slow down to fifteen miles per hour for the next series of switchbacks flew past. The van tilted ominously as she entered the first curve. She braked, trying to both steady the van and slow her momentum into the even sharper curve ahead.

Bam! Metal shrieked, and she flew forward, the seat belt catching her. Slamming the brakes, hoping the idiot behind was doing the same after smashing into her rear bumper, her teeth smacked together as a second, even greater impact shook the van. Metal ground against metal, the chassis wrenching impossibly, the SUV behind her pushing the van toward the edge of the road.

The edge that led into a sheer drop.

She twisted the steering wheel and risked hitting the gas, trying to get away from the SUV. The van flew free for a few hundred yards. Then the SUV plowed into the back on the passenger's side, shoving her totally out of her lane and into oncoming traffic. Thankfully, there wasn't any, but the curve reversed, and now she was facing the drop off the side of the mountain once again.

Before she could react, a final impact sent the van smashing through the flimsy wooden guardrail and flying off the side of the mountain.

As Ellings stalked closer, all those street-wise self-defense courses I'd taken at the Y seemed meaningless. Plus, I'd broken the first rule Randy had ever taught me about walking in the woods: Always carry a knife. Not necessarily for defense—a knife came in handy for so many things. Marking your trail, scraping mud from your boots, whittling a stick. But self-defense, yeah, that would be nice right about now. I didn't even have my Leatherman anymore—had lost it somewhere during the chaos of the morning when we rescued the boys.

So it was just me and my big mouth against a six-foot-something, two-hundred-plus, hulking, purebred bully. I didn't like my odds. Of course, I wasn't about to let him see that.

"You lost, Ellings? Need me to show you the way home?"

"I'll show you—" His hand went to the knife clipped to his belt—it was a Buck, just like the one my dad carried, three-inch, carbon-steel blade, opened with a flick of the thumb. Ellings didn't open it, but he unclipped it and twirled it around his palm, thumb poised to unleash the blade.

"Dickie Ellings, is that you?" A woman's voice came from the grave-yard, startling us both.

Ellings turned, and I used the opportunity to edge closer to the lane leading to my truck.

A tall black woman, her hair spun around her head in an intricate coil of silver-streaked braids, stood up from where she'd been clearing a grave of fallen leaves. Ty's mother, Chantelle.

"I'm so glad to have run into you," she continued, climbing over the wall of brambles surrounding the graveyard and ignoring the knife in Ellings's hand. She wore jeans, a USMC sweatshirt, and work gloves. "Do you think your mama can swap me out some ramps for a basketful of morels? I want to do them up for the church social on Sunday. You'll be there, right, Dickie?"

His face reddened as he glanced down, shuffling his boots in the dead leaves. "Yes, ma'am. I'll ask her."

"Thank you kindly." She dismissed him with a smile and turned to me, giving me a big hug—not even worrying that this placed her back to Ellings. I watched him warily over her shoulder, but he was already stomping away, shaking his head like a bear in heat. "Angela Joy." She drew my middle name into a sigh. "It's been too long. Come on with me so we can catch up on everything."

She held on long enough for Ellings to move out of sight, then released me. "I see you haven't lost your touch, AJ. You should know, the best way to handle a bully like Dickie is to let them wear themselves out fighting against nothing. Let 'em think you're no threat, make them feel good."

"So, what, I should have given him a smile and flashed him my tits?"

She laughed, the sound ringing clear. "Ah, I've missed you, child."

We continued down the path to where Chantelle's ancient Ford pickup, still sporting the same powder-blue paint job it had when I was a kid, was parked alongside Jeremy's newer model.

"Maybe I should have flashed him." All four tires on Jeremy's truck had been slashed. Damn Ellings. How in the hell was I going to make this up to Jeremy? Much less pay for new tires.

Chantelle scowled, glanced down the road after Ellings as if angry that her generosity had been abused. "Just you wait until I tell Emma Ellings what her son's been up to. That Dickie Ellings is going to get the tongue-lashing of his life."

"That's not going to buy Jeremy new tires."

"One thing at a time. Usually I think folks should handle their own business, but I'll bet Ty might just find some fingerprints or something that would put Dickie behind bars a few days. Long enough to think twice about threatening women and destroying private property." She checked her cell phone. Like mine, it had no service here. "C'mon, I'll give you a lift. Long as you don't mind a few stops along the way."

The back of her truck was filled with five-gallon water jugs. "What's with all the water?"

"Lots of folks have the blackwater, but my spring's still clear." She climbed into the truck, and I joined her. The cab smelled of herbs: lavender, rosemary, something more earthy—probably morels. I inhaled deeply, enjoying the way the scents swirled through me, rich and complex and comforting, soothing my worries.

"I think I could live in here," I sighed happily. Chantelle smiled, cranking the wheel—no power steering for her—and turning the truck around. "What's blackwater?"

"When they started blasting the top off Black Mountain," she nodded in the direction of the devastated mountain, "it was like being in the middle of a war zone—explosions day and night. Some of the wells around here started turning sour. More coal they processed, more blackwater. Then, when they filled Jacob's Hollow, it happened to almost everyone downstream. The state came out, did some testing, said it wasn't drinkable. Some of the streams they posted, said folks shouldn't even come in contact with the water, it was that dangerous."

"Why didn't they stop Masterson?"

"Said there was no proof the blackwater came from Masterson's mining activity." A look of contempt crossed her face. "Like you were meant to find coal dust, arsenic, mercury, and all sorts of other poisons in your well water. Blamed it on the hundred-year floods we had the past three years running. But that flooding came because of the erosion—even a fool could see that taking the top off a mountain is going to lead to flooding, not to mention burying miles of stream under the fill."

"So you're supplying folks with clean water?"

"Half the miners are laid off since Masterson shut down the underground mine. They can't afford bottled water or fancy filtering systems. Of course, it's only going to get worse when that new coal-washing plant gets built."

That was the part I still didn't understand, even after Elizabeth's lecture yesterday. "Why? Doesn't the waste from the plants go into the impoundment with the other toxic sludge?"

"You seen that thing? Sitting right above the school?"

"Yancey flew me over it yesterday."

"Did he tell you about all the kids made sick by it? Those chemicals are leaking into the groundwater—starting with the school." We pulled up in front of a double-wide trailer with a pretty trellis and half-moon gate leading from the driveway up to the front deck. "Wait, let Trisha tell you herself. She's got three at that school, and they're all sick most days."

Tree branches snapped and cracked against the van in a lightning storm of sound and color. Elizabeth flew forward against her seat belt, forces of gravity yanking her in every direction. She didn't even have time to draw in a breath before the van bounced against solid ground—lifting her out of the seat until the seat belt grabbed her again—then lurched, bounced one more time, and rolled forward.

The windshield was starred and cluttered with branches and dead leaves, but there was enough visibility for Elizabeth to see the wall of rock a split-instant before the van hit it.

Then her world turned to metal crying out in pain, the explosion of the airbag inflating, and the slam of a moving object against an immovable surface.

It happened so fast there was no chance for her life to flash before her eyes—or maybe it had been such a short and uneventful life that the movie ended without her noticing, she wasn't sure. But the fact that she could think such thoughts was a calm oasis as the world around her shook.

Finally silence. Except for water lapping at the van and the wind whistling through the open rear door. Elizabeth heaved a breath in. It hurt, but not too bad. She moved her arms and legs. Everything working properly. Unbuckling her seat belt, she pressed her palms against her belly, not sure what she was checking for but thinking it was best to check before she climbed out of the seat. No pain.

Lucky. Damn lucky.

Her mind was as foggy as the smoke the airbags left behind. The van had landed upright—thank God—in a stream gushing down the side of the mountain. She couldn't decide between trying to push the door open and climbing out that way—but she'd get her shoes wet—or staying inside the van and waiting for help. Surely the driver of the SUV would— oh no, they wouldn't, not after causing the accident. Stray thoughts collided with an explosion of clarity . . . this was no accident. That driver had tried to kill her.

Her stubborn mind didn't want to admit the idea. She shook her head, as if arguing with someone other than herself, but all that did was make her headache worse. As she massaged the bump on her forehead she tilted the rearview mirror so she could get a clear view out the open rear door of the van. No one was coming.

She wasn't sure if she should be relieved or panicked. No one meant the other driver wasn't coming to finish the job. But no one also meant she had to figure out a way out of this godforsaken wilderness on her own.

Think, Elizabeth, think. Panic sluiced through her, leaving her trembling so hard, she couldn't have opened the door if she wanted to, much less escape through the water. She rested her head against the steering wheel, using the remnants of the airbag as a pillow. A minute, she just needed a minute. To think. To calm down. To decide what to do next.

Celine Dion sang out from the cell phone holstered at her belt. Phone! She grabbed it, then fumbled as it took her two tries to answer it. Three bars!

"Hello?" she said, her voice as shaky as her hands.

"Miss Hardy? This is Dr. Voigt at the medical examiner's office. I just wanted to let you know that we did test your father's remains for organophosphates and found a significant concentration in his stomach contents. I won't be able to tell you which specific organophosphate compound it is until we have the results of further testing. But I thought you should know that I'm revising the cause and manner of death."

Frowning hurt too much. She propped the arm holding the phone up on the window's ledge to stop it from shaking. "Excuse me?"

"You were right. Your father was poisoned."

TWENTY

Cole was pretty cool, but after his mom left them alone, David felt awkward. What did kids talk to their dads about? When they didn't even know their dads and their dads didn't know them?

Now he knew why so many of his friends complained about being shuttled off for a weekend visit after their parents divorced.

They were out on Flora's back patio, enjoying the afternoon sun. Cole kept sitting, then standing, then realizing how much taller he was than David, then sitting down again, but the Adirondack chair made him sink too low and he had to heave himself up and perch on the edge of the seat to be anywhere close to David's eye level.

David watched, hiding a smile. It was weird, a grown man, so nervous around him. "Guess I'm not exactly what you expected."

Cole wrung his hands together like he was washing them. "I didn't know what to expect," he confessed. "I never spent much time around kids. My wife and I, well, she really wants them, and so do I, but we've never. . . ."

"Don't worry, it's not genetic."

"What? No, I never—your mom explained." He frowned, his cheeks flushing, and he shifted his posture again.

"Is that why you ran out onto the field? Because Mom told you about me?" David asked. "Like, would you have done that even if I wasn't your kid?"

He was glad that Cole didn't rush to answer, but instead thought it over. "I think I would have done it anyway—I want to think that. But when your mom spotted you out there and I knew you were in danger. . . ." A knot formed between his eyebrows, and he rubbed it with his finger, not looking at David. "I never want to feel like that again. It was like my insides had been turned inside out, like nothing made sense, or would ever be right again, until I knew you were safe."

"Mom acts like that every time I have to go into surgery."

"Surgery?" Cole sounded tentative, as if he was afraid to ask.

The last thing David wanted was to remind his father that his kid was less than perfect, so he brushed past it. "Yeah. Sometimes she even cries, but she pretends like she's just allergic to hospitals."

"Your mom cries? She never used to as a kid—not even with Indian rubs."

"Ugh, I hate those." They both looked out over the ridge, watching the play of wind and cloud and shadow across the tops of the trees. "Must have been pretty cool growing up around here."

"Best place in the world. Especially if you're a kid."

"So why are you trying to blow up all the mountains? That's you, right? Masterson Mining?"

Cole took his time answering that as well. David had the feeling that his dad didn't often have to talk about difficult stuff. Not like David and his mother did—they debated all of her cases and stuff in the news and things David read—like the attack on Pearl Harbor, which he was reading about now. It was cool the way she treated him like his opinion counted as much as any grown-up's.

And it was pretty cool that Cole seemed to feel the same way. Like he cared what David thought. "You know how dangerous underground coal mining is, right?"

"Your mine had a fire in it from methane. And you use short-wall mining, so that's more dangerous. Two men died in a ceiling collapse three years ago—"

"I know our safety record, thanks. That's part of the reason why we closed down the underground mine. I want to convert it to continuous mining, but that costs money. And the country needs coal. So surface mining seemed a way to solve all our problems. At least that's what my dad thought."

"He's wrong."

Cole's head whipped up at that. "He's your grandfather. Show him some respect."

"He's still wrong. Mountaintop removal isn't the answer. Not the way you're doing it—you're just causing more problems from erosion and groundwater contamination and getting only a fraction of the coal out in return. Plus, not as many people get jobs."

"How do you know all this?"

"Hello, it's called the Internet. I looked it up last night after Yancey flew us over your mining site."

"Not mine. My wife runs the MTR site. I'm in charge of reclamation."

"Right. I saw the pictures of what that looks like—you'll toss a few grass seeds, plant a few trees, and in a few years they'll all be dead or washed away by erosion."

"That's because no one took the time to evaluate the environmental impact of MTR—or suitable uses for completed mining sites. If the government had stricter regulations and guidelines, then maybe we could still get the coal without hurting the people or the environment."

"I thought mining companies didn't like the government interfering with their business. That's what your dad said in one of his speeches."

"Let me guess. You went to his website."

David didn't bother answering. While he'd waited in the library for his new teacher to decide which assignments she wanted to give him, he'd used the outdated school computer to do some research. Cole didn't appear anywhere except as a notation on the subsidiary site for Masterson Mountain—the MTR mining was a separate company from Masterson Mining.

But Cole's father, Kyle Masterson, was everywhere. At political rallies speaking against unions and federal regulations, at banquets discussing how he was single-handedly saving West Virginia and its hardworking families, even at a revival preaching about God giving man dominion over the animals and plants and land.

David didn't agree with him, but he had to admit that Kyle Masterson had charisma. People listened to him and believed him. David suspected that happened because Masterson was telling them what they wanted to believe, something he'd never understood. His mom raised him to face the truth and, if you didn't like it, to work to change it. He couldn't figure out why people would prefer to ignore reality and just do nothing, hoping the world might magically change. Seemed illogical.

He hoped Cole wasn't like that. "So you're waiting for new regulations to change the way you do surface mining?"

Cole stood up, stretched, as if uncomfortable. "You are so like your mom. She always asked the tough questions as well."

"But you didn't answer."

Cole's grin was wide enough that David wasn't sure if he was really smiling or if he was angry. But then he laughed, and David relaxed. "Okay, but you have to keep it a secret. You can't even tell your mom." He crouched before David, one hand on the arm of David's chair. "Promise?"

"Okay. I promise."

"I'm working to change how we do everything—not just Masterson Mining, but the entire industry. Zach Hardy was helping. We were working on better regulations, more options for waste disposal and reclamation, options that could create jobs and protect the environment."

"But why do you have to keep that a secret? Doesn't everyone want that?"

"They do, but they don't want to sacrifice any of their profit, so the mining corporations will never do it voluntarily. They can't—their investors won't let them."

"But you can?"

Cole shrugged. "We have enough money. And if I can make this work, it will be a chance to do something, I mean really *do* something. Make a difference. Can you understand that?"

"Sure. You want to go down in history."

"Something like that. But now that Hardy's dead, I'm not sure how I'm going to make things happen. At least not the way I want them to."

"My mom will help. Just ask her. She's good at making things happen." He paused, thinking of the guy who killed himself on the radio. "Well, she tries, anyway."

"I might just do that. But now I have to think of you."

"Me? What do I have to do with it?"

"No use having a son if you can't make him proud, give him a future." Cole threw the words away as if they were meaningless, just two guys shooting the breeze, but he was staring at David like he meant everything he said.

Then he stood again, opening and closing his hands like they were cramped. He cleared his throat and gestured to the path leading up the mountain. "Your mom take you to the wishing rock yet?"

David craned his head up at the path. It had rope handrails along both sides and curled back and forth up the mountainside, but was still too rough and too steep for him to navigate on his own. "No."

"You know," Cole said, sitting on the chair's arm so he was at David's eye level, "one of my fondest memories of my dad is him carrying me on his shoulders."

"Why? Did you hurt your legs?"

"No. It was during a big company picnic. Masterson Mining had blocked the union again, and we were celebrating."

"I thought unions were a good thing. Mom says they protect workers."

Cole chuckled. "Someday you'll have to talk to my father about that." His gaze tracked the path of a big bird circling overhead. "Anyway, he carried me on his shoulders as part of a race. Father-son thing, you know. We had to get through all these obstacles without him dropping me. So many times I thought he would—he was going so fast, I don't know how I hung on. But he kept telling me, 'Just hang on, just hang on, that's all you have to do, I'll do all the rest.' And so I did."

"Did you win?"

"Did we ever. My father still has that trophy in a place of honor in his study. Anyway, what do you say? Trust me enough to take a ride up to the wishing stone? You won't regret it. I promise."

I'd gone to school with Trisha McPherson—Trisha Tierney, her name had been then. How easy it was to remember the freckle-faced, always smiling girl who sat beside me in homeroom. But the woman who emerged from the trailer looked nothing like the girl I remembered. She'd gained weight—a lot, maybe a hundred pounds or more—and lost the smile in a sea of worry-wrinkles. Only the freckles remained.

She had a toddler on her hip and was trailed by three more kids, two boys and a girl, as she trudged down the path toward us. "Chantelle." A smile colored her voice, although the corners of her mouth stayed down as if they'd been super-glued into a perpetual frown. "It's good to see you. I haven't had time to finish that coverlet I been promising you—"

"That's all right," Chantelle replied, interrupting before Trish could refuse the water. "I'd rather have it done right more than fast." Chantelle was a master quilter. The only reason she'd be accepting a coverlet from someone like Trish would be to make Trisha feel like she wasn't taking charity.

I scrambled around to the back of the truck to haul down one of the water containers. It weighed a good forty-some pounds. No wonder Chantelle was in such good shape if she'd been hauling these around all day.

"AJ," Trisha said, switching the baby to the opposite hip, "hear you're responsible for the school closing. Dennis is none too happy about the kids coming home early, interrupting his day."

She jerked her chin toward the trailer. Through the window I saw the back of a man's head and the glow of a TV.

"Sorry about that," I mumbled, not sure how I came to be assigned the blame.

She shrugged. "Almost rather them home, myself. Seems like not a week goes by that one of them doesn't get sick."

"Chantelle was telling me. Said you all were worried it was the school making them sick?"

"Oh yeah. They're fine come summer. And over Christmas break, even with all the colds and flu running around that time of year. But get them back in school and this one's belly aching and tossing her cookies every night, that one's asthma starts up, the other complains of rashes that just won't heal up no matter what the doctor gives me to salve them with. It's never-ending, I tell you."

"Do other families have the same problem?"

"Everyone I know." She turned to Chantelle. "The Haigs down the way, their Betsy had blood in her pee. Again. Doctors can't figure it out."

My brain revved into hyperdrive. Elizabeth hadn't mentioned any of this. Her legal strategy was based purely on the environmental impact of Masterson's mountaintop removal. What if we went another route? Made it personal? If I could tie the kids' symptoms and the contaminated well water to Masterson, we could bring a class-action suit. Not only would that stop Masterson, but we might be able to get some compensation for the people of Scotia.

The more I thought about it, the more I liked it. Yeah, there was also the whole coming home and being a hero, rescuing the town that despised me, but that was only the tiniest part. The idea that Masterson could affect so many people, destroy their properties, their health, wreck their families, and get away with it—I couldn't even think of words to describe the fury that burned through me.

"Trisha, do you think you could help me get some other parents together? I'd like to hear about the kids who are sick."

Her eyes narrowed in suspicion. "Heard how you worked with fancy city lawyers, suing companies and losing folks their jobs—"

"Not anymore. I just want to see if we can figure out what's making the kids sick and help them."

She looked at Chantelle. Chantelle nodded. "AJ's right. This has been going on long enough. Time to do something about it. No reason why us mothers can't get together and see if we can figure something out."

Trisha gave a snort, her gaze cutting back to her husband sitting watching TV. "Guessin' you're right. Not like we can rely on the men to do much. They're too worried about losing any chance of a job with Masterson."

"It might not even be Masterson," I said, trying to be fair, although I knew it had to be him and his toxic sludge. Still, one thing I'd learned from the Pinehurst Chemicals case was to not leap to conclusions until you had concrete proof. "But how are we gonna know unless we start looking?"

TWENTY-ONE

Chantelle drove us through the hollow to several more homes with wells affected by the blackwater. The more I talked with folks—mainly the women struggling to cook and clean and provide their kids with clean drinking water—the angrier I got. It was bad enough to see Masterson destroy his own land, but for him to destroy the water these people depended on—that infuriated me.

One elderly couple who lived alone in a single-room cabin showed us their makeshift attempts to filter the water for washing so they could save the bottled water for drinking and cooking. Their once-pure spring water was an opaque oily brown, reminding me of the toxic sludge filling the impoundment above the school. They strained it through an old whiskey barrel they'd filled with sand, and it came out the other end the color of sweet tea. Then they filtered that through layers and layers of muslin, leaving behind a greasy residue that, when I dared to touch it, burned my skin.

The worst thing was that most of them, even the older couple, defended Masterson, or at least didn't blame him. They all worked for him, now or in the past, or were hoping to work for him in the future, so they didn't dare.

But I did. If I could prove that he and his mining practices were behind the blackwater, I'd make him pay for everything he'd done. How could he abandon the people who kept his mines running?

Of course, that was a big "if." I was half-tempted to start taking samples then and there, but figured it would be best to see what the scope
of the contamination was first. Map it out, document every step, so I
wouldn't have a repeat of the Pinehurst Chemicals fiasco, where all my
efforts had led to nothing usable in court and I'd ended up letting everyone down, especially our clients.

By the time we'd left the fourth home, word of the meeting that
night was spreading. Reverend Thomson, the Methodist minister, called
to volunteer his church for the meeting, and it was starting to sound
like we might need a place that big. I'd thought maybe there'd be a few
moms hauling along their sick kids and calendars scribbled with notes
from doctor's visits, but it seemed like everyone we talked to knew at
least half a dozen other families with problems.

We were headed down Route 60 when my phone rang. The connec-
tion was spotty, but I could make out Elizabeth's voice.

"Someone killed my father!"

By the time Chantelle and I arrived, two sheriff's cars and a fire rescue
truck were already on scene. The guardrail was splintered, the pavement
stained with skid marks, and broken branches littered the road like con-
fetti. I climbed out of the truck and stood staring into the open space
beyond the guardrail. Water gurgled nearby. The edge of a metal culvert
buried under the road was visible just beyond the wrecked railing. A
pair of climbing ropes marked where the rescue guys had climbed down
to bring Elizabeth up.

Finally I spotted her, draped in a blanket, sitting on the rear bumper
of the rescue truck, talking to a deputy. The other deputy was down the
road taking pictures and measuring distances with a wheel.

"She was lucky," Chantelle said. "Broke through at the culvert where
there aren't any trees."

"Lucky is an understatement." We walked past the broken guardrail.
Twenty yards below, my van sat in a stream, its front end crunched up
against a stack of boulders, rear door hanging open, water lapping at the

belongings that had slid out. Boxes and bags and books were scattered along the creek bed. One of the garbage bags I'd used to pack my clothes had split open, and I spotted my Rolling Stones T-shirt swirling in the current, snagged on a branch.

It wasn't the loss of the possessions that bothered me. It was the fact that Elizabeth had been targeted while driving my van. But whoever had hit the van couldn't have been after me—the only person I'd pissed off that much was Dickie Ellings, and he was busy pulling his knife on me and Jeremy's truck about the time this happened.

How had the driver known Elizabeth would be behind the wheel of my van? It had to be someone who saw her at the hospital or followed her from there.

"Are you okay?" I asked her, interrupting the deputy and not caring. "What happened?"

"I'm fine," she said, grimacing as she pushed her hair back and touched a knot forming on her forehead. "Thanks to your van having every safety feature known to man."

"Hey, my kid rides in that van."

"Not anymore he isn't," Chantelle said. "Looks pretty near totaled."

"I've got George McCoy coming with his wrecker to haul it up," the deputy put in. "You were lucky, Ms. Hardy. Sure you can't remember anything else about the driver or the vehicle that hit you?"

"Like I said, I couldn't see much. His high beams were on and the sun visor was down. Plus, he wore something drawn up around his face, maybe a hooded sweatshirt." She frowned, concentrating. "I think it was gray."

"Gray hooded sweatshirt, black SUV, unknown make or model." The deputy didn't sound very hopeful.

"Maybe a pickup truck—something jacked up high like an SUV." Elizabeth hung her head. "I'm sorry, I wish I could be more help."

"If you think of anything, please give us a call." He handed her a card and left.

"You're sure you're all right?" I asked again. "Maybe we should get you checked out at the hospital."

"I'm fine. Really. I just want to go home—" Her face drained of color. She looked at me, stricken. Reality had set in. "I can't go home. Can I? It's real. It's really happening. Someone wants me dead."

Chantelle drove us back to the protest site, where Elizabeth and I switched over to her Subaru. I drove; she was still too unsteady. She kept apologizing for losing all my stuff in the crash, totaling the van, and dragging me into things.

"It's not your fault." I steered back into town. We were headed to her father's house to pick up her things and then to Flora's. "It's Masterson's."

"I'm not so sure." She told me about what her PI friend had found out about Yancey. "He said Yancey could resort to violence."

Yancey had been at the hospital. But still . . . I pulled into her dad's driveway. "What would he have to gain?"

"Media attention. Lots of it. Maybe a TV deal."

"Not if anyone gets hurt and they learn it's his fault."

"All I know is that he has those girls armed to the teeth, and he was at the cemetery when that threat on my life showed up." She frowned as if something else had just occurred to her, then shook her head.

"Half the town was at the cemetery. Plus all those news people. You have no proof." I might not like Yancey, but I couldn't see him as a killer.

She led the way inside and went upstairs to grab her bag. When she returned a few minutes later, she dangled a set of car keys in front of me. "My dad drove a Ford Escape. Think it's low enough to the ground that David can transfer in and out okay?"

"Are you serious?"

"If you want it, it's yours. Least I can do."

Shock and surprise ambushed me, leaving me speechless. It was the most generous thing anyone had ever done for me—and I'd only known her for a day. I followed her back outside. She opened the garage door, revealing an electric blue SUV. It was a hybrid and looked practically brand-new.

When I tried to protest, she shook my words aside, climbing into her Subaru and closing the door. I settled into the Ford's driver's seat and turned the key. Wow. The emergency brake worked. And the defroster too probably. David was going to flip.

We pulled up in front of Flora's house and found Cole and David out front throwing a football. Pulling up in a nice car, to a nice house, nice guy out front with his oh-so-very-nice son, made me realize how much both David and I had missed out on during the past ten years. A strange nostalgia for what-never-was collided with anger at the fairy-tale ending that had been stolen from us.

The grin of absolute delight on David's face laid those feelings to rest, replacing them with something so light and joyful, my heart skipped like a rock tossed across a still pond.

"Mom," David called as I emerged from the car, "Cole taught me how to throw a spiral—watch!" He launched the black-and-yellow Nerf football in my direction. It flew through the air in a perfect arc, no hint of a wobble, and all I had to do to catch it was to take a single step forward.

"Nice job," I said, lobbing it back to him underhanded. I'd never mastered a spiral and didn't want to make a fool of myself. Especially not in front of Cole—having him around still felt like company. "Is Jeremy here?"

I needed to tell him about his truck. I'd called George McCoy, who suddenly was getting a lot of business from me, and he'd promised to replace the tires and have it back by tomorrow. Of course, I still had no idea how to pay for it. After Elizabeth just gave me a car, it didn't seem the time to ask for an advance on my pay. If she even wanted to continue the case after everything that had happened.

Who said life in the country was boring?

Elizabeth carried her things into the summerhouse, Cole and David helping her, while I went to face the music with Jeremy. He didn't take it too bad, especially when I told him he was getting four brand-new tires out of the deal.

"Sure there isn't a way to make Dickie Ellings pay for the damage?" he asked as he drew up Flora's afternoon dose of insulin.

"I called Ty, and he said they'd try to get some fingerprints, but not to hold your breath. Said this wasn't like TV."

"Yeah. I just hate the thought of that idiot getting away with it."

I told him about Elizabeth and the premature demise of my van. "She gave me her dad's car to drive, but you can use it until we get your truck back."

"Sounds good."

"How did Cole and David do?" I didn't want to appear to be spying on them, so I tried to sound casual. Jeremy wasn't fooled.

"They were great. Cole even took David up to the wishing stone. David came back grinning to beat the band, saying it was 'superlative' and 'awesomely awesome.' You've got nothing to worry about."

"David let Cole carry him all that way?"

"Yep. Piggyback. Didn't seem to bother him at all."

Jeez, I carry him out of a field polluted with toxic scum and he practically tears my head off, afraid of being embarrassed. But still. It was a relief to know Cole and David were getting along so well.

Not too well, I hoped—I hated the twinge of jealousy that rippled through me. I wanted David to have everything, including a father who cared for him, but I had had him to myself for ten years and I found myself suddenly reluctant to share his affections.

I rolled my eyes, laughing at my own childishness. Cole appeared at the back door, and I choked my laughter back. "Hey there," he said. "I thought maybe we could talk?"

We walked up the path to the wishing stone. It was the first time I'd been there in ten years, and I'd all but forgotten how breathtakingly beautiful it was. The stone was an ancient limestone outcropping hanging off the side of the mountain just below the peak. If you climbed out to the edge, you felt like you were suspended off the edge of the world, sky all around you. Some folks got scared at the immensity of it. Barely anchored to the earth, you could see wave after wave of rolling mountain stretched out beyond.

Not Cole. He'd stand as far out as possible, on the very edge, where the rock was eroded by the wind and constantly crumpling. He said the view made him feel powerful, majestic.

Me? I felt safest up here. Anchored. Like this vein of rock running through this mountain from the center of the earth and threading its way up here to touch the sky was where I was meant to be. Nothing bad could ever happen to me here—in fact, the very best thing in my life had happened on this very spot.

"I heard you brought David up here."

"He's a good kid, for a Ravens fan." Cole stood on the edge of the precipice, just like he had when we were kids, and spread his arms wide, letting the wind hold him in place.

I stood beside him, shaking my head at how little he had changed. "Hope you didn't tell him everything that happened up here."

He laughed, a throaty sound shredded by the wind and rearranged into music. "Someday we'll tell him. When he's old enough."

"Ugh. The sex talk. I'll leave that to you—it's a father's job."

"And I'm a father!" He shouted the last word, leaning his entire body into the bellow. The echo returned as the world sounded its approval.

I couldn't help myself. He looked so young and happy and, well, so like the Cole I'd known and loved. I took his hand in mine, swinging it in time with the gusts of wind, just like when we were kids.

Cole intertwined his fingers in mine and turned toward me. He brushed my hair out of my face with his other hand. Let his palm linger on my cheek. God, it felt so familiar. So right.

Except for the cold touch of his wedding ring.

Jerking away, I stepped back and turned around, letting the wind whip my hair into my face, hiding from him. "We can't."

His sigh echoed into my heart. "I know. I know." He sank down to sit on the rock. "This is all so confusing."

I didn't sit down. Instead, I remained standing, keeping my distance.

"Tell me about Waverly." The woman was going to be in my life whether I liked it or not. I wanted to know why he'd chosen her. What was so special about her that she deserved the sacrifice we were making? Because right at that moment it was taking everything I had not to fling myself into his arms and kiss away all his worries and my own.

"I'm not sure what to tell you." He stared out over the valley, eyes crinkled by the wind. "Waverly is Waverly. She saved me."

Ouch. I wanted to be the one who saved him—thought I had been, that last night together when he was torn up with grief over his mother's passing. That night we'd spent right here in this very spot, sheltered by stars. "How? How did she save you?"

"When I left for college, I was lost. I had no idea what I wanted, spent my time drinking and partying."

"What do you mean you had no idea what you wanted? You wanted to travel, to see the world, protect it—"

A sad smile crossed his face. He turned his head away to hide it, but it was too late. "No. I didn't."

"That's all you talked about as a kid. All those maps and pictures of exotic places—"

"Who got me those maps and pictures?"

I thought about that. Remembered rescuing a bunch of old maps and *National Geographic*s from the library trash bin, wrapping them up as a birthday present for him. "But—"

"That's all *you* talked about. I went along for the ride. Just like my dad thought I wanted to be a mining engineer. And Mom thought I wanted to be a writer. Waverly was the only one who was okay with me doing the only thing I was ever any good at."

The Cole I remembered had been good at everything. "What was that?"

"Football. Once I got my act together, I ended up starting tight end for three seasons at West Virginia. Didn't get picked in the draft, but Waverly saved me again. We went to Canada, and I played a few seasons with the Edmonton Eskimos. Then I blew out my knee and after rehab had to face the truth—much as I loved football, I was at best a mediocre player. I didn't have a future there. So we came back home. Turns out, Waverly is not only a great engineer, she's also really, really good at running stuff. She's the right-hand man my dad always dreamed of."

"But . . . what about you?"

He shrugged. "I'm doing what I always did. Taking my dad's paycheck. Bumming around the forest, hunting, fishing. I help out with the Pop Warner and JV football teams—assistant coach. Not everyone has ambitions, Angel. You and Ty, you were always the ones with dreams. I was perfectly happy with the way things were back then—football in the fall, hanging out with you guys the rest of the year, nowhere to go and no particular time to be there."

"And Waverly, she's cool with that?" Didn't fit my impression of the Queen Bitch, but I had to admit a little bias.

"She's got enough ambition and smarts for both of us. Talk about driven. I can relax and just go along for the ride."

We were silent. And as far apart as we'd ever been, the wind cutting between us like a knife.

He cleared his throat. "My dad wants me to get a paternity test."

"No surprise. I'll bet he'd be even happier if it came with two one-way tickets to Antarctica for David and me."

"Actually, he wasn't as upset as I thought he might be. Started talking about his legacy again, all that jazz. Said, since Waverly and I haven't had any luck—"

Ugh. I so didn't want to know about his and Waverly's love life. "I'm not letting David have any paternity test if the results are for your father. We don't want anything from him. Or you."

"I want David protected. You know, for the future. Kid like him, he deserves the best. College, help with his disability—whatever it takes, I want him to have it."

I had to make sure I wasn't imagining his words, they were so close to the words I'd dreamed a thousand times over the past decade. "You're serious?"

"Yeah. If David's okay with me being part of his life—I mean, I thought we had a great time today, connected, but if he doesn't think so, I can just help out behind the scenes." He sounded scared, uncertain—not the Cole I knew.

"David had a great time today," I reassured him. "I think the adjectives he used were 'superlative' and 'awesomely awesome.'"

"Great. Good. I was hoping maybe I could pick him up from school tomorrow? Take him over to Hawk's Nest—it's such a spectacular view of the gorge. And then after that, we could—"

"Relax, relax, we're not going anywhere." It wasn't until I'd spoken the words out loud that I realized they were true. We were staying. Scotia was David's home now. And he'd finally have the one thing I'd never been able to give him: a dad. Better—a dad who cared for him. Maybe even loved him. "You've got all the time in the world."

Elizabeth sat alone in the summerhouse. David had gone back up to Flora's house, Cole and AJ were off somewhere looking earnest and speaking in hushed tones, and she had the cottage to herself. She liked it that way. Not just for the privacy—being able to relax and drop her guard—but also for the solitude, the chance to regroup.

Calming down wasn't an option, not after learning that her father had been murdered. And almost dying herself. She bounced back up from the overstuffed chair she'd plopped down on less than a minute ago and walked through the small house, orienting herself, checking the windows and doors. Movement did nothing to soothe her jangled nerves.

A few moments later, she found herself back in the chair. This time she knew what she needed—not peace and quiet, but answers. And there was one person who might have them.

She dialed out on the old-fashioned rotary phone, impatient by how slow it was, waiting for the dial to reset after each number—how had people lived like this? As the phone on the other end rang, she hoped they had reception. It was frustrating that the rest of the world was well into the twenty-first century, but here in Scotia she still had to worry about cell coverage and rotary phones.

Finally the call connected. "Hello?"

"We need to talk," Elizabeth began, uncertain how to steer the conversation.

"What about?"

"For starters, maybe you can tell me everything you know about my father's murder."

TWENTY-TWO

Elizabeth listened carefully, wishing she was having this conversation face to face. But she'd given in to impatience.

Charity paused before answering. "Your father was killed?"

"Didn't you know that already? After all, you wrote that note threatening to kill me too." It was a hunch, but the best one Elizabeth had—and it made more sense than Yancey writing the death threat.

"Me? I'm a reporter. That would be totally unethical, trying to influence a story."

"Not to mention illegal." Elizabeth noted that Charity didn't deny writing the threat. "Yancey couldn't have left the note. He was surrounded by Ladies and the press. But you could have slipped away and no one would have noticed."

"Why would I do something like that?" The note of righteous indignation in Charity's voice sounded forced, confirming Elizabeth's suspicions.

"You were trying to drum up more interest for your story—you were worried that it would die with my father if I didn't take up his case. So you decided to bully me into it."

Another long pause. Elizabeth waited her out, remembering the reporter's mind games from last night.

"I know nothing about your father's death—other than how he appeared when I found him."

"But you suspected something?"

"Yes. At first he refused to grant me an interview, then suddenly he was all gung-ho, acting like he had some key new evidence against Masterson. And then he was dead. The timing seemed too perfect."

"Where were you? Do you have an alibi?"

"Like I told you, I was sitting in that restaurant in Charleston. You can ask anyone who worked there that night—I waited over two hours, so I was pretty obvious. Then I drove back and joined Yancey and the others."

Elizabeth was certain the police would check it out. She also had a feeling that Charity was telling the truth. Finally.

"What makes you think your father was killed?" Charity's voice held an undercurrent of excitement, a reporter about to reel in a big story.

"The medical examiner found traces of the same insecticide that poisoned those two boys this morning."

"So whoever has access to that insecticide would be a suspect. Do you know where it's used?"

"No. AJ said it's old, been banned since 1987."

"All the better—should be easy to track down."

Elizabeth didn't like the eagerness coloring the reporter's voice. The last thing she needed was something else on her conscience in addition to AJ's van and her stuff. "Let the police do their job. I only wanted to know if you knew something you weren't telling me about my father's death. Or if maybe Yancey does."

She could almost feel the reporter's "spidey sense" tingling. "Yancey?" Charity responded. "You're kidding. Why would he want to hurt your dad? Your dad's case was his key to fame and fortune."

"So you haven't seen anything suspicious?" The reporter obviously hadn't discovered the secrets of Yancey's shady past.

"No. But I'll keep my eyes open."

"Be careful."

Elizabeth wasn't very happy when I told her about my idea to switch our legal tactics to a class-action lawsuit.

"Do you have any idea what that involves?" she asked. "The resources a class-action suit takes? I wouldn't even know where to start."

We were finishing dinner—greens wilted with black beans, roasted corn, and tomatoes, along with Flora's cornbread, a recipe I lusted after but she kept secret, telling me only that she'd leave it to me in her will someday. Which I was perfectly fine with as long as she kept on fixing it while she was alive.

"Kinda." I answered Elizabeth with my mouth full, saw David's eyes on me, and quickly swallowed. "But these folks I met today—they could really use the help. And if the school is making their kids sick. . . ."

"Okay, I'll think about it."

"Good, because there's a bunch of them coming to a meeting tonight."

Elizabeth dropped her fork. "Tonight?"

"They just need someone to hear them out. We can at least do that."

"Can I come along?" David asked eagerly. "Will Cole be there?" He'd been upset when Cole had to go home to his own family for dinner. While I was happy that David and Cole had hit it off, I didn't want David's heart breaking every time Cole had to leave.

"No. Cole won't be there. And you need to get to bed early tonight. You look exhausted." His eyelids were droopy, and muscle spasms shook his legs. "Maybe a long, hot tub first. Let your muscles relax." Spasticity was the bane of David's existence, and the main reason why he used his chair more than his crutches. Too much exertion and his large muscles would begin to scissor together uncontrollably.

It was a measure of how tired he was that he didn't even argue. "Okay. But I get to see Cole tomorrow after school, right?"

"I'm not sure about you going back to that school." Not if it might make him ill.

That woke him up. He lurched forward in his chair. "Mom. I'm going to school tomorrow. I have to. Otherwise they'll all think I'm a wuss."

"It doesn't matter what anyone thinks. The water at the school might be contaminated. I can't risk it."

"*You're* not." He rested his fists on either side of his plate. "I promise, I won't drink any water. You can pack my lunch. Heck, I can maybe do some detective work for you, sneak some samples—"

"No. You leave the detective work to me."

"But I can go to school tomorrow." He made it sound like a fait accompli.

"You can go to school. Just for tomorrow. Then we'll talk." Tomorrow was Friday, and as much as I hated the idea of him anywhere near that school again, I didn't have many choices. At the next closest school, over the mountain in Smithfield, I'd have to get him enrolled, figure out how to get him there and back again every day, and how to fit that into my work schedule. I glanced at Elizabeth. *If* I still had a job, that was.

"And I'll see Cole tomorrow," David added, pushing the limits, as always.

I turned my hands palms up in capitulation. "He'll pick you up from school."

"All right!" He popped a wheelie, almost up-dumping the table.

When Elizabeth and I arrived at the Methodist church, there was already a crowd waiting inside. Reverend Thomson greeted us warmly, gave his condolences to Elizabeth about her father, and thanked her for staying on to help. He barely glanced at me—I wasn't sure if it was because of the whole unwed mother thing, the rumors about my mental instability and suicide attempt, or the fact that I'd busted one of his church windows way back when and still owed him the money to repair it.

When he glanced over my head at the stained-glass portrait of Jesus with the loaves and fishes, the apostles' faces replaced by a cheap pane of clear glass, I had my answer. Good. A broken window I could fix. The other stuff, not so much.

The church door opened, and I was surprised to see my father standing there. He didn't enter; instead, he caught my eye and beckoned for me to join him outside.

"What are you doing here? Are you okay?" I asked as he led me around the corner to the side of the church. "Shouldn't you be home resting?" A spark of hope flared inside me. Had he come to watch me work?

"You need to stop this. Now."

So much for hope. "Why? Talk to me like an adult and give me a good reason. Because I don't take well to threats or demands."

His eyes grew wide, revealing bloodshot whites. He drew in his breath, triggering a rumbling cough. As he coughed, he glared at me—as if his coal miner's lung was somehow my fault. I wasn't buying it. I straightened, crossing my arms in front of my chest, and waited him out.

"Angela Joy." Suddenly he was pleading. "Think of your mother. She could lose everything."

"How? Masterson told Cole he has no problem with David and me being here—I mean, I'm sure it's not in keeping with his perfect little well-controlled universe, but he's okay with it."

"You don't understand. That man can destroy us all. Starting with your mother. What would she be if we lost the house?"

"Why would you lose the house? Surely it's paid off by now."

He hung his head. "We don't own the house. Mr. Masterson does."

"You sold our home to Masterson? Why?"

"Initial payment. We owe him a lot more."

Figures. Masterson was a genius at getting his hooks into everyone.

"How much more?" I was already mentally deducting what I owed Flora and Jeremy from what Elizabeth was paying me, hoping the remainder was somewhere close to what my parents needed. I couldn't let them lose our house—Randy's home. Dad was right about that. My mom would never survive.

He drew in his breath, this time without coughing. "Almost half a million dollars."

I choked. "Half a million—how the hell—"

He turned away. And suddenly I realized how it happened. Two LifeFlights. Seven months in a hospital, one of them in intensive care, all those doctors and tests and surgeries and specialists. I'd been so overwhelmed with fighting to survive and then fighting for David that I never really added it up. Assumed the insurance covered it and never questioned how.

Now I knew the truth. The price was more than the house and money—Masterson had demanded my parents' collusion as payment. When they lied to everyone about my imaginary psychosis and suicide attempt, they hadn't betrayed me; they'd been trying to make sure I got the care I needed. They'd been trying to protect me.

"God . . . Dad . . . why didn't you tell me?"

He shrugged, still not facing me. "What's to tell? A man takes care of his family. Or he isn't much of a man."

We stood in the shadow of the church, the voices and footsteps of the people entering around the corner surrounding our silence, placing us beyond an invisible boundary. I lowered my arms, my hands open at my sides, empty. Need churned through me, mixed with regret and sorrow—a profound grief echoing back ten years and returning to pummel me as if it was fresh. My mouth tasted of oil and acid, a memory from that night when everything had changed.

And I realized, finally, that everything *had* changed. There was nothing I could do to fix it. Not now. Not ever.

"I'm sorry," I said, straightening my arm to touch him, but he was too far away, beyond my reach. "We'll find some other way to save the house. I can't let Masterson continue to hurt these people. I can't give up."

A flinch roiled through him even though I hadn't touched him. I dropped my hand.

"Not can't, Angela Joy. Won't." He walked away, leaving me in the shadows.

TWENTY-THREE

I'd thought the meeting would be fairly informal—gathering information, listening to folks, and deciding if the case had enough merit that we should investigate. I hadn't counted on the anger.

Before either Elizabeth or I could do much to explain the process, people began standing up and airing their complaints.

"Why should we get involved?" George McCoy shouted. "Now that Yancey and his Ladies are here, they're the ones getting their faces on TV. No one cares about us."

"You're not doing it to become a TV star, now, are you?" I retorted. "Not with that mug of yours, George McCoy."

"Look," Elizabeth said, "we needed Yancey's ability to pull in the big media, broadcast our story to as many people as possible. But I see no reason why locals can't take it from here. If you're willing."

"I don't understand," a woman I couldn't see in the back called out. "Why are we suing the government instead of Masterson?"

"Because it's the Army Corps of Engineers and the Department of Environmental Protection that approved Masterson's permits," Elizabeth explained.

"So, even if we win, all Masterson will do is move on and try again? Who's to say the next time it won't be my mountain or my hollow he wants to fill up with rubble?"

"Exactly," Elizabeth said. "That's why we need to set this precedent. So we can stop not just Masterson but all the mining companies from getting their permits approved. And that's why we're going after an injunction against the government."

"What's in it for us then? Who's going to pay to repair my foundation?"

"Or fix my well? At least buy my family bottled water until this mess is all cleared up."

"Someone's gotta pay!"

Shouting resumed, drowning out Elizabeth. I climbed onto the organist's bench and used my fingers to whistle them quiet. "Shut up and listen!" Suddenly ninety pairs of eyes were staring at me. I climbed down again, not enjoying the spotlight at all, but it was, as Elizabeth kept telling me, a necessary evil. "Why do you think we're doing this?"

"To save our mountain."

"To stop Masterson."

"No." I shook my head vehemently. "No. This is about saving your kids. Trisha, how many days of school did your son miss last year because of his breathing problems?"

"Forty-eight. They about took me to court over it."

"And Mary, what about your little girl? Didn't you tell me she's gotten ulcers since starting here at this school?"

"Sure 'nough. Wakes every morning with stomachaches. But she's fine soon as summer comes and school's out."

"I can't prove it, not yet, but I think Masterson's coal slurry has seeped into the school's water supply. If—and mind you, it's a big if—we can prove that it has and that it's making your kids sick, then we might be able to go after him."

"There's lots of 'ifs' and 'mights' in that sentence."

"You're right. There is. But with a class-action suit you could claim damages."

"You mean, we'd win money?"

"Enough so we could pay the doctor and buy medicine?"

"And get the school fixed?"

"Or moved. Just move the school—away from that damn slurry pond hanging over our kids' heads like a guillotine."

"Right! Move the school. Save our kids!" They began to chant. The room vibrated with enthusiasm.

I made the mistake of looking over my shoulder at Elizabeth. She was frowning and lowered her voice so only I could hear. "We don't have the resources for a case like this. It could drag on for years, and none of these people would ever see a dime. Not to mention the money we'd be out. Masterson has tons to burn—enough appeals and stalling tactics and he'll win no matter how good a case we have."

The door opened and Cole entered. I couldn't help my smile—that's how fast old habits take over when you go home again. And I didn't care. It felt good having him in my life, even if he wasn't mine.

That point stabbed home when Waverly followed him inside. And behind her was Old Man Masterson. My smile drifted into uncertainty, lost in the implications. Cole believed in what we were doing, he hated the MTR mining, I knew he did. So why would he join his father and come here?

The conversations hushed. Old Man Masterson tugged his leather gloves off, finger by finger, and slapped them into his palm. People looked everywhere but at each other's eyes, resistance fighters trying hard not to be able to identify each other if they were captured and interrogated by the Gestapo.

"I understand we have some problems going on around here," he said in a calm tone, quiet enough that it forced everyone to strain to listen.

Elizabeth scowled and opened her mouth to protest. I jumped in first—no sense both of us getting crucified. "The only problem around here is you."

He paused, then looked me up and down as if deciding whether or not I was worth his notice. To my dismay, Cole stepped forward and defended his father. "You owe him the courtesy of listening." He raised his voice. "All of you do."

A few nods from the crowd, enough to cow any other protests. "Hear him out," someone shouted.

"All right. What's your solution to these folks' problems, Mr. Masterson? Their wells are poisoned, their kids are sick, and their land is being flooded away."

"Actually, you just nailed the heart of the matter right there." His voice was condescending, as if he was surprised I could manage basic English, much less elucidate a complex situation. "Land. But it's not their land. Not most of it anyway. It's my land. Masterson land."

Most families in Scotia were land-rich and cash-poor. When times were hard, they'd sell land and mineral rights to the Mastersons at rock-bottom prices—a decision they often regretted later when they realized what they'd sacrificed. Obviously, the practice had continued since I left. From the number of people looking down and shuffling their feet, I guessed that Masterson had bought up a lot more family holdings.

"Now, I've always been willing to have my workers—past or present—live on my land at no charge. Some places there's generations of Masterson workers living off the same land. Seems the right thing to do. The Christian thing to do."

Rustling and murmurs tumbled through the room in a wave. Folks around here didn't like being beholden to anyone—they liked it even less when they had their noses rubbed in it.

"If anyone here has a problem with living where they are, they're welcome to move. But I think we'd all agree that I have every right to do what I want, when I want, with my land."

The murmurs died away. More nodding. We were losing the crowd. I nudged Elizabeth, hoping she'd have some legal words of wisdom that would refocus the issues.

"What about the school, Mr. Masterson?" she asked.

"I deeded that land to the county school district. How they maintain the property is their concern. I suggest that if you're looking for a villain in all this, you start there. Not by bad-mouthing a company that has kept this town alive for seven generations."

That sounded the death knell. People began leaving, sidling out the doors, not looking back. Masterson, Waverly, and Cole stood beside the exit, shaking hands with some, nodding to others as if they'd just hosted the social event of the year.

I spied Cole slipping out. I rushed after him, cornering him in the parking lot.

"Cole, how could you?" I wished I didn't sound so heartbroken, but couldn't help it.

"What do you mean, how could I? How could you? Don't you see that it's David's legacy you're risking with this foolishness?"

"Foolishness?"

"Yes. As usual, you're rushing into something you don't understand. Couldn't you leave things alone without riling people up?"

"I thought you wanted to stop the MTR."

"Making sure there are better regulations on future MTR permits is one thing. That's only common sense. Destroying my family's business with a civil suit—David's family business, his future—is another. I saw what happened when you went after Capital Power. I can't let that happen to us."

As we stared at each other, both leaning forward from the hips, my fists balled, his hands stretched wide open as if trying to fling his anger aside, I had a flashback to ten years ago. Only it was Old Man Masterson I was screaming at then.

Like I'd been caught in some kind of karmic time-loop. One certain to end badly.

I took a step back, grabbed a breath. "Cole. I don't want to argue with you."

He jerked his chin up, gaze snapping in surprise. "So you're giving up? This idea of suing us?"

"I didn't say that."

His father and Waverly came through the doors on our side of the building. He straightened, tension still coursing through his body. "Then we've nothing to talk about."

He walked away.

My cheeks burned as if he'd slapped me. I wanted to run after him, fight back—but realized I'd be wrestling ghosts. We lived in two different worlds. Always had, I guessed.

Still, I waited for him to come back to me.

Cole kept on walking toward his wife and father. A cold wave of despair rolled through my belly. I waited. Couldn't help the hope flickering in my heart.

He never even looked back.

TWENTY-FOUR

I remembered how I'd felt back ten years ago when I'd woken up in the hospital. The first words I could comprehend were my dad's as he told the doctors to kill my baby if it meant saving me. I couldn't talk—there was a breathing tube stuck down my throat—but I remember lying there, helpless, hopeless, feeling betrayed. And alone. So very alone.

I hadn't felt that way again since David was born. Not until tonight. Scotia, the place where dreams come to die.

"Why didn't those people tell you they were living on Masterson's land?" Elizabeth asked as I drove us back to Flora's. "Instead, they let us make fools out of ourselves."

"Probably they hadn't told anyone." A city girl like her wouldn't understand. "Most of those holdings had been in their families for generations. To admit that things had gotten so bad that they had to sell out—"

"It's a betrayal?"

"Exactly. Not for them, for their kids. Kids who would have at least had land to their names even if they didn't have much else."

"That stinks. I'm starting to see why you hate Masterson so much. And why my father hated him too."

There was an edge to her voice I hadn't heard before. "I don't think even Masterson would stoop to murder," I said, "if that's what you're thinking."

"Someone did." She sat in silence, her head turned to the window. Then she sighed. "Maybe it's for the best, anyway. We'd never have the resources to pursue a class-action suit. We'll just stick with my father's original strategy."

"Which you said would fail."

"Maybe not. I need to talk to Cole"—it took everything I had not to flinch at his name—"about this mysterious Environmental Impact Survey he was hinting at." She paused, obviously uncomfortable with being the one giving a pep talk. "There's still hope. We haven't lost yet."

I grunted in response. Sure felt like losing. All those folks cowed by Masterson. Cole betraying me—and using David's future as an excuse! Implying that I was a bad mother for not kowtowing to his family's greedy moneymaking machine.

"Am I wrong?" I asked Elizabeth. "Not giving David everything that Masterson's money could buy?"

"I don't know. Like you said, kids change everything. So what does David need that more money would take care of? Seems like he has everything a kid could ask for: people in his life who care, he's happy, it's obvious he thinks you're the biggest hero since Wonder Woman—"

"He said that?" I asked, amazed.

"Didn't have to. You should have heard him bragging about the cases you guys have worked on together, the way you figured out about the toxaphene poisoning this morning, the people you've helped."

I shrugged off the unaccustomed praise—but saved it for later, to reflect upon and cherish in private. "Still, think of all the opportunities Masterson's money could give him. A big house, college of his choice—"

"Kid's smart enough to get into any college he wants. Do you know what he's listening to on his iPod? *At Dawn We Slept*. I didn't read that until it was assigned in my college history class. And he seems pretty happy with where you're living now."

"But—"

She turned in her seat to face me. "Is it how much *David* has that worries you? Or how much *you* have to give him?"

I didn't have an answer for that. Thankfully, we pulled up in front of the summerhouse, saving me from the need to reply. We walked inside and woke Jeremy up from where he'd fallen asleep reading on the couch. "How was David?"

"Crashed and burned as soon as you left. Haven't heard a peep from him since he went to bed."

"Thanks, Jeremy."

"No problem. See you in the morning."

I insisted on Elizabeth taking my bedroom while I bunked on the couch out front. She looked wrecked, and I was glad she'd be in the middle room. Now that we had no idea who we could trust, including so-called allies like Yancey, it seemed prudent that one of us stand guard. After everything that had happened tonight, I doubted I'd be getting much sleep, anyway.

While she was in the bathroom, I checked on David. He was deep asleep—so deep that he wasn't even snoring. I resisted the urge to nudge him. I missed hearing his snoring—somehow the noise was reassuring. Like when he was a baby and I used to stand at his crib, listening to his tiny, sweet noises.

I contented myself with watching. The light from the hallway landed on his face in one golden shaft, contrasting with his dark hair. He resembled Cole far more than he did me.

I'd forgotten how infuriating Cole could be, always doing as he pleased, never mind discussing things ahead of time. Although I was sure he *had* discussed this decision . . . with his father. Not with me, the mother of his child.

Old Man Masterson had been crowing about his precious legacy and keeping the business in the family ever since we were kids, and he'd expected Cole to be the perfect son living up to the Masterson name.

The thought of him anywhere near David made me clench my jaws so tight my ears popped. This afternoon I'd been so happy about Cole accepting David. Now I had to figure out how to pay the price.

Including getting my folks' home back from Masterson.

I crept forward and planted a soft kiss on David's forehead. Then I left. I had a sinking feeling I knew what Masterson would demand in return for freeing my parents: David.

TWENTY-FIVE

I never dream. Not since I almost died ten years ago. The doctors said something in my brain was damaged. Said I was lucky I hadn't lost more.

Losing my dreams meant losing Randy. I used to see him in my dreams after he died. He was always frozen at sixteen, but still my big brother, teaching me stuff or just walking with me through the woods as I wrestled with problems. Listening, joking, making me smile—that's what I lost when I lost my dreams.

Now, instead of sleeping deep, I toss and turn most nights, waking every few hours to check on David, get caught up on work—everything takes me twice as long to read as other people, so I take a lot of work home with me—or just sit at the kitchen table and stare at the pile of bills on one hand and the empty checkbook on the other.

I'd much rather have Randy. Especially nights like this when I could have used some big-brother advice. What to do about Cole? My folks? Masterson? Who killed Zachariah Hardy? How could I help the people of Scotia without destroying the one industry that kept the town alive?

Most important: What was best for David?

Let's face it, it sucked to have a child with special needs—not his cerebral palsy or medical needs, but the need to cultivate all the miraculous potential resting in his mind.

As far back as second grade his teachers had salivated over David's potential. Before we left D.C., his principal begged me to reconsider, maybe even leave David in the care of someone else while I went to find work. She said he was "more than gifted." Hell, I could've told her that.

I wanted him to connect with more than just books and abstract ideas. I wanted him to see what impact ideas could have on people's lives, how real people lived, what it smelled like to be surrounded by nature, how big and bold and beautiful everything was, how he could play a role in changing the world.

Most of all, I wanted him to feel safe and secure and loved. The way I'd felt when I was his age, before Randy died. Which seemed impossible in the city, where gunfire and sirens provided constant background noise and we never knew when we'd be forced to live out of the back of the van.

As I lay on the couch, surrounded by the crackles of the wood burner and the scent of the lavender sachet Flora used to keep her quilts fresh, I thought about David. Wished I could dream and see his future, ask Randy what I should do.

The sound of footsteps crunching on gravel catapulted me to my feet. The sound repeated. I wished I'd found time to stop by my parents' house and pick up a shotgun or hunting rifle.

Instead, all I had was an iron poker.

I crept to the front door, snuck a peek through the curtains. A man-sized patch of darkness flowed between the vehicles parked below the summerhouse.

The lights were off inside, but I knew he'd hear me as soon as I opened the door. Which maybe wasn't a bad thing—let him know we were awake and ready. Not the easy targets he expected.

I hit the porch lights just as I flung the door open and stepped out. The shadow straightened. I caught a glimpse of white skin, but his face was shielded by a ball cap pulled low.

"Hey!" I shouted, hoping he'd take the bait and turn toward me so I could see his face better.

Instead, he turned and ran.

I took two steps after him before stopping. Not because it was foolish—fury and adrenaline had leached the common sense right out of me—but because a dog barked once and raced past me.

Ty got up from the porch swing and followed Nikki. He was dressed in jeans and a flannel shirt under his deputy's parka. "Wish you would have had the sense to stay inside. Nikki and I were all set up for an ambush."

"What are you doing here?" I asked, surprised but glad to see him.

"After the show you put on at the meeting, I thought it was best if someone kept an eye on things around here tonight."

Nikki had caught up with the intruder and was circling him, trapping him on the side lawn beside the summerhouse.

"Good girl," Ty said, unsnapping his holster and approaching the intruder. I waited at the edge of the lawn. Nikki stood at attention, glaring at the man. He froze, his back to me. Ty circled around, then relaxed. He gestured to Nikki and she sat back on her haunches.

"Call the dog off, I didn't do anything," a woman's voice carried to me.

I joined Ty and Nikki, still clutching the poker. Finally I saw the intruder's face. "Charity?" It was the reporter from Yancey's crew. "What are you doing here at three in the morning?"

"Only time I could sneak away without drawing attention," she said. "I wanted to talk to Elizabeth about the meeting tonight. You too."

Her speech was fast—too fast. She was lying. Or maybe just didn't like dogs and they made her nervous. Whichever it was, she turned to Ty. "Can I go now? I haven't done anything wrong, you have no right to detain me."

He gestured, and Nikki moved away from Charity and joined Ty. Charity began jogging toward the road. "Wait," I called. "Thought you wanted to talk."

She stopped, and glanced pointedly at Ty. He looked to me and I nodded, then he and Nikki returned to the porch, watching from the steps.

"What?" I asked the reporter, not too happy about the panic still jazzing my veins. Was everyone connected to Yancey addicted to drama?

"I did some research on you," she began. Her eyes glittered in the faint moonlight as if she was an animal getting ready to pounce.

I merely shrugged. "You and half the world know my story. It's old news."

"Not the Capital Power story. The story behind your almost dying ten years ago."

I must have flinched because both Ty and Nikki took two steps toward us. I waved them back. "What's that got to do with anything?"

"What if it wasn't an accident? What if someone sent that truck to force you off the road?" Her voice rose with anticipation.

Even though he was too far away to hear her, I looked to Ty. The sight of him, so solid, ready to defend and protect me, was a comfort.

"Why would you think it wasn't an accident?" I asked, struggling to keep my voice level. I didn't sense Ty behind me until his hand joined mine, holding me tight, returning the warmth to my frozen fingers. Charity looked at him, then smirked at me.

"We'll talk more later," she said. "A full interview. On the record." She turned toward the road and began picking up speed.

After my accident, I'd have been a fool not to suspect that Masterson played a role in it—after all, it'd been one of his trucks that forced me into that impoundment pond. But I'd never had any proof.

I watched Charity go, puzzled. And suspicious—after what Elizabeth found out about her dad being poisoned, I was suspicious of everyone. Did Charity really have proof that Masterson had tried to kill me? Or was she just using me?

Ty and I returned to the porch. He plopped down on the swing, but adrenaline and residual fear kept me pacing. Nikki sat at Ty's side, her head swinging as she followed my movements. Her ears were canted at attention, and Ty laid his hand flat against her shoulder, keeping her still even though it was clear that she was as agitated as I was. He patted her, whispered something to her, and she relaxed. Wish it was that easy for me.

"Three in the morning seems a strange time for a reporter to come for an interview," he drawled. I didn't have an answer to that. We both knew he was being facetious, and I was in no mood for small talk.

"Guess it was a good thing you're a light sleeper," he added.

I whirled on him, certain he was reprimanding me for my foolishness—racing out armed with only a fire poker. Instead, he pushed over and patted the space beside him. After taking one more circuit of the porch, scanning the darkness and seeing nothing, I slumped down, rocking the swing violently.

Nikki, on the other side of Ty, lowered her head to rest it on his thigh, and looked up at me as if she shared my misery. He scratched her between her ears. "What happened tonight at the meeting?" he asked, his gaze on the dog, giving me space, reading my emotional state better than I could myself. "I've never known you to walk away from a fight."

I took a moment. My stomach was still running, chasing after an intruder, my heart galloping after it.

"I don't know what I'm doing here," I confessed. "I'm being pummeled from every direction—more a beating than a fight. Flora talks like she thinks she's dying, my dad talks like he wishes I was dead—or at least gone—and I haven't even seen my mom yet."

"Maybe that's where you should start. Your mom."

"Right. The same woman who convinced me we could stay with her and then wouldn't even come out to meet her only grandchild."

He pursed his lips and wrapped his free arm around my shoulder as if settling me like he had with Nikki. Hate to say it, but it worked. Ty has such a soothing presence—steady, like nothing bad can happen when he's around.

Pretty much the opposite of Cole, who always seems to have a whirlwind of activity around him, people trying to please him or get his attention or just be near him, as if his charisma is contagious. Randy was like that as well.

Ty doesn't need charisma. He has something more, something deeper, quieter, stronger. Not sure how he does it, but I wish someday he'd teach me. I could use more quiet and less passion and turmoil in my life.

"Maybe there's a good reason why your mom couldn't bear to see you and David." His voice was low, thoughtful. "But aside from that, she's still Masterson's accountant, even if she works from home now. Maybe she knows something that could help you and Elizabeth with your case."

I blinked. Why hadn't I thought of that before? I'd been so distracted by my dad and his defense of Masterson that I forgot about Mom's job. But it wouldn't work. I explained to Ty about Masterson owning my family's home. "She'd never divulge anything confidential. Not if it meant risking the house."

"Why not let her make the choice?" he suggested. "You might be surprised."

Probably not pleasantly surprised, I thought, remembering two nights ago, standing in the cold and rain, barred from entering my own house, David being denied the chance to meet his grandparents. But maybe it was worth a try.

Not like I had any other options.

"In the meantime," he said, "I think first thing tomorrow I should do some checking on your reporter friend."

Ty and I spent the night keeping watch. And Nikki, of course. He caught me up on his life since I left Scotia, and I shared with him the roller-coaster ride I'd been on for the past ten years. Mostly we just sat in silence, trying to stay warm. Nikki helped with that, sprawling across our laps like a big furry blanket.

He left as the sun was rising—refused my offer of breakfast, saying he had to get home and changed since he was on the day shift. He at least let me refill his thermos with some coffee I brewed that had been supplied by Jeremy when he stocked our kitchen. As I sipped my coffee, watching Ty and Nikki drive away, I felt off balance, and not just from lack of sleep. It was unsettling, drinking coffee I hadn't bought, in a house I didn't own, after sitting up all night with an old friend I hadn't spoken to in a decade.

I was used to standing on my own, taking care of David and myself. It was overwhelming and humbling to suddenly have all these helping hands—even Elizabeth and Jeremy, strangers both just two days ago.

The sun rose, blossoming like a schoolgirl's hair ribbons unfurling across the sky, and I made a promise to myself not to forget these uninvited but much-appreciated blessings, to not take them or the people behind them for granted.

Another huge difference between life here and life in the city. In the city, it would have killed me to ask for help. When I'd called Flora and asked about coming home after I couldn't make the rent, that about broke me. I'd never have done it if it was only me, but I had David to watch over.

In D.C. it was all about the stuff, the money, everything in our world tugging constantly on my purse strings: medical bills, clothes for David, rent, groceries, keeping the van running. A never-ending juggling act with me waiting to see which ball I'd drop and shatter.

Here, I wasn't worrying about breaking. I'd find a way to repay all the people who'd helped us. More than repaying them, I'd let them know how much their help meant to me. And I'd try my best to help someone else, keep the generosity flowing.

I surprised myself by smiling at the thought, finally understanding something Flora had been trying to teach me ever since I was a kid. "What goes around comes around," she'd always said, and I'd taken that to mean, if I was bad, then bad things would happen to me—it was all my fault.

But that wasn't the lesson at all. She'd been trying to get me to see the many good things that came my way, to pay attention and appreciate them. Not just things, but people.

The thought energized me enough to pull out some eggs and sausage and actually pretend to cook—if swirling stuff around a frying pan could be called cooking. The outcome could never rival Flora's breakfast, but it must have smelled good enough because soon both David and Elizabeth were at the table, forks in their hands, eager to dig in.

"What's the plan for today?" Elizabeth asked, scraping the charcoal off the toast I'd burned and using it to season her eggs.

"I still get to go to school, right?" David asked.

"You do." I tried to hide my trepidation. "If you're sure you want to." He nodded vigorously, his mouth full. "I'll take you this morning, and Cole will pick you up this afternoon."

"Good." He folded an entire piece of toast into his mouth, cheeks bulging like a chipmunk's.

"Human bites, please," I said with resignation, receiving an eye roll in return. I turned to Elizabeth. "I thought we could go see my mom. See if she can tell us anything about Masterson's land deals."

"Your mom? Why would she know anything helpful?"

"She's Masterson's bookkeeper. Been working for him thirty years."

She looked wary. "Maybe that's not a good idea, putting her in the middle. Yesterday, when I met her, your mom seemed a little, well, fragile. And after your dad getting sick—"

I waved her words aside. My mom had always been "fragile"—ever since Randy's death. I'd been thinking about approaching her ever since Ty left. Maybe I could use a little blackmail of my own—like the chance for her to see her grandson. Although I didn't have much hope of it working. It was an idle threat. I'd never prevent her from seeing David if David wanted to meet my parents. But I was a pretty good poker player—maybe I could bluff her.

If it didn't work, at least I'd have tried—if nothing else, it would give me a chance to see what was going on with her and why my dad was being so overprotective, more so than usual.

"You have a better idea?" I asked her.

"I want to check my father's computer for that file Cole was talking about."

"We can do that after we see my mom." She bristled at that, but I ignored her. I wasn't about to let Elizabeth head out by herself, not after someone tried to kill her yesterday.

An hour later we dropped David off at school. The hazmat team had stripped the playing field of its topsoil, dug a runoff ditch around the field's perimeter, and anchored a tarp over it. I'm sure the sight of the bright-blue tarp was meant to reassure, problem taken care of, but I was leery. This was going to be David's last day here even if I had to bribe the school officials to let him into Smithfield instead.

I ran in to tell the office that Cole would be picking him up instead of me. The secretary and Letta Nowicki looked at me like I was deranged. Apparently they didn't worry about child abduction here in

Scotia—in fact, Letta's main concern seemed to be the possibility of having to stay late to watch over David since didn't I know it was a Friday night and people had plans.

I shot her down with a glare and a muttered reminder that it was her school's lack of supervision that had landed two students in the hospital and could have injured my son as well.

"I'm sure you'll have all your documentation ready when my attorney calls," I said over my shoulder, hoping that I'd wrecked her day. Payback's a bitch.

I ran back out to the Escape where Elizabeth waited. A circle of kids surrounded David on the playground, all wide-eyed as he regaled them with his adventures while trapped in the toxic sludge. He didn't even wave good-bye as we left.

The protest site was quiet today—the only signs of activity were the tree-sitters' banners whipping in the wind. Storm clouds were rolling in, and I hoped they'd hold off until after Cole took David over to Hawk's Nest.

"Looks like rain," Elizabeth observed.

"Might blow over," I said, mainly just because, after my encounter with Letta, I was feeling contrary. "You never know around these parts."

Her phone rang just as I turned onto Main Street. "You're breaking up. What?" She listened for a moment, then straightened in her seat. "We'll be right there."

"What is it?" I asked after she hung up.

"That was Charity. She thinks Yancey's the killer, said she has proof. She's scared that he's after her. We need to get over there now."

I spun the wheel and headed back out of town toward Yancey's place. "Call the police." I handed her my phone. "Ty's number is in there, call him direct, he's on duty."

She dialed. "No service, it starts to ring, then drops the call."

"Try nine-one-one. I read somewhere you can get through to them even if there's a weak signal."

Thumbs of both hands dialing, she jerked her head to look at me. "Why the hell would that work? It's still the same equipment."

"I don't know. Just try. We're almost there."

"No luck. Now it doesn't even try to ring. Maybe we should go back to the school, we know there's a signal there."

It would mean turning around and losing time. Yancey's place was just around the bend at the top of the ridge. "Did Charity say why she thought he was the killer?"

"I couldn't make it out, she kept breaking up."

"They have a landline, she would call the police directly if she felt she was in true danger."

"I guess. Maybe she was just being dramatic—you know she's the one who left the death threat for me at the cemetery."

"Really?" I added that to my skepticism about the reporter's 3:00 AM visit to me. "Okay, then we keep going. I'll go in, get Charity, and we'll leave, see what she has to say."

As we sped around the final bend in the road and turned down the drive leading to the main house, Elizabeth said, "How do we know Charity isn't the killer? We only have her word that she's actually a reporter. She could be anyone."

I didn't have an answer to that one. "What motive would she have to kill you and your dad?"

"What motive does anyone have? Masterson's the only one with a motive that we know of."

I slowed the car a hundred feet short of the main house. The meadow was empty, and I didn't see any movement around any of the smaller outbuildings at the edge of the woods. "What do you want to do?"

She gave me back my phone. "We'll go in, ask for Charity, and use their phone. If possible, we'll stick close to all the Ladies—no one's going to try anything with a dozen witnesses."

"Unless they're all involved."

"And you said I was paranoid."

We parked in the circular drive in front of the house. I was tempted to leave the engine running for a quick getaway, but that also left us vulnerable to someone stealing the car, so I took the keys with me, keeping them in my hand as we walked to the door.

"Wait, I've got a signal." I dialed Ty's direct number. Faster than chancing being put on hold by the 911 operator and losing the signal again. Elizabeth hesitated in front of the door while I told Ty what was going on, but someone inside must have seen her because just as I hung up the door opened.

Yancey stood there, holding a machine gun.

"Elizabeth, AJ," he said with a grin verging on Rasputin maniacal. "Welcome to the party."

TWENTY-SIX

To her credit, Elizabeth didn't run or even flinch. Instead, she straightened and assumed what I could only imagine was her courtroom demeanor, staring Yancey straight in the eye, ignoring the weapon in his hands. "Where's Charity?"

He frowned. "I don't know. I'm looking for her myself. Why?"

"She was going to tell me about finding my father," Elizabeth bluffed. I was impressed. Her poker face was almost as good as mine. Maybe even better.

Yancey stood aside to allow us in, but no way I was going to let him at my back. Elizabeth went ahead, but before I could move, from outside came the sound of gunfire, followed by women screaming.

Yancey bolted past me, racing toward the woods at the far edge of the meadow. I took off after him. A toolshed lay halfway between the house and the trees, but he passed it, his gun raised. More gunfire, more screams and shouts. There was movement in the trees, women running and ducking for cover, all wearing camo and carrying weapons. A few lay in the grass, motionless.

A siren sounded just as Yancey and I reached the first woman. She lay facedown, the back of her camo jacket splattered with crimson.

I glanced over my shoulder and saw Elizabeth stopping Ty back at the drive, pointing in our direction. Ty glanced our way, spotted Yancey with his gun—now aimed at the trees. I realized too clearly what was about to happen if I didn't stop it. Fast.

"Yancey, give me the gun," I yelled.

He whirled, the gun pointing at me. "What?"

"Give me the gun. Now!"

His eyes grew wide as he saw Ty take Nikki from the rear of the Tahoe. "Aw, hell!"

He threw the gun down. "Hold still," I ordered. "Hold very, very still." I turned and called to Ty. "It's okay."

Too late. Nikki was already hurtling toward us, a brown-black blur against the green grass.

Yancey's too-tan skin blanched the color of turnips cooked too long. He turned and ran.

"No!" I cried. "Yancey, don't run!"

Too late again. Nikki careened past us, a bullet aiming for a kill shot. With a leap worthy of Nijinsky, she hurled herself at Yancey and dropped him to the ground.

When Yancey fell, the woman on the ground before me screamed and scrambled to her feet, racing in the other direction, back toward the house. The other Ladies emerged from the woods, brandishing weapons, some running to help Yancey, others running away.

"Stop!" Ty shouted to the women. He reached me, his gun drawn, aiming at the Ladies. "Drop your weapons!"

"Ty, it's okay." I tried to intervene. But the hand I held up to him was covered in crimson from the Lady who had miraculously recovered and run away.

"AJ, are you hit?"

"No, no. Ty, call Nikki off. It's paint. It's only paint." I repeated myself, trying to break through the shouting and yelling coming from the women, Yancey's screams as Nikki kept him pinned to the ground, and Ty's own adrenaline. Not that I blamed him. The guns looked real—too real. If I was a cop and had them aimed at me, I'd have already fired. It was a testament to his instincts that he'd held off.

Ty hesitated. I used the time to turn to the Ladies. "Yancey's fine. Put your guns on the ground."

"Do it," Ty added when they hesitated, his gun still drawn as the Ladies whirled in confusion. "Now!"

Finally his words penetrated, and they began to slowly lower their weapons to the ground. Elizabeth came up behind us with the first Lady I'd found on the ground.

"Release," Ty called to Nikki, who immediately leapt off Yancey and returned to Ty's side. Her ears were at full alert, her balance poised for action.

"They're paint guns?" Elizabeth said. "But—"

"You didn't really think we'd be running around with real guns, did you?" Yancey asked, rolling onto his knees, keeping a wary eye on Nikki. His face was streaked with mud and grass and fury. Or embarrassment, given the wet stain that spread out from his crotch. "I ought to sue your entire department," he continued. "Bunch of Nazis. We have every right to—"

"Aim a realistic-appearing weapon at an officer of the law while he's performing his duty?" Elizabeth answered for Ty. "I don't think so. Where's Charity?"

Yancey climbed to his feet and looked over his shoulder, scanning the crowd of Ladies. "She's not here. I don't know where she went. Why?"

"She called me. Said she was in trouble. And that you killed my father."

For the first time anger colored Elizabeth's voice—I had the feeling more lay buried beneath her calm-lawyer facade.

Yancey took a step back. "Me? I never—"

The door to the toolshed popped open and Charity emerged. "In here!" she called. "It's in here!"

Unlike the other Ladies dressed in paint-splattered camo, Charity was dressed in a flowing gown, makeup and hair carefully arranged, camera-ready. There was no way she could have missed the commotion, but she'd waited until now to announce her presence. Elizabeth was right—Charity had a definite flair for the dramatic.

She held the door to the shed open, gesturing Vanna White–style. "There, look."

We all turned. Hanging from a rafter was a white Tyvek full-body suit complete with hood and face mask. Below it were several large containers marked—TOXAPHENE.

TWENTY-SEVEN

Charity's discovery quickly devolved into a media feeding frenzy. Ty called for backup, and several more deputies showed up, as well as a pair of detectives, the county prosecutor, the state police evidence team, and the sheriff himself—just in time for some quality on-air socializing with the press.

News trucks from as far away as Charleston arrived in record time, leading me to wonder if we were the first people Charity had called after she found the toxaphene—and done her hair and makeup. They took Yancey away in handcuffs, still wearing his soiled clothing, protesting his innocence, threatening to sue everyone involved, and appearing more like Charlie Manson than ever. His Ladies flocked around him, trying to block the police, screaming vows of undying love while flouncing for the cameras.

Once they got a warrant, Ty took Nikki through the house and found stashes of illicit pharmaceuticals. Several of the Ladies also quickly found themselves in handcuffs and being driven away in the back of squad cars.

Through it all, Elizabeth sat in the front seat of the Escape, slowly deflating. "Why?" she kept saying, her gaze unfocused as she watched the forensics guys cart the evidence out from the shed and load it into a van. "I just don't understand. Why?"

I didn't have an answer. In fact, I wasn't convinced that Yancey was the culprit. Elizabeth's PI friend had depicted him as a devious thrill-seeker who craved attention, but why would he resort to killing? Especially when he was already getting the spotlight he desired? It seemed too risky. Plus, I knew he wasn't stupid enough to leave the evidence in plain sight.

Finally, we each took our turn with the detectives, telling what little we knew. By the time we were dismissed, it was past lunchtime, although neither of us was hungry.

"I guess we should still go see my mom," I said as I steered the Ford through the parked police cars and news vans and headed away from Yancey's house.

"What for?" Elizabeth sounded devoid of hope. "When it comes out that my father paid Yancey, our case is doomed."

I almost gave in to temptation—I'd have loved to keep avoiding my mom and whatever was going on with her. But that was a coward's way out. I turned onto Maple and pulled up in front of my parents' house for the second time in three days. Hard to believe it had only been three days—but it was just as hard to fathom that I'd been back in Scotia for that long and had yet to lay eyes on my mom. For some reason it made me feel guilty. Like I'd been avoiding her instead of the other way around.

We had made it to the front porch steps. Before I could knock or ring the bell, the door opened.

"You again," my mother snapped at Elizabeth. She stood in the door, looking angry but otherwise fine. Her hair was pulled back in her usual French twist, and she wore a blouse and a pair of slacks—my mom never wore jeans, not even to picnics. "I told you to go away, leave me alone."

"Mom." Finally she turned to me—as if she hadn't even noticed me standing there in front of her. "What's going on?" She blocked my path just as my dad had done when I first arrived home. "Let me in."

"We can talk on the porch."

"It's freezing out here and getting ready to storm."

She turned to glance over her shoulder. I took advantage of her movement and slid past her, inside the house. The doors to the front parlor and dining room were both shut—something I could never remember happening when I lived here—and there was a new doorway behind the stairs, closing off the kitchen hallway.

Puzzled by all the closed doors—what were they hiding?—I yanked open the door to the dining room.

"No, Angela, don't."

Too late. As I pulled the door toward me, an avalanche poured out. Cartons of soda, bags of clothing, boxes of papers cascading down from a wall of stuff that came to the top of my shoulders. Past the mountain of debris, as far as I could see, was more stuff, all the way back into the farthest corners of the room. The chandelier, once my mom's pride and joy (and my nemesis since it was my job to stand on newspapers on the dining room table and polish every single crystal) hung sideways against an overturned desk chair and tangled up with a pair of hockey sticks.

We didn't know anyone who played hockey.

I stood there. Frozen. Shocked. Afraid to even look at my mom for fear that I'd sense some kind of madness behind her eyes. This was nuts—no one could live like this. "How—"

My voice drifted away on a landslide of Archie comic books, Jughead laughing at me from the topmost cover.

Elizabeth came to my rescue. She disengaged my hand from the doorknob and pivoted me away from the view. Her eyes mirrored mine, wide with surprise and a hint of fear.

My mom stood on the bottom step, arms crossed over her chest defensively. I was sure she was going to throw us out.

"Mom, what's going on here?" I asked, debris still settling around my feet. I stooped to pick it up, then stopped halfway. Where would I put it?

"Don't do that." My mom's voice was strained, as if I was about to break something fragile and precious. "Just don't touch anything."

I straightened, blood swimming behind my eyes, trying to focus, almost giving up, the scene was so surreal. "I don't understand. How—"

Instead of answering, she jerked her chin, her lips twisted in distaste, and led the way upstairs.

I followed, too shocked to speak. The steps were clear—but the hallway at the top was a labyrinth of debris. Clothing and books and sporting goods and stuffed animals piled like termite hills verging on collapse.

Disoriented, I stepped on a wayward Ben Roethlisberger bobble-head, cracking it. The noise sounded like a gunshot. Mom whirled around, saw what I'd done, and fell to her knees, cradling the broken dime-store toy like it was a priceless treasure.

"Be careful, Angela Joy," she snapped. "I got this special for Randy when I went into Charleston to file some deeds for Mrs. Masterson."

"Mrs. Masterson has been dead for ten years, Mom," I said gently. I didn't add that Randy had been dead for fifteen years—since long before Pittsburgh signed Big Ben as quarterback.

She folded the broken football player into her handkerchief. "The new Mrs. Masterson. Cole's wife. I'll have to find my super-glue and try to fix it."

Elizabeth touched my arm and shook her head in a "forget it" gesture that made me brace myself for worse to come. Mom looked fine on the outside, but clearly something was broken on the inside.

"You're the Masterson Mining accountant?" Elizabeth asked my mom, diverting her attention from the broken bobblehead she was mourning.

"Have been for thirty years. I handle the books, the payroll, all their dealings. Mr. Masterson won't trust anyone else."

I exchanged glances with Elizabeth. Whatever was going on with my mom, her mental faculties couldn't be too far gone. No way Master-son would let her continue to have access to such important dealings otherwise.

My mom opened the door to Randy's room. There was no mess or clutter here. Instead, everything appeared normal—too normal.

My heart felt yanked back fifteen years, leaving my chest aching with the emptiness Randy's death had left behind. His room hadn't changed—not a single thing was out of place, everything waiting for him to walk through this door.

Waiting, wanting Randy. Not wanting me.

My breath ricocheted between my hollowed-out ribs. I was twelve again, Randy was going stir-crazy recuperating from his mono, cooped up inside on a glorious September day. And me, brat that I was, made it my mission to torment him. I'd climbed the maple tree outside his win-dow and taunted him until he'd used his fly rod to try to knock me off the branch I hung upside down on, chortling like a monkey.

I glanced up, moving only my eyes, not wanting to break the spell—I swear I could smell his deodorant, hear his laughter followed by swearing when he scraped the rod against the ceiling, then snagged the curtain rod, pulling it from its bracket. The black streak was still visible on the ceiling and the curtain rod still sagged, hanging by one screw on that end.

Nothing had changed. Not a thing. Randy still lived here, trapped forever in Scotia, in my mother's shrine.

Turning around, fighting for balance, I held my arms out. As I spun, thunder cracked outside and the wind rattled the windows. The storm had broken.

"Mom—" I tried, failed to find words, and tried again. "What—"

She shook her head at me in annoyance, her lips pursed in a silent *shush*, and turned to Elizabeth. "Why do you want to know about the Mastersons?"

Elizabeth hesitated, obviously not sure how to handle my mom. I had no idea either. "Well, you know my father was trying to stop the mountaintop removal mining expansion."

"You taking over for your father?"

Elizabeth nodded. "Yes, ma'am. I am."

Mom twisted her mouth as she considered. Then she left the room.

Elizabeth and I exchanged a glance. I shrugged, I had no idea what was going on. We followed. Mom was down the hall in my old room. The door was propped open by a stack of document boxes taller than me. Inside were more stacks and crates and trash bags brimming over with papers and two filing cabinets with drawers crammed so full they hung open.

All of my furniture was gone. As were all of my belongings. Even the band posters and maps I'd papered my walls with. All missing.

I'd been erased. Or more precisely, replaced.

"Thirty years of Masterson Mining," my mom announced, spreading her hands. "On paper, disks, and"—she sat down at a TV tray that held a laptop, the only furniture besides the filing cabinets left in the room—"online. . . . Here you are," she clicked on the keyboard and a spreadsheet popped up. "Zachariah Hardy. Payment in full. Services rendered."

"Wait. Masterson was paying my father?" Elizabeth leaned over Mom's shoulder, reading the screen. She glanced at me, forehead wrinkled in puzzlement. "There's payments to Yancey here as well."

"Why would Masterson hire your dad and Yancey?"

Mom tapped the screen impatiently. "The payments came from the MTR reclamation account. Authorized by Cole Masterson."

"Cole?" I asked, trying to see past them to the screen. The figures were lined up like toy soldiers and just about as meaningless to my eyes—but not as confusing as the idea of Cole hiring Yancey and Hardy.

"Cole is in charge of the reclamation phase of the MTR site," Mom told us, bringing up another spreadsheet. "He's planning to build a wind farm up there. Should bring in as many jobs as the mountaintop mining, but it'll also generate income for the town with the electricity."

"He'd have to have an Environmental Impact Survey for that." Both Elizabeth and I stood straight, staring at each other as the puzzle pieces dropped into place. I continued. "Cole said he wanted the government to change the MTR regulations. He hired your father to force them into it."

"And when my father's legal strategy failed, Cole gave him the EIS to use to halt the MTR expansion." Elizabeth raised her hand to her mouth, then lowered it again. "That was the smoking gun my dad was so excited about before he died."

"Did Masterson know that Cole wanted to get stricter regulations on the mountaintop removal permitting process and was working with your dad?" I asked. Maybe Old Man Masterson had arranged for Hardy's murder. It was a tempting scenario.

My mom was typing again. Her gaze had emptied as if she was lost in cyberspace, a world of well-ordered numbers and transactions. No emotions, no clutter, no dead son, no estranged daughter. "Not sure Mr. Masterson worries too much about the MTR," she replied in a monotone. "Mrs. Masterson is the one in charge."

TWENTY-EIGHT

If there was anything worse than being called to the principal's office, it was being called there after everyone else had already escaped for the weekend. Not to mention the trepidation of keeping his dad—his dad!—waiting for him. David bounced his front wheels impatiently as Mrs. Nowicki closed the door and took her seat at her desk, looking down on him like a cat ready to pounce.

Make that a fat cat. No. One of those dogs with the folds of skin and drool and beady eyes that popped out.

"Mr. Palladino, we need to have a little chat," Mrs. Nowicki said, her double chins jiggling.

David stifled his groan. In his experience, "little chats" with grown-ups usually turned into long, boring monologues with him paying penance. Like cleaning his room *plus* the entire refrigerator after he'd re-created Alexander Fleming's discovery of penicillin in his sock drawer.

"I know you face a difficult transition into our school system," Mrs. Nowicki continued. "After reviewing the materials from your old school, I'm debating how we can best help you. Your teachers are quite worried that you'll be bored with our curriculum here."

She paused, her eyes glittering, and David knew she'd come up with something even worse than placing him in the Support Unit. People like Mrs. Nowicki never actually "helped" anyone—they just used their power to make others squirm as much as possible. Like ants under a magnifying glass.

"And," she finished triumphantly, "I think I've found the perfect solution. You're going to be our school's very first official student orator."

"Orator?"

"Yes. We've been trying to come up with a way to interest the students in subjects outside the realm of the standardized curriculum. This will be perfect. You'll be giving oral reports on independent study subjects to all the classes—of course, you'll have to vary your reports according to age level, so that might make for some extra work." Her eyes crinkled in delight at the thought of David toiling long into the night. "But you're such a smart boy, I'm sure you're up to the task. The older kids might challenge you—they might not care for a fourth-grader trying to teach them—but you'll do fine. Here's a list of subjects to start with."

She handed him a page jam-packed with topics like "The Impact of the Magna Carta on Western Religion" and "Geologic Survey of the Appalachians as Recorded by Fossil Evidence Unearthed in the New River Gorge."

Great. Somehow she'd made his favorite subject, history, sound boring. "I'd be working with a teacher?"

"Oh no. You'll report directly to me."

"Ah. Of course." He had a sudden flash of an illustration he'd once seen depicting a man on the rack facing the Spanish Inquisition. This felt almost as bad. Not only would he be committing social hari-kari as soon as she began parading him around the classes—probably wearing some kind of silly costume, maybe a court jester?—but he wouldn't have any time to read his own books or help his mom with her research or do anything fun like tossing a ball with Cole.

He stared at the paper, seeing his future dive-bombing into oblivion faster than a Japanese Zero on a kamikaze mission. Before he could figure a way out of it, the secretary poked her head into the office.

"I'm leaving now," she said. "But there's a man waiting."

"Waiting for me?" Mrs. Nowicki said, smoothing her hair.

"No. Waiting for him." She nodded to David and left.

Cole! He was here to rescue David. Having a dad around was already paying off. David pushed back from Mrs. Nowicki's desk. "I guess that's my dad. I'd better get going."

"Cole Masterson?" Mrs. Nowicki stood. "You wait here. I'll go get your—dad."

He wasn't quite sure why she made the word "dad" sound like a curse word, but he did as he was told. Although he did ease closer to the door and pulled it ajar so he could listen to what Cole said. He couldn't help it—it just felt so cool to have a guy like Cole call him his son and say it like David was someone special.

The kids back home who didn't have dads made it seem like it was no big deal—some of them didn't have moms either, only grams. But these past two days he was learning it was a big deal, even if Cole and his mom weren't together—although it was easy to see that they should be. Maybe he could figure out a way to make that happen and they could be a real family.

Now that would be outstandingly awesome.

He leaned his ear against the crack, listening.

"I'm here to pick up David Palladino." That wasn't Cole's voice, it was some other man. David snuck a peek. It was the guy who'd gotten his mom arrested, the one with the knife.

"And you are?" Mrs. Nowicki's voice was the same "I'll squash you like a bug" voice she'd used on David. Sickly sweet and deadly all at once.

"You know damn well who I am, Letta Nowicki."

"Don't you take that tone with me, Dickie Ellings."

"Is everyone else gone?"

"Yes. And you know I can't release a student to you without parental permission."

"My instructions come from Mrs. Masterson. And"—he raised his hand, a knife flashing in the fluorescent overhead light with the movement—"this is all the permission I need."

As David watched in horror, Mrs. Nowicki screamed, then crumpled to the ground, blood spurting from her neck.

The man's expression never changed—it was the same twisted smile David had seen on the video when he'd tried to hurt the tree-sitter lady. He wiped his knife blade on Mrs. Nowicki's blouse and pulled a cell phone from his pocket.

"It's started. Did you make the call? I'll get the kid. No, don't worry, I'll be done with him by the time she gets here. Yeah, I know. It'll look like suicide."

TWENTY-NINE

The words on the computer screen were fuzzy, jumbled, as I tried to make sense of them. "Wait. Waverly's in charge of the MTR?"

"It's a separate company. She's CEO of the MTR subsidiary," Elizabeth said, effortlessly reading over my mom's shoulder. "Is that right, Mrs. Palladino? Any injunction that prevented expanding the operation would cut into her profits, not Masterson's main corporation."

"Right. And she's out of capital. Been spending it buying up options to new mineral rights on land for MTR. But those options expire in a few months if they don't get their permits."

"So if we win the injunction and stop the MTR and they expire—"

"Waverly's company goes bankrupt," Elizabeth finished for me. "She'll lose everything."

"Including her father-in-law's support," I said. Things were finally making sense. "I'll bet she doesn't even know about Cole undermining her efforts—he sees it as protecting both the community and his family's business. All he wanted was for your father to get the permitting process better regulated so there'd be less environmental impact from MTR."

"It'd eat into his company's bottom line—"

"Cole doesn't care about that."

"But they'd still be able to profit, especially if he developed alternative energy sources like the wind farm in addition to the profits from the coal. Why didn't he say anything?"

"He doesn't want his father to know, of course," I answered. Cole never could stand up to his father. It was his greatest weakness.

I began pacing the space between a stack of boxes and the window. The idea that Cole had been unwittingly undermining Waverly's greedy attempt to scoop up all the MTR sites in the area tickled me. What can I say? I was jealous—not just of her polished good looks and college education but of the way Cole admired her. How I wished that just once he'd ever spoken of me the way he'd talked about Waverly.

Then I stopped short, staring out the window as the storm whipped the branches of the hemlocks beyond. "If Cole hired your dad and Yancey, then who used the toxaphene to kill your dad and try to poison the protesters? There'd be no reason for Yancey to do it."

"Unless my dad discovered something in his past he wanted covered up?"

"Toxaphene?" Mom clicked the laptop's keys again. "Mrs. Masterson ordered ten drums of it a few weeks ago. Paid for it with funds from the MTR subsidiary."

"Mrs.—you mean Waverly?" I wove my way back to the computer. It was right there on the screen. An invoice for toxaphene signed by Waverly Masterson. I glanced at Elizabeth. "Waverly killed your father?"

"Or had someone do it for her." She was a lot calmer than I was. Or was just hiding her emotions better. But I saw her hand clench as she stopped it halfway to her mouth and knew she was fighting to stay in control. "Why?"

"To stop his appeal so that she could move forward with the mining expansion before her options expired." Lightning flashed in the distance. But it was the realization that shook me, not the thunder.

"My father died to save her company money?" Elizabeth stood rigid, but her voice rattled with fury.

"She's crazy."

"No. She's trying to protect her family," Mom said, her voice spooky the way it sounded like it was coming from a far-off place. She spun in the chair and looked right at me for the first time in as long as I could remember. Not a glance, not a vacant gaze like I was a piece of furniture she'd forgotten to dust. Really at me, into me. "That's what I'd do. Why do you think I'm telling you all this?"

I remembered what my dad had said. "Mom. You know Masterson will try to take the house. We'll fight him, I promise we will. But I can't not use this information."

"I know." She raised her hand from her lap. Waved it at me in dismissal. "Don't worry, he won't be taking this house. Not over my dead body. Or his."

Elizabeth gasped at her harsh words. Before I could think of a response, my phone rang.

"Mrs. Palladino?" A woman's voice, nasal and whiny, came through the line. "Is this David Palladino's mother?"

"Yes. Who is this?"

"This is Mrs. Warden, the school nurse. We need you to come right away. David fell and hit his head."

Panic surged through me. "Is he okay? Did you call the ambulance?" Oh God, I knew I should never have let him go back to that school.

"He's fine. But we need you to sign some forms—"

"I'll be right there." Forms? My baby was hurt—again!—and she was worried about paperwork?

"What is it?" Elizabeth asked.

"David's hurt. I need to go to the school." I glanced at my mom. She was back in her cyberspace trance, clicking through to a shopping site, looking at model airplanes, mumbling something about Randy liking a new Spitfire. I shook my head, unable to cope with her problems on top of everything else.

"I'll drive," Elizabeth said, leading the way out to the car. I handed her the car keys and climbed into the passenger seat. I'm not sure my mom even knew we'd gone.

David's heart leapt into his throat and lodged there like a fat wad of bubblegum throbbing and pounding and urging him to run, run, run. . . . He choked down his panic, tried to think. First, he needed something between him and Ellings, the man with the knife. The big, bloody knife.

He eased the door shut, holding his breath as if that would help the latch not make a noise. Locking it, he rolled across the room to the door on the wall leading to the main hallway. He pushed through it just as a loud thud rattled the office door behind him.

Escape lay to the left, where the main school doors were. He turned that way, but before he could get up to speed, the outer office door swung open and the man appeared.

"Hey, David," he called, one hand behind his back, a smile that was meant to look friendly plastered on his face. "Your mom sent me to pick you up."

"Okay," he yelled to the man, trying to sound nonchalant, "let me grab my books." David pushed back, one hand turning his chair as the other reached into his bag for his cell phone. As soon as he had it, he flipped it open and hit the big center button, the one marked 911. He shoved it between his legs so he'd have both hands free.

Then he took off, pushing as fast as he could. The man paused, but soon followed, his footsteps echoing through the empty halls. At first just a quick walk, then a more urgent thudding as the man realized David could move faster than he could.

"Nine-one-one, what's your emergency?" a bored-sounding lady answered on the third ring.

"A man, at Scotia Elementary. He stabbed Mrs. Nowicki."

The lady kept asking questions, but it took all David's energy to push the chair and figure out where to go He knew the layout of the school—hopefully better than the man. Because of the different ages, the three wings had been partitioned into clusters of classrooms and lockers, with central areas like the gym and cafeteria connecting them. He turned one corner, then another, circling around to the fifth- and sixth-graders' classrooms and lockers. As he whipped around the final corner, he careened off an open locker door.

"Hey, watch it!" a girl yelled.

David spun, one wheel tipping off the floor for a gut-wrenching moment. His cell phone slid shut, but he squeezed his legs together and caught it before it fell. Ellings's footsteps slowed at the intersection behind them, then sounded again, going in the wrong direction.

"Come with me." He grabbed the girl's hand.

"No. I have to get my English book, I forgot it—" He recognized the girl from the fifth-grade class, her name was Abby. She had brown hair and hazel eyes and freckles that showed up when her nose turned red in the cold while playing dodgeball outside during recess.

"There's a man. He just killed Mrs. Nowicki. We need to hide."

She hesitated, one hand still reaching into her locker, while he held on to the other.

"Now, Abby." He yanked hard, just as footsteps thudded nearby.

She whipped her head around at the sound, eyes going wide, and nodded. He let go of her hand, and together they took off.

"Where?" he breathed. They couldn't keep going around in circles forever.

"In here." She pushed open the door to the girls' locker room. David rolled over the threshold. He'd never been in the girls' room before—it looked just like the guys', only no urinals and it smelled better. The graffiti was different too. More colorful instead of just blue and black. Before he noticed any more, Abby raced back beyond the toilets and sinks and into the locker area.

"I can't," he protested. "My chair won't fit." The lockers were far enough apart, but there were benches between them, blocking his path. "You hide in a locker. I'll lead him the other way."

Abby shook her head and backtracked. "This way."

She led him back through the showers to a wide door about half the height of a normal door. "There should be room—push in," she said, moving behind him to give him room to maneuver.

It was the closet where they kept the laundry bins. He pulled one outside to make room for his chair, thankful that the hamper wheeled easily and quietly. He rolled in, turning so he faced the door. Abby pulled the basket within reach, moved behind the door, and tried to crouch down and back up inside the small space.

"You'll have to sit on my lap," he said, pulling his cell phone free.

"You're sure?" she whispered. "It won't hurt?"

A noise came from the locker room. He tugged her onto his lap, almost banging her head against the low ceiling. She reached outside the door, sliding the laundry bin as close to the door as possible—camouflage.

Then she closed the door, leaving the smallest crack so they could hear and see outside.

"I know you're in here," Ellings shouted, banging lockers. "Get your ass out here now! Damn crippled freak. Don't you waste my time!"

Abby wrapped her arms around David. "He's going to kill us," she breathed into his ear.

"I called the police. It's going to be okay, I promise." She curled herself against him, and the weight of his words hit him. He had to get her out of here, she was just an innocent bystander. It was David that Ellings was after—although he had no idea why.

His cell phone began to vibrate, the slight sound jarring both of them. Abby pulled back as he opened the phone. It was Cole. He lowered the volume before answering, not sure how far Cole's voice might carry, and held the phone against his lips, barely whispering. "Cole, we're in the girls' locker room. There's a man—he wants to kill us."

Just as David was about to risk saying more, a shadow fell over the crack in the door, blocking the light from the locker room.

Abby squeezed his hand so tightly he felt his bones grind together. They both held their breath.

Ellings paced in front of the door. Then he stopped.

"I lost him," he said, talking to someone on his phone. "No sign of Palladino, and I think the kid called the cops. I have to get out of here." There was a pause. "What do you mean you'll take care of burying the evidence? How are you going to stop the kid from talking to the cops? Oh, okay. Yeah, that will work. I'll take care of the kid and wait here for you."

David and Abby huddled together as Ellings hung up and walked away. They heard the door across from them open, the one leading into the gymnasium.

David relaxed, but then both of them jumped when a new voice sounded. "Ellings, what the hell are you doing?"

It was Cole. He'd come. They were safe.

"It's okay," David told Abby. "He's one of the good guys."

Then a gunshot sounded. Metal crashed. The sound of two men grunting and slamming into the lockers shook through the closet. A gun spun past along the tile floor, whirling just out of sight.

"You're an idiot, Cole." Ellings's words were punctuated by the rattle of a locker door, followed by a thud. "You have no freakin' clue."

The men were immediately outside the laundry closet. Their breath was loud and hoarse, two great animals fighting to the death.

"What the hell are you talking about?" Cole said.

"Waverly. She loves you. Enough to get me to kill to protect you and your damn company."

"Kill my son, you mean. You're crazy. Waverly would never—"

"Shut up! You don't deserve her!" Another collision, this one against the wall beside them, feeling so close that David expected the men to crash through the drywall and land on top of them. Then the sound of flesh striking flesh.

Finally, silence.

The door opened. Cole stood there, holding Ellings's knife with one hand, a pistol with the other. "It's okay. Everything's okay."

David wheeled out, barely noticing Abby's weight until Cole lifted her off. Cole's eye was swollen and his knuckles were bloody. Beyond them, slumped against a set of lockers, lay Ellings. He looked worse than Cole.

"He"—David's voice failed him and he tried again—"he killed Mrs. Nowicki. I saw him."

Cole crouched down and hugged him hard. "I know. It's okay, David. He won't hurt anyone again." His nose dripped something slimy onto David's hair, but David didn't care. He held Cole tighter, trying not to shake and cry like a baby and failing.

"I'm proud of you," Cole said. "You were so brave." He gently disengaged David. "Now let's see about getting this guy to the police."

David nodded and wheeled back to where Abby stood staring, pressed against the wall of the showers, as far away as she could get from Ellings and still keep Cole in sight. Cole hauled Ellings up with one arm as if he weighed nothing, even though Ellings was a lot heavier than Cole.

"Let's go." Cole shoved Ellings out in front of him, away from the children, holding the gun on him.

They'd only gone a step when the entire building shook.

THIRTY

I was glad Elizabeth was driving. I tried to call David myself, since the idiot school nurse had hung up on me, but his phone was busy. Which was irritating as hell, because he was only supposed to use his phone in case of emergency, and if the nurse was right there with him, who could he be calling? Oh. Me.

I hung up and stayed off the line, waiting for us to clear the dead zone between town and the school, expecting him to call.

My phone went from two bars to no bars to one bar to none again. Frustration had me bouncing in my seat, urging the SUV to move faster. I tried my voice mail, thinking David might have left a message, but nothing.

Not wasting time with any gentle sprinkles, the clouds opened up with an out-and-out deluge. Elizabeth pushed the wipers to high, and I got a chance to see firsthand how much better the SUV's defroster worked than my van's. We were just up the mountain from the school, close enough that I could see Cole's red Cherokee in the parking lot. Alone except for a black SUV. No ambulance, no other cars—was it just him and the nurse with David?

My cell coverage returned, and I called Cole. It went to voice mail. I didn't bother with a message—we were almost there.

Elizabeth slammed on the brakes.

I tore my attention away from my phone, wondering what she had stopped for.

"What the hell?" she said, leaning forward, craning her face up as she stared through the windshield.

Then I saw it.

Overhead, above the school, the dragline, the massive crane used to rip the tops off of mountains, had come to life. But it wasn't digging. Instead, its huge payload bucket was swinging over the edge of the ridge, catapulting directly toward the earthen dam holding back millions of tons of toxic coal slurry.

It moved faster than I imagined it could, like a rattlesnake striking. A thunderous boom sounded, and the earth shook beneath the car.

The dragline had swung its bucket directly into the dam. The dam didn't burst, but a landslide of rock and dirt shook loose, tumbling down the side of the mountain.

My gaze dropped from the dam down to the school lying directly below.

"David!"

David pushed Abby into the showers, hoping the extra thick walls would protect them. She yelled something, but he couldn't hear it over the rumble and crashing all around them. An earthquake? He didn't have time to think about it. Smoke and dust choked the air, the ceiling buckled, raining plaster down on them, and the shower pipes began to burst, exploding one after the other, drenching them in water.

Then it stopped. He hadn't realized it, but he'd pulled Abby back down onto his lap, sheltering her with his torso as best he could. She pushed back, gasping for air. Her face was smeared with plaster and water, but she seemed okay.

"You're bleeding," she gasped, touching his cheek.

He raised a finger. A small chunk of tile had embedded itself in his cheek. He pulled it free, barely felt it. Abby climbed off of him and helped push him clear of the rubble that blocked his path. Nothing too large, he rolled over most of it easily.

"Cole?" he shouted into the dust, his words almost swallowed by the sound of the water behind him.

A man ran past. Ellings.

They emerged from the shower area and turned to where they'd last seen Cole.

He lay face down, only his face and one arm visible, the rest of his body buried by the row of lockers that had dominoed down on top of him.

"Cole!"

To my relief, Elizabeth restarted the car as I dialed first Cole, then David, to warn them to get out of there. Neither answered. I called 911 and told them what was going on, hanging up just as we made it to the turnoff to the school. The black SUV plowed past us, almost ramming into us, going so fast I couldn't see the driver.

The earth shook again as the dragline smashed into the dam once more. More rocks and dirt slid down, this time accompanied by medium-sized boulders unearthed by the shock. The dam still held, but who knew for how long.

Elizabeth slowed for the turn but bypassed the school parking lot, bouncing onto the dirt road heading up to the mining site.

"Stop!" I shouted. "I need to get David!"

I undid my seat belt and popped the door open. But instead of slowing down to let me out, she sped up. The momentum swung the door shut before I could jump.

"Elizabeth!"

"If we don't stop whoever is in the dragline, they're both dead," she shouted. "And so is the entire town."

My phone rang. David. The SUV bounced over the ruts and puddles as Elizabeth pushed it even faster. I fumbled my phone open. "David, are you all right? Where are you?"

"In the school."

"You need to get out. Now. The dam is about to burst."

"Mom, it's Cole. He's hurt. Real bad."

"I called the police, they're on their way. You need to get out of there, David. *Now.*"

He sucked in a sob. "No. I'm not leaving him."

"Give Cole the phone. Let me talk to him."

Elizabeth steered us past the tree-sitters—they were roping down from their trees, scrambling to get away, slipping in the mud as they ran.

"Angel?" Cole's voice was heavy, like he was carrying something that took all his strength.

I had so many questions, but they didn't matter. Not now. We were almost to the dragline. Through the rain I could see two figures struggling in the cabin overhead. Now was our best chance to get on board before it swung into motion again.

"Cole, the dam is coming down. You need to get out of there. Make David leave."

"The dam?" His voice whistled, a strange gasping noise. "Don't worry. David will be okay. I promise." Another gasp.

There was a clattering noise, and the line went dead.

I tried redialing Cole and David, but neither answered. Elizabeth pulled the SUV level with the metal ladder leading to the entrance hatch of the dragline. Frustration clawed at me, each breath snagging on my fear. I needed to be two places at once.

But I was only one person. Elizabeth jumped out of the car, not bothering to close the door, wind and rain pelting her. I followed but had to pause and look down the mountain at the school. A third of the building closest to the mountainside was buried in rubble. I couldn't see if it had collapsed or not.

Elizabeth had a hard time climbing up the ladder, her pumps slipping on the wet rungs. There was another ladder not far from me, so I ran through the rain and grabbed on. I swung up to the metal gantry leading to a hatch just as the dragline began to move again.

It was surprisingly quiet for such a monstrous-sized machine. Instead of the grind of gears and engines, there were intermittent *poofs* and *puffs* and *pssts* like a dragon belching.

I got to the hatch and wrenched it open. Elizabeth was just behind me, ducking through the opening and shaking water from her hair.

"The controls will be this way, up these steps," I told her, getting my bearing in the dimly lit belly of the massive crane. All around us were large cables threaded through various machines, punctuated by metal boxes and controls and thick air hoses. It was like being inside a submarine—or at least what a submarine looked like in movies, all metal ladders and gantries and narrow passages.

As the machine swung there was no lurching, but my balance system didn't buy into the idea that we were at the center of the centrifugal force and thus immune to falling. Instead, I felt dizzy, forced to grab on to a guide bar as I climbed up a steep set of metal steps and through a hatchway. Elizabeth lagged behind, trying her best to keep up.

Remembering the trick of momentum that had gotten me over the two-line rope bridge in the trees, I surged forward and my vertigo passed. A metal door barred my path—the control room.

Swinging the door open, I rushed inside. A large recliner-like chair took up most of the center of the glass-walled room. But what grabbed my attention was my father's body lying on the floor in front of me, blood oozing from his side.

"AJ. Should have known you'd screw everything up," Waverly Masterson said from behind me. I whirled as she raised her gun and slammed it into my face.

THIRTY-ONE

David watched in horror as Cole passed out, the phone falling from his grasp and spinning beneath the fallen lockers. "Abby, check his breathing." He inched the chair as close as he could to Cole's hand while Abby knelt at his head. "Is he breathing?"

"I don't—yes, I hear him. Barely," she said. "David, what do we do?"

"My mom said the dam is going to burst. You need to get out. Now." He leaned down and took Cole's hand. It felt so cold. That couldn't be. Superheroes didn't die.

"No. You need to come with me."

"Don't argue. Just go."

He turned his head and swiped a tear with his knuckle before she could see. This was no comic book. This was real life. But still, he couldn't give up, not his dad, not after waiting so long. He squeezed Cole's hand once more, hard, like the first time he'd met his father and they'd shaken hands like men. Cole had treated him like more than a son—he'd acted like David was someone he was proud to know.

"I'm staying with my dad."

Cole raised his head, his hair hanging over his eyes, plastered to his forehead with blood. "Both of you," he gasped, "need to leave. Now."

Cole collapsed again. That was okay. Because David had just figured out how he was going to save them all.

The blow spun me around so my back was against the console. Pain sparked through me, fueling the adrenaline bonfire begun when I'd realized David was in danger. Ignoring the gun, I pushed off from the console and tackled Waverly.

She fired. I didn't even hear the shot, but felt it singe past my neck.

My legs were yanked out from under me, and I landed on top of my dad. He twisted his body to put himself between the gun and me.

Waverly shoved the door shut behind her, but it stopped before it closed the whole way. She didn't seem to notice since she was facing us. I struggled out from behind my dad's arm.

"I tried," he gasped. "Tried to stop her."

"I know," I said, hoping it was only the shadows from the storm clouds that made him look so gray.

"I'm thinking," Waverly said—her tone so casual she could have been talking about a lost umbrella, but her eyes darted back and forth like she was a cornered animal frantically searching for a way out— "that after I bury the school and unleash the toxic sludge, there might be a little accident here as well. Not enough to harm the dragline, of course—this machine cost fifty million dollars. Everyone knows you and Frank have been arguing—just like you and Letta Nowicki, AJ. Hmm. Seems like you fight with just about everybody. All the better for folks to understand this tragic accident. You two arguing, the dragline runs amok, your dad can't save the dam, the school is buried with your son in it, and AJ, you turn on your dad. Shoot him dead. Then you kill yourself."

She smiled, nodded in satisfaction at her new scenario, and raised her gun, aiming at my dad.

Before she could pull the trigger, I launched myself at her. I rammed her into the instrument panel on the side of the console chair. The door behind her opened, and Elizabeth ran in, grabbing her from behind. Waverly tried to scratch and claw at us, but I twisted her wrist until she dropped the gun while Elizabeth held her in a bear hug. As soon as the gun fell, I scrambled after it.

Waverly screeched in frustration and broke free from Elizabeth, wheeling on her and hitting her with a closed fist. Elizabeth staggered against the chair, her hands flying to her face. Waverly ran out.

I took a step to follow her but realized there was more important work to do here. "Dad, can we plug up the damaged area, save the dam?"

He moaned. "Help me up."

Elizabeth, whose nose was bleeding, helped me get him into the operator's chair. He flicked a switch, and a television monitor came to life, giving us a close-up view of the damage. To my dismay, I saw that there was now a crack in the dam, with dark ooze slipping through. More cracks began to appear nearby.

"We can fill it," he said, "but I can't do it alone." His left hand dangled at his side, useless.

"Tell us what to do," I said, hoping David had listened to me and escaped. Fear threatened to blind me, but I forced myself to stay focused. What other choice did I have?

Before Dad could give us instructions, an alarm sounded.

"What's that?" Elizabeth asked, jerking her hands away from the instruments.

"Waverly. She's crazy!" Dad said, turning the alarm off. "She's climbing up the boom. She's going to get herself killed."

Seemed like easy justice to me. But Waverly hadn't struck me as the suicidal type. And she knew this machine, probably as well as my dad. "Could she stop us from up there? Sabotage the dragline so we can't plug the dam?"

Dad thought, his eyes going wide. "Yes. If she makes it up to the cable drum, she can jam the load cell. The entire machine will shut down. It's a safety measure to prevent accidental overload."

"How do I stop her?"

"You'll need to go down to the bottom. Go out onto the boom—there's a catwalk up the middle. It'll be rough—the tip of the boom moves over forty miles an hour once we get moving, and I can't wait for you, I have to bolster the dam wall now or it will go."

"You do what you need to do," I said, shoving Waverly's gun into the back pocket of my jeans. I opened the door.

"Don't let her throw anything into the load cell—it looks like a tin box just below the cable drum. And Angela," his voice grew stronger, "be careful!"

After AJ left, it took everything Elizabeth had not to vomit all over the dragline controls as blood dripped from her nose onto her hands. She turned to Mr. Palladino, and her vision went dark at the sight of his blood staining his shirt.

"I can't do this alone," he snapped at her as she sagged down to her knees, leaning against the cold metal of the base of the instrument console. She waved a hand at him weakly, fighting to breathe. Her skin was drenched in sweat as she shivered, her vision swimming. She never did well with blood—not her own or anyone else's.

Hardys didn't faint. They didn't panic. And they never, ever ran away from their duty. Her father's voice drummed through her brain, squelching the nausea.

Elizabeth climbed to her feet. She joined Mr. Palladino, leaned over his left side, and fit her hand into the joystick controls there. "Tell me what to do."

The alarm sounded again. "Angela made it out," he said. "Hope she's ready for one helluva ride." He toggled some switches on the right-hand side, and the cabin began to spin—not only the cabin, but the entire dragline. "All we have to do is fill up the bucket, swing it over the dam breech, and drop it into place. Easy as pie."

Right. So why were all these switches, buttons, and knobs here? Elizabeth began to ask for a more complete explanation when a blurry figure appeared on the other side of the windows. Rain whipped by wind streaked the view, but it was someone climbing inside the boom, clinging to cables on either side of a catwalk as the machine spun. Not AJ—this person had dark hair. Waverly.

"Damn, she's moving faster than I thought," Frank said. "Angela better hurry." He worked a few more controls, and suddenly the huge bucket suspended from the boom plummeted, dropping beyond the edge of the cliff they were on.

"Did you mean to do that?"

"Fastest way to get fill—won't be pretty, though." Sweat gathered on his brow as he manipulated the controls, nudging her with his shoulder. "Red toggle, release the hoist brake."

She did as instructed, then looked up to see AJ rushing up the catwalk after Waverly. AJ's blond hair was whipped by the wind, and it was clear she was struggling to keep her footing as she tried to outpace Waverly.

Lightning struck close enough that the dragline rocked with the force. AJ lost her grip and slid back, teetering at the edge of the catwalk, suspended sixty feet in the air, her arms flailing for a handhold.

Another jolt of lightning blinded Elizabeth for a split-second. When her vision cleared, AJ had vanished.

THIRTY-TWO

David glanced beneath the lockers that had knocked Cole down and realized that the only thing keeping Cole trapped was one metal door that had fallen open and been jammed against Cole by the weight of the rest of the lockers, pinning Cole against one of the benches. It was like a three-dimensional puzzle. All he had to do was move the right piece and Cole would be free.

Of course, if he moved the wrong piece, he'd be trapped under there with Cole. "Help me get down there," he told Abby as he locked his chair in place.

She followed his glance, then shook her head. "You'll never fit. I'll go."

Before he could protest, she was down on her hands and knees, squirming under the rubble. "His leg is trapped against the bench," she called back. "I'm afraid to move it."

"Don't," he shouted. Cole stirred at his voice, eyes fluttering open. "Hold still, Cole, we're getting you out of there." David slid down from his chair, the better to examine the problem. He reached behind his chair to pull his maglight from his backpack. His mom insisted that he carry it along with his cell phone—she was paranoid about emergencies. Guess maybe he wouldn't tease her so much about that anymore.

He shined the light, focusing on the door pinning Cole's leg. "Don't move Cole's leg," he told Abby. "Can you push that door instead? All it will take is an inch or so."

She grunted and shoved at the door. Getting nowhere using her arms, she twisted around the confined space and used her legs instead. The door moved—then the entire pile of debris shuddered, the metal wailing like a lost child.

"Stop! That's enough!"

Abby scuttled back until she was safely beside David. She grabbed his hand as the locker door moaned, folding in on itself a quarter of the way. The rest of the debris shifted with it, settling into a new configuration.

One that left Cole's leg free.

Cole grabbed on to David's chair, using it to leverage himself out from under the rubble. "Thought I told you two to get going," he said, his voice a bit stronger, but not by much. Doubled over as he worked to breathe, he couldn't stand up straight and kept both hands pressed to his left side.

"Couldn't," David said, his heart buoyed by the fact that Cole was still alive. "Not without my dad."

Cole said nothing, but gave David a twisted smile as he led the way to the door.

Just like climbing a tree, I told myself as I hauled ass up the catwalk. The boom itself was at least twenty feet square, its supports massive and spaced so far apart that the catwalk felt flimsy, floating above the ground, the only support coming from my sheer, stubborn unwillingness to fall.

So just don't fall, I heard Randy taunting me as he challenged me to climb higher, faster, than he could.

The wind kept trying to topple me off the slick metal steps. I kept both hands on the safety cables, hauling myself up with my arms as much as I was propelling myself with my legs. Climbing, climbing, not looking down, instead focusing on the ever-dwindling distance between myself and Waverly.

Loud *pssts* and puffs of steam came from all around me as the crane moved, but those sounds weren't nearly as loud or frightening as the thunder and lightning gathering above us. The dragline was a natural lightning rod, I realized. Maybe this hadn't been such a great idea after all.

The dragline jerked to a halt, and I was wrenched to one side, banging my chin on the cable as I caught myself. The cable was cloaked in some kind of grease that came away black on my hand. While the dragline paused, I wiped my hand dry—as dry as possible—and looked up for a split-second.

We were now facing away from the dam and toward the school. Cable whistled as it spun out above and below me, the bucket lowering to scoop up earth for fill. As distracting as the movement was—the catwalk was swaying in unpredictable directions that threatened to make me seasick—I focused on the school.

It was so far away that I couldn't make out details. Sirens sounded, and a police SUV pulled into the school lot. Where was David? Had he made it out? And Cole?

A bright white light filled my world, hurtling down at me like the hand of God, shaking the entire dragline, and I was knocked off my feet, tumbling into the void, blinded.

With Elizabeth's help, Frank steered the dragline back around to face the breech and position it for the drop. "It's giving way," he muttered, his gaze on the monitor. "But this will plug her."

"Are you sure?" Elizabeth asked, trying to match his movements with the joystick she held. The ride was jerky—she hated to think how that translated out on the boom, battered by the wind and rain. If AJ was still somewhere clinging to it . . . if she was still alive and not crushed beneath them.

Waverly was almost to the big round steel drum where Frank said the load cell was located.

"Hurry," Elizabeth urged.

"Should have never let Angela come home," he gasped as he worked. "Keeping her away was the best way to keep her safe."

"You couldn't have known that Waverly would resort to murder," Elizabeth said, trying to comfort him, hoping it would help him to focus on the job at hand.

"Doesn't matter. All my fault. Edna, Angela Joy, Randy . . . all my fault."

"Your fault?"

"Y-yes. My fault." His voice faltered, faded into silence, then strengthened. "I sent Randy to practice that day. I told him it was okay to play. I killed my only son."

She stared at him. The cascade of events stemming from that one decision appeared inevitable from the viewpoint of Frank Palladino's twisted, guilt-stricken logic. His decision had sent his son to his death. Plummeted his wife into a grief so deep she couldn't climb out, so instead she had buried herself inside their own home. Alienated his daughter, driving her into Cole's arms—just in time to almost die herself ten years ago.

No wonder he could barely look at AJ, much less welcome her home.

God, what a twisted family, Elizabeth thought. And she thought her parents were screwed up.

"It's okay," she squeezed his hand. "Everything's going to be okay, Frank. We just need to save the dam."

His grip went slack in hers. Slid away from the dragline controls. "Frank?" She turned. His eyes were closed. Blood saturated his shirt and dripped onto the metal floor at an alarming rate. "Wake up, Frank! You need to help me. I can't do this alone."

She shook him, slapped his face. His head lolled to one side, but his eyelids didn't even flutter. He still had a pulse, but it was weak and very fast, skittering beneath her fingertips. Maybe it wasn't even his pulse, maybe she was feeling her own panic.

She didn't have time to figure it out. She had to translate the dragline controls and figure out how to dump the payload and plug the breech before the dam burst.

Alone. It was all up to her now.

THIRTY-THREE

I pitched over the side, the cable burning against my palms as I struggled to hold on. I slid a good ten feet down it, as if it was a zip line, before slamming into the edge of a metal support. The breath flew out of me, and I almost released my grip. The gun fell from my pocket. Metal clattered against metal, the sound quickly swallowed by the storm.

Somehow I managed to hold on—through reflex more than thought, because at that moment I was in so much pain and filled with so much terror that all thought was banished.

The only thing that saved me was the panel at the base of the catwalk—designed to prevent wayward tools from dropping into the cables, I guessed. It provided a toehold, stopped my falling. Wedging my feet against it, I swiveled my weight forward, back onto the catwalk, and hung on for a second, my face pressed against the metal rung, hugging it tight.

Once I caught my breath, I dared to look up. Waverly was almost at the cable drum. The dragline had reversed course and was now whipping back toward the dam.

I had to stop her before she could sabotage the crane and stop Dad from dropping the payload that would plug the breach. Which meant I had some catching up to do.

Clawing my way back up to my feet, I resumed my hauling-pushing motion, this time fighting to move faster, skipping rungs even though that increased my chances of slipping and falling, forcing my muscles to work double-time. It was windier, and the crane less steady, the higher I went—forces that slowed Waverly but that I refused to allow to slow me. Every time I stole a glance she was closer to me—but also closer to the cable drum.

The dragline swayed violently, like some kind of crazy bucking-bronco carnival ride. I didn't think it all came from the wind and movement since we'd stopped over the breach. We were eighty feet above the bucket and three times as high above the ground. Close enough to see the wind churning the coal slurry below, whipping it into a frenzy.

The bucket hovered maybe a dozen feet above the widening breach, the cables that held it jerking and straining, and I wondered what the hell my father was doing.

No time to worry about it—I was almost to Waverly. And she was only a few feet from the metal box that held the load cell.

Thankfully, the load cell was nestled below the massive cable drum, which was aligned on the outside of the boom, out of reach. There was no gantry or walkway to cross over to the load cell. But that didn't stop Waverly. She climbed over the safety cable, stepping off the catwalk and onto a ten-inch-wide support beam.

"Waverly, don't!" I shouted, my voice tearing through the wind.

A loud *psst, psst* devoured her reply. I rushed closer, almost slipping and falling. Gripping the safety cable with her back to it, she fought to find her balance on the crossbeam.

I was almost close enough to reach her. "Waverly!"

She glanced over her shoulder at me. "All I ever wanted was Cole. Do you understand that? What it means to love someone so much that you'll do anything for him?"

"I do. If you love Cole, then give it up." Two more steps and I was close enough to grab her arm. Using my weight as leverage, I tried to wrestle her back over onto the catwalk. "Waverly, don't you understand? Cole is down there. He's in the school."

Her screech was inhuman, something born of a nightmare. Releasing her grip on the safety cable, she reached to claw at my face. Leaving me holding her entire weight. The dragline shuddered violently. The bucket tilted and released its payload.

Waverly used the distraction to push away from me—and the safety line. As the machine lurched, she slid backwards, arms flying out to her sides.

She almost caught herself—I thought she would, her arm circled around the support beam, anchoring her body. For just an instant she looked up, met my eyes.

Gone was the haughty expression of the woman who'd won Cole's heart and stolen the life I was meant to have. In its place was only pain and despair. She blinked once.

Then she let go.

Cole staggering behind them, Abby started out trying to push David, but it was soon clear that he could go faster than she could. Once they were out in the main hallway, she jogged beside him, then fell behind. David stopped and hauled her once again onto his lap. Then he began to wheel as fast as he could.

David wasn't sure if it was sweat or blood slipping between his palms and the wheels. He couldn't stop to think or find his gloves or look. All he could do was breathe, grab, push, repeat, breathe, breathe, keep breathing, grab, don't slip, push harder, harder, faster. . . .

He fought the urge to look back for Cole and concentrated instead on finding a clear path through the darkness and rubble. The entire building groaned and swayed, a giant getting ready to topple right down on top of them.

Abby. He had to focus on her, not Cole, he had to save her, couldn't fail, couldn't let Cole down, Dad, he couldn't let his dad down, not now . . . his grip slipped and the chair lurched, flying forward on one wheel, ramming against a fallen light fixture. Abby cried out, but she did the right thing—leaned into David using her weight to right them before they lost momentum.

The doors. They were just ahead. They were almost there.

A loud crash shook the building. Metal screamed, wood burst, glass shattered, as the building gave a final gasp and collapsed in a wave of brick and mortar and smoke rushing right at them.

Waverly was gone in a blink, the dark waters of the impoundment pond burying her. I couldn't stop to think about it and tried hard not to remember what that water felt like, how eager it was to suck the life out of a person. Instead, I flew down the catwalk, my feet barely touching the rungs.

By the time I made it down to the school, the back half of the building had collapsed. Ty was there along with a fire truck, an ambulance, and two other police cars.

But they weren't going into the building. Their attention was focused on the dam. They were radioing to others, whipping maps open and examining them, one of the police cars and an ambulance leaving just as I arrived. They headed up the hill toward the dragline. Help for my dad.

"What are you doing?" I shouted as I sprinted past the men. "My son's in there!"

Ty raced after me, splashing through the rain puddles. "AJ, stop! It's too dangerous."

He caught up with me just as I wrenched the door open. His radio sputtered something about an evacuation of the entire valley, but the rain drowned it out. He plowed into me, trying to pull me away. I twisted free.

"AJ, let me. Wait outside where it's safe." He grabbed my arm, and I punched him in the gut in response.

Free for the moment, I ran into the school.

Disoriented by the near-darkness, I began coughing on the dust and almost immediately tripped over a pile of fallen ceiling tiles. Then a beam of light pierced the shadows.

"Mom?"

I made a noise that sounded more like a squeal than any adult woman should admit to, but I didn't care. "David!"

Ty and I reached him together. He had a girl about his age sitting on his lap, both of them squeezed into a corner of the alcove that hosted the water fountains. Apart from a few scrapes and bruises they seemed fine.

Ty lifted the girl free while I unstuck David's chair from where it'd gotten wedged. "Are you sure you're okay?" I asked as I pushed him through the debris to the doors. I didn't have time to do my own inventory of him, but would as soon as we were safely outside.

"I'm fine," he said, pushing his wheels himself. I gasped when I saw his palms, bloody and shredded. "Mom, stop. You've got to help Cole. He was right behind us, but I didn't see him after the lights went out."

I looked beyond him—total darkness, no movement. The wall to the office had collapsed, creating a small mountain of twisted drywall, ceramic tiles, and metal supports. If Cole was in there, somewhere—I turned my back on the sight. I had to get David to safety first. Cole would agree, I knew.

We made it to the door, and David insisted on wheeling through it himself while I held it open. Ty had turned the girl over to the firefighters and was running back to help us.

"You okay, David?"

"Just get my dad," David said. "Promise me you'll get him—or I'll go back myself." He turned to me, smoke-colored tears streaking his cheeks. "Mom—"

"You head out to the fire truck. Now," I added when he opened his mouth to protest. "Ty and I will take care of Cole. I promise."

He stared at me. Hard. Then he nodded and pushed through the door and down the ramp to the parking lot.

Ty handed me a flashlight, a small one, barely larger than a penlight. Then he unsnapped his duty flashlight and turned it on. Strange sounds echoed through the building: water dripping, wood creaking, electricity sparking.

Cautiously, we approached the wall of rubble where David said he'd seen Cole last. "Cole?" I shouted.

We stopped and listened. A low moan, barely audible, came from the edge of the rubble. Ty and I raced over. Cole lay there, face up. He was in a clear area, only a few pieces of drywall and lots of dust covered his body. But he wasn't moving.

Ty set his flashlight down and radioed for help. I knelt at Cole's head. "It's okay, Cole," I said, my words garbled by tears. I stroked his hair, uncertain of what else I could do to help him. "It'll be okay."

His eyes fluttered open but couldn't hold their focus. "David?" The effort of speaking seemed too great. His eyes closed again.

"He's okay. He's fine."

"Good." His hands were clasped to his belly. I laid my hand over them. Too late, I realized that his shirt and jeans were soaked with blood. I tried to move his hands, to press my own against the blood streaming out between them, but he moaned. "Don't. Please."

"Hang on, Cole. Help's coming." I saw the firefighters hauling their gear up the steps beyond us.

"Tell David . . ." His voice drained away, but his lips kept moving. I lowered my ear to his face. Even his lips were gray. I tried to tell myself that it was only dust, but I was never very good at lying, not even to myself. "Love you. Both."

My tears splashed onto his cheek, but he didn't seem to notice. "Cole. Don't. You hang on, damn you. Don't leave us. Not now. You can't—"

Ty pulled me away as the firemen slid into position beside Cole. Tears sparked in the dim light, coating his cheeks. He held me tight, his hand buried in my hair, arms wrapped around me so I couldn't see anything. I didn't have to. I could hear the men working, hear their frustration as they began CPR, calling out ideas to each other as they tried one thing, then another.

My body shook against Ty's. Adrenaline chased away by fear and grief, leaving in its wake a numb despair. This wasn't happening, it couldn't be happening, not after I'd finally found him again . . . David's face forced its way into my vision, and the thought of him losing Cole stole away my remaining strength.

I slumped against Ty, relying on his arms to keep me from falling.

A sound like a wild animal caught in a trap raced through Ty's body—a subsonic, primal keening. I was the only one who heard. Not so much heard it as felt.

Cole was gone.

"We're sorry," one of the firefighters behind me said. The building was still groaning around us—as if it was mourning Cole as well.

Then the mountain of debris began to shudder and shift as water tumbled through it, pushing it. Sparks flew overhead, accompanied by pops as loud as gunshots.

"We need to get out of here," Ty shouted.

I couldn't move, my body was too drained. For one short moment, I'd have been happy to collapse there, stay with Cole forever. It would have been so much easier than facing David.

"AJ!" Ty shook me hard. "Now. I'll get Cole."

In a haze of sparks, water, and smoke, Ty knelt and lifted Cole's body into his arms. The firemen grabbed their gear and scrambled as the smell of fire billowed from the rear of the building. I stumbled to the door and held it for open for Ty and Cole.

As it slammed shut behind us, the entire building shook like a death rattle.

THIRTY-FOUR

My father was just as stubborn a patient today as he was yesterday, I discovered. The bullet had torn through several muscles and caused some bleeding in his spleen, but it was all fixed fairly easily—if the surgeon could be believed.

Only problem was that he refused to say who shot him. Said he couldn't remember.

I didn't understand why he would protect Waverly after she'd almost destroyed the entire town and everyone in it. Until I saw Masterson leaving his room. Guess Dad was protecting his job and Masterson's reputation—as usual.

Hoped it was worth half a million and our house.

They gave up dragging the toxic sludge in the impoundment, searching for Waverly's body. Figured they'd never find it before the chemicals turned it into unidentifiable mush.

The police caught Ellings at a truck stop on I-64. He wasn't so particular about protecting Waverly's reputation, although he tried to place some of the blame on me and Cole and David. Even blamed Elizabeth for driving my van, saying Waverly was only trying to get rid of "the bitch and the bastard."

Seemed like since coming home, I was inspiring those kinds of feelings in most everyone I met. Including Charity, who had lost her job when word of her sending Elizabeth the death threat got out. As well as Yancey, who had gotten the green light for his TV series, *Yancey's Girl Power Eco-Army*, but was livid when I refused to sign a release allowing him to use footage of me and David or to use our names or any personal information.

"But that's, that's, like, everything," he whined, sounding more like a nine-year-old than David.

"It's that or a lawsuit," Elizabeth had informed him cheerfully, handing him a nondisclosure form to sign on our behalf. Which he had, grudgingly. Then he and the Ladies left.

Leaving me and Elizabeth to fight Cole and Zachariah's battle.

Three nights later, we were at her house, packing up her dad's stuff, alternating cleaning with sips of wine. It was better than the alternative—trespassing on Masterson's land to watch Cole's funeral from a distance, since I'd been banned from attending. I wasn't sure I'd have gone even if Old Man Masterson had let me. Seemed to me that the best revenge against him and the greatest tribute to Cole was to simply keep raising David the best I could and stay far, far away from anything to do with the Mastersons.

After the scare with the coal slurry, the DEP tested the groundwater near the destroyed school and found it contaminated. The DEP and the Army Corps of Engineers also reviewed Cole's Environmental Impact Survey and decided—with a little help from the press, not to mention a public sit-in of all the Scotia parents and school kids—to halt MTR mining throughout the state until better guidelines could be developed.

I couldn't help but hope that the moratorium might become permanent. Masterson must have seen the light as well—or at least glimpsed it. He was allowing Cole's wind farm plans to continue and had shut down the other MTR sites that Waverly had planned. Instead, he was reopening the underground mine—the mine that seven generations of Scotia men had worked in and some had died in.

My dad got his old job back and was ecstatic, despite his doctor's warnings. My mom just smiled, and I had the feeling that even though they now owned the house free and clear, she might still be looking for payback from Masterson. Flora was livid, of course, especially since the mine was still non-union. Elizabeth was happy her dad had won his case.

And me? Me, I was too numb to care. I didn't even care that I was now out of a job. All I cared about was figuring out what to say to David to help him heal. Cole's death had rocked him, hard. He barely slept, barely ate, barely spoke.

Control freak me, I threw all my energy into finding a way to fix it for him. Ty helped, spending a lot of time with David, letting him work with Nikki. He said sometimes having a canine to talk to was better than pouring your soul out to another human, but I was skeptical.

And worried. Mostly because I had no idea how best to help David.

"You know when Cole said it was all his fault?" Elizabeth broke our moody silence by pouring more wine. We needed to organize the files scattered over the office table, but our hearts weren't really in it.

"Yeah." I wasn't up for conversation, much less talking about Cole, but she didn't take the hint.

"I figured out what he meant."

"What?"

"He's the one who called Yancey. The biggest, loudest media circus money could hire. A bit of overkill for one little injunction, especially when he had the EIS to use. I think he wanted to get caught doing it— it wasn't hard to trace the money. Any good journalist would have found out with a little digging if Waverly's antics hadn't distracted everyone."

I thought about that idea. It fit. And was just like Cole. He'd held back the EIS until the last possible moment since it would then be public knowledge that Cole had commissioned it and he knew his father would disapprove. "Poor Cole. He never could stand up to his old man. This was his chance to become the man he wanted to become."

Elizabeth raised her hand to her mouth, but instead of tapping her teeth, she simply lay a finger against her lower lip, considering. "He did in the end. Don't you think?"

I couldn't answer her, my final image of Cole etched into my vision.

"David has a father to be proud of," she continued, the statement an offering.

She was right. I needed to talk with David, help him mourn in a healthy way—not get mired in grief like my mom.

"And so do you," I told her.

She stared sorrowfully into the depths of her wineglass. Then she tilted it in my direction. "To Cole and Zach."

"To Cole and Zach." We clinked glasses and sipped.

"And to continuing their good work."

I looked up at that. "Are you serious?"

She smiled and nodded. "But I can't do it alone. Want a job?"

I clinked my glass against hers in answer. "I think your dad would be very, very proud."

"Thank you. To Hardy and Palladino, Environmental and Consumer Advocates."

"To Hardy and Palladino." That was definitely worth another sip of wine.

Later that night, I sat with David up on the wishing rock. It was a testament to how miserable he was that he hadn't argued at all when I asked Ty to carry him up with me. After Ty left, we looked out across the abyss, the mountain draped in shadows except for a sprinkling of stars overhead.

I waited, hoping he would start talking on his own.

"Why does everyone keep dying?" he finally asked. "Is it something I did wrong? Is it my fault?"

"David! No, never. How could you think that?"

"You almost died because of me, when I was born. And now. . . ." He couldn't finish, shaking tears away.

"What Cole did, he did because he loved you."

"But loving someone is supposed to be good. People aren't supposed to die. Especially—"

"Especially not fathers you've been waiting your whole life to meet?"

"Yeah." Anger lanced through the syllable.

"I wish things were different—"

"Wishes are for babies. Stupid fairy tales. They never come true, not the way they're supposed to."

"Or the way you want them to?"

He jerked his chin in a nod.

"That shouldn't ever make you stop wishing. Not for the really important things. I spent nine months wishing and wishing for a perfect baby—"

"Yeah, look how that turned out." He banged his fist against the rock.

I hugged him fiercely, hoping my body could speak louder than my words. "My wish *did* come true. I got my perfectly perfect baby boy, and I wouldn't trade him in for the whole wide world."

He fought at first, then stiffened, then finally relaxed in my embrace. His tears quickly soaked through my flannel shirt. I kissed the top of his head and squeezed him even tighter. "Your father was a good man. A brave man. And that's exactly the kind of man you'll be someday."

"How can you be sure?"

"Because that's the kind of man you are already."

He shook himself free, back to being a nine-year-old untouchable boy. He rolled his eyes. "That's the kind of thing moms always say."

"Doesn't make it any less true." I kissed him again, this time on the forehead, just to irritate him and remind him who was boss. And mostly because I wanted to. The thought of him ever facing the doubts and guilt I'd lived with—I had to do better, give him more than I'd had. "Don't you ever forget that."

Again with the eye roll, but this time a smile accompanied it. Not a smirk. Rather, one of his secret smiles, the kind he got when no one was looking and he'd spotted something beautiful that no one else noticed.

"Mom, can we go home?"

My heart lurched—I'd thought he'd want to stay here in Scotia, but maybe the trauma with Cole had been too much. God, how could I have been such an idiot, making plans to stay just because it was what I wanted?

"You mean to D.C.?"

He looked puzzled, a knot forming between his eyebrows, just like Cole used to have. I resisted the urge to soothe it away with a kiss. "No. I mean home. The summerhouse. I'm getting cold."

"Oh, right. Home." I felt so light I could have flown right off the side of the mountain. Instead, I anchored myself by hugging him so tight he squirmed.

We were home. For good.

A Conversation with Erin Brockovich

Author of *Rock Bottom*

Q: What inspired you to write fiction, and particularly, a suspense thriller?

Erin Brockovich: I noticed something happening in courts of law when juries deal with environmental issues like groundwater contamination. The repercussions of a case might be riveting but the scientific jargon, the parts per million—it's dry and becomes overwhelming. In fiction, that same story can be told in a way that maintains its dangerous and heroic elements. People can get caught up and intrigued by it, and perhaps start thinking, "Hey wait a minute, that could be me." I think that's the exciting side of writing a book—that you can draw a reader in, and open a door to people who want to learn or to ask questions. It enables them to become aware, to believe that they can make a difference, and to become their own hero. If I can tell a story and a person can close the book and say, "Wow, this is really happening," then I'm all for it.

I'm learning that the more I can create awareness, the more we can teach people that no superman is coming to save them. Government agencies are without funds, industry could change and undo its damage but they haven't decided to do that yet, and we have litigation but it takes 5 to 15 years, so we've got to learn to rely on ourselves and our communities. Some of the issues that the story covers are daunting and depressing, but through our creativity and imagination we can turn a nightmare into awareness and make it a dream—a good dream—for restoration, action, and rebuilding. I think that we have great strength in joining together.

Q: Readers will believe they see much of you in AJ. How is she like you and how is she different?

Erin Brockovich: She's similar in many ways. At some level, she's uncertain of herself, she's been behind the eight ball, and has to deal with a child with a serious medical condition. She doesn't really have anyone to rely on other than herself, and she has great compassion.

I don't know that she is very different from me! In some instances she might be a little gutsier than I am. Sometimes she shocks even me, she does things and I think, I don't know if I could have done that. She has that edge that I had when I was younger and at times still have, but now that I'm older there are other things on my mind. I think I've found a more spiritual level, maybe a bit of a calmer level. As I mature and grow wiser, there's a part of me that handles things a little bit differently. But, even at fifty, if I'm pushed the wrong way, that AJ in me will come back out.

Q: Has your life ever been threatened—a situation AJ faces—in the course of your work uncovering environmental crime and health threats?

Erin Brockovich: In the early days, there were threats—implied and blatant. These have fallen off, now that people know my name. Not that they all respect me, but they know where I stand. I don't worry about it.

Q: In your book, you weave together family, ecological, and legal themes in a compelling page-turner; do you find the same mix in your work as an environmental and consumer advocate?

Erin Brockovich: People come to me with worker's comp and whistleblower issues, environmental problems, pharmaceutical and disease issues like this new lung disease. They turn to me for corrupt government issues, and international concerns, as well; I hear from people in Australia, Canada, Ireland, and South Africa. I think people trust that I actually listen. I was sitting for an interview and the reporter asked a caller, "Why do you go to Erin?" And the woman answered, "Because she actually cares, and she listens. No one listens anymore." They trust that maybe I'll do something with their information.

Q: Rock Bottom centers on environmental crime and greed; do you think our country's challenges in this area go under-reported? What do people need to look for and know to better protect themselves?

Erin Brockovich: Our challenges and risks are very under-reported. I just had a community meeting regarding a huge chromium VI case (hexavalent chromium is most commonly produced as a byproduct of industrial processes). The people were all excited because the EPA was going to list them as a Superfund site. And I had to tell them that that might be all that was going to happen; the EPA has 1,200 other Superfund sites they haven't cleaned up. Agencies and industries are playing the shell game; agencies are unstaffed, overburdened, and the country is broke. They were shocked, and I felt terrible. A large part of the population really thinks that the government or some agency is going to save them, but Superman's not coming. It's scary and very daunting.

This is a perfect example. I remember when I started working on the Hinkley, California, case in 1991, and talking with a geologist about how it might take 50 to 75 years of effort to get the chromium VI out of the water. Then he said, for that chromium VI to naturally attenuate, it would take 1,000 years; for Pacific Gas & Electric to clean it up, worst-case scenario: 250 years. And now, PG&E has said it will buy up those one hundred homes, but they still don't know where the plume of tainted water runs, and what other homes may be affected over time.

It's a major wake-up call. We don't want to make the association between our electrical power and the shiny hard finishes on our cars with what we've done to the environment. Awareness is key, and you don't have to be a doctor or scientist to understand that water is a precious commodity. Any action is better than no action, and every single community can start to take action.

We raised millions of dollars for disaster relief in Haiti. We need to do that for our own country. At local levels, we can have fundraisers to take care of groundwater contamination. It will make a difference. I am hoping this series of books will prompt people to want to take action, whatever the cause may be, from clean water to breast cancer. Let us all be our own AJ; let's begin to save ourselves.

Q: As president of Brockovich Research and Consulting, you are currently working a number of cases. Can you tell us a bit about them—their locations, the issues you face?

Erin Brockovich: Here are some of the cases we are currently looking at:

Camp Lejeune, North Carolina—More than forty male veterans are reporting breast cancer and an estimated 22,000 have been poisoned from the tainted water supply used by up to a million Marines and family members. The water was contaminated with chemicals from an off-base dry-cleaning company and industrial solvents used to clean military equipment. Despite a 1974 base order requiring proper disposal, solvents were dumped or buried near base wells for years. So, our young Marines who have completed two or three tours of duty successfully are poisoned on our own soil. This is a true sore spot for me; these men and women risk their lives in service to our country and their water is tainted?

West Palm Beach, Florida—This case is a reminder that these challenges are everyone's issue; carcinogens poison us all, regardless of race or income. There is an inquiry into a potential "cancer cluster" in a rural suburb of West Palm Beach. State and county health officials have launched a Level II investigation in the Acreage community after finding a potentially higher rate of pediatric brain cancer there in their initial research.

Beverly Hills High, California—More than 450 kids who attended the school have cancer. We had found dangerous levels of toxic gases such as benzene, toluene, and methane being emitted; there is an oil-production facility underneath the school, which sits on an oil-rich site.

Midland, Texas—I never thought I'd see another Hinkley, California; I'm afraid I might be wrong. Hexavalent chromium (chromium VI) is now being found in significant amounts in the water of over forty homes in Midland. The only difference between here and Hinkley is that I saw higher levels here than I saw in Hinkley. People using well water fell off the grid and were subject to some of the poorest environmental protection laws anywhere in the country.

Q: How did you become involved with these cases?

Erin Brockovich: I get thousands of e-mails and when I start seeing one or two e-mails about a similar problem and then it grows to five or ten, that's a flag for me that something's wrong so I start paying attention. I started noticing people reporting that they appeared to have a higher number of individuals in their neighborhood, building, or area with cancer.

When I started mapping all these e-mails and where they were coming from, I ended up with 422 red dots on a map of the United States—my "cancer cluster" map. Each one of those is an e-mail, a person telling me that they're concerned not by one or two cancer cases, but by seven or ten or twelve, sometimes unusual strains or younger populations with cancer—kids. This startled me.

I'd like to start working with federal and local agencies, and at the congressional level, and encourage people to get back to common sense in taking care of our environment and of ourselves. The system is broken, litigation is not a quick response, and it takes years. We can find millions to bail out banks but nothing for EPA testing and site clean up. I think it's a tragedy for all of us. Let's put our economy to work by cleaning up these sites.

Q: What do you find most challenging about your work? Most fascinating about it?

Erin Brockovich: Just when I think I can't take anymore disheartening news, there's hope. You find one person, one company stepping up to the plate, and I think that's what I find helpful. I find human beings fascinating. When they see the true, underlying issue and they understand it, they respond and act to make a change for the better. My challenge is to help bring people to that point of taking action.

Q: This thriller is the first in a series; can you give us a hint of what is in store for AJ and her son?

Erin Brockovich: AJ has plenty of adventures ahead of her. And I like to think that there is a little bit of AJ in each one of us. Communities are getting angry, and taking action into their own hands. Superman is not coming, so we need to get busy. I want this series to be solution-driven, enabling people to start a process themselves. I have a map of 422 communities with potential cancer cells, and we're not listening. If a few people close the book with a renewed sense of what can be accomplished, and become proactive in taking on accountability and responsibility for spreading the word about environmental issues and clean up, the AJ in all of us will be here for a good long time.